THE DISMEMBERER'S HANDBOOK

THE DISMEMBERER'S HANDBOOK

KIMBERLY LOVE

THE DISMEMBERER'S HANDBOOK
THE HARLEY WOLFHART SERIES BOOK 1

Copyright © 2021 by Kimberly Love

All rights reserved.
Printed in the United States of America.

No part of this book may be used or reproduced in any manner whatsoever without written permission except in the case of brief quotations embodied in critical reviews or articles.

This book is a work of fiction. Names, characters, businesses, organizations, places, events and incidents either are the product of the author's imagination or are used fictitiously. Any resemblance to actual persons, living or dead, events, or locales is entirely coincidental.

Cover Design and Interior Design by We Got You Covered Book Design
WWW.WEGOTYOUCOVEREDBOOKDESIGN.COM

First Edition: November 2021

THIS BOOK IS DEDICATED TO THE READER WHO ASKED ME
IF I WAS OKAY AFTER READING THE FIRST DRAFT

PROLOGUE

THE BLOOD RAN ALONG THE wooden tabletop, seeping through the cracks and staining the wood. He liked to watch it pool, to follow the lines as it dipped into the cracks, disappearing from sight. There was something thrilling about the way that blood moved away from the body as if looking for a means of escape from its prison.

It was quiet around him. If he went outside, he would hear the woods whispering around him. The shed that he was in was behind his home where he lived, and no one was around. He didn't worry about this place—no one ever came there—so he had the freedom to do as he pleased without worry of interruptions.

He looked down at the golden retriever he had on his table. Cutting its throat had been satisfying in ways that he could never fully explain to anyone. Man, the dog could bark though. Every time he had gone near it. Bark, bark, bark. It had been fucking annoying. The best thing he ever did was shut it up. He knew how to dismember the body, since he had been taught at a young age. He disposed of the bodies easily—there had been a lot of them.

People in the neighborhood were starting to whisper, wondering where all the neighborhood pets were going. He would have to collect from further away in town. There were too many whispers close by.

There was a creak behind him caused by the shed door opening. That was not supposed to happen. There was a gasp, and his hand clenched around the blade in his hand. He was a sight, he knew that much. His shirt was covered in blood, the blade glistening crimson.

He turned to find her standing there. Judgment was on her face. She would never scream; she would deal with him in her own way.

She tried to hide it but it was so obvious: she smelled of fear as it emanated out of every pore. He couldn't read her expression—she kept that from him. He had not expected fear from her. It was not her way. What would he do with her now?

ONE

MURDER REMINDED HARLEY OF HER mother sometimes, and she didn't know why. Murder haunted her dreams. It left her listless and feeling helpless. Unfortunately, it was her job to be immersed in it.

She sat on her couch, bent over as she read through a file. It was a file that had been troubling her for some time. It was a failure of hers, one she never had quite got over. She had a hard time letting go of things that went wrong in her life—she could thank her mother for that.

The file was an obsession of hers, one that her partner, Chris, kept reminding her to let go. The photo attached to the file was of a young girl, only sixteen years old but who had been caught up in a world she didn't belong in. Her name was Sam, and Harley was haunted by the picture. A runaway from home, she had been turned by a local pimp who was also part of a drug ring the department had been trying to bring down for a while. When Harley had run into her on the street, she had been lucky enough to find the girl sober and remorseful about the life she had come into. She had convinced the girl to become a Confidential Informant for the department and to turn over information they needed to bring down the drug ring.

Harley rubbed her heart through her shirt as a burning sensation hit her. Sam had been too young to be involved with the guys they had arrested. She was someone's child, and she belonged in a classroom learning algebra—or whatever it was kids learned nowadays in school. She didn't belong in some dive of an apartment, giving blowjobs for her next hit.

No kid deserved that kind of lifestyle, and yet so many of them were lost to it every single day. Harley couldn't help but feel responsible for the girl and every other lost soul who fell into a life of drugs. It was her mission to eradicate the city of drugs, something her partner often told her was a pipe dream. Well, hell, pipe dream or not, it was her job to at least try. If she didn't, she would see Sam's face in her nightmares for the rest of her life. Harley believed that she could have given the girl a second chance at her dreams, and God only knew she could relate to the girl and her problems.

She shivered suddenly, feeling cold all over. It was either luck or fate that had Harley determined to live a different life than her mother. She had never spent a night on the streets, but she had come close. She could have easily ended up with a life just like Sam's, hustling her body away, and her mother wouldn't have cared even half as much as Sam's parents cared about Sam.

The pain burned in her heart once again—her mother still affected her after all these years. She didn't hate her mother. She would have loved to have known her in the way that some of her coworkers knew their parents, but that was never going to happen. Her mother was an addict and that lifestyle had always been more important to her than carrying for her young daughter. It was a miracle that Harley had got out at all. A wave of sadness close to depression rolled over her, and she closed her eyes as she thought of her lost mother.

A knock on the door startled Harley out of her thoughts, and she jumped. *You're supposed to be a cop, slick*, she thought to herself. She got up from the couch and went to the door. She swung it open to find a delivery boy with a package that caused her to start salivating on sight.

"Officer Wolfhart, you are looking lovely this evening."

Harley rolled her eyes. It was probably a strong indication of her depleted social life that the delivery boy knew her by name. "Curtis, I've asked you to call me Harley multiple times. Let's not make this weird. How much do I owe you?"

"$22.45. You're not eating alone, are you?"

She smirked as she dug out the money she needed from her wallet. "You know I don't have any friends,

Curtis; my work is my life. I don't have time for friends."

"Do you want some company?"

"Absolutely not! Are you even legal yet? Get out of here before I make up a reason to drag you into the station," she said, laughing as she handed him money.

She closed the door before he could argue, and she shook her head as she returned to the couch. She set the Chinese food that she had been thinking about all day on the coffee table in front of her. She thought about what Curtis had said and wondered if she should have invited Chris over. He was probably already entwined with his bimbo of the week, and he would have only got mad as soon as she would have brought out the file on Sam. They were both about to take their detective's exam in order to go to the next level in the department, and he didn't like the fact that she was making waves. She was on the cusp of her thirtieth birthday and her life was starting to go places.

But shouldn't somebody have to pay? They had been partners for a few years as officers and they were hoping to move to the homicide department or even Special Victims Unit if everything went well. They wanted to do it together—partners for life, and all that. She had personally been offered to take the exam because of her discovery of Sam. The department felt like she had what it took to become a detective. She wanted that more than anything, mainly so that she could help take down the man responsible for putting Sam on the streets.

There was nothing we could have done; we weren't even there. It was something that Chris had reminded her of so many times that she hated it every time that he said it. The department had come close to cracking the drug trafficking case; they had got a tip from Sam about a deal going down and they took the opportunity to do a bust. *If only I had been there.*

That was what haunted her the most: that she hadn't been there. Maybe things would have turned out differently. Maybe Sam wouldn't have been shot. She was so young. Harley could have helped her into a better life; she didn't need to die a drugged-out prostitute with no future. Harley had wanted so much more for her. She took the news personally, blaming herself for Sam's death even though Chris thought that was ludicrous. But she was the one that had convinced Sam to become a CI in the first place. She could still be alive had Harley not got involved in her life. She should have been there during the bust, whether she was a detective or not. Sam had trusted her, and Harley had failed her.

Harley had been surprised when she met Sam's parents; her mother was a pediatrician and her father was a local pastor. They were devastated by her death—they had never stopped looking for her after she had run away, and the police had not been much help. There were so many runaways, and some were simply never returned to their parents. Sam's parents had no idea about the life that she had become involved in and had always wondered if she was already dead. It may have made a difference in Sam's life to know that her parents loved her and wanted her to come home. In the end, they had only wanted what was best for her.

When Sam's parents had come in to talk after identifying the body, her mother seemed shell-shocked. She had asked for Harley personally, and Harley was sure that she was going to get an earful. She had walked out into the squad room and had been shocked when she first saw them. The mother had been dressed conservatively in a short-sleeved dress down to her ankles and the father had looked like he was ready for a Sunday morning sermon. She had expected to see a mother strung out on meth and a father who stank of beer. That was usually the case in these situations; there was usually a good reason why a child ran away from home. But in this situation, sadly, the parents had been too strict.

"I'm so sorry for your loss, Mr. and Mrs. Scripps."

Harley had been shocked when Mrs. Scripps had crumpled into her arms sobbing. She had expected them to be mad at her, to blame her for the loss of their daughter, but instead, they were grateful.

Harley had patted Mrs. Scripps on the back uncomfortably, unsure of what else to say. It was never easy giving bad news to parents.

"Thank you so much," Mrs. Scripps had whispered.

"For what?" Harley had asked, confused.

"For trying to help her. Your Captain told us the whole story, about how you tried to help her, to get her out of there."

Tears had welled up in Harley's eyes. "I wish that I could have done more."

Mrs. Scripps had looked up at her. "You did what you could. Sam was always headstrong, believing that she knew what was best for herself. She wouldn't have left until she was good and ready. What you did was to give Sam hope, and that was more than I could have offered. I just wish she would have come home; I would have done anything to have her home."

"For kids like Sam, they feel like there is no forgiveness at home," Harley had answered.

"I know, and that's something we have to live with. We should have made sure that Sam knew that no matter what she did, we would always love her. After she was gone, we looked for her, but we never knew where to look. I prayed for so many nights that she would just find her way back to us. We didn't care what she had done; we just wanted our daughter back."

"I know and I'm so sorry for the pain you must be going through right now."

Mrs. Scripps had wiped at her tears and looked at her husband who smiled sadly at her. "We are just so thankful for what you were willing to do for her, Harley, and we wanted to tell you in person."

Harley had just nodded and watched as they left the station. Two broken souls with a lifetime of regret. Sam had been dead for three months, though, and they were still trying to find the lead to bring down her killers.

It was true: Sam had felt shame about the hooking and the drugs, and she had felt like she could never go home again. Harley ran into girls like that almost every day on the job, and she always wished that she could take them all home with her.

Harley started opening takeout containers of fried rice and Kung Pao chicken. She had a feast before her and she wondered how she was going to eat it all. She took a big bite out of an egg roll, the flaky crust breaking off into her mouth. She savored the sweet taste as she thought about the detective's exam. It would be life-changing, for sure—she would no longer be just a beat cop. She could be part of cases that really made a difference. That was why she had become a police officer in the first place.

Her personal life had been a disaster and it was any wonder that she hadn't ended up in the same place that Sam had. Her mother was just fucked up enough to name her after The Joker's psychotic girlfriend. *Thanks, Mom.*

The last time she had seen her mother was during a random stop at the grocery store to grab milk. As Harley was checking the expiration dates on the jugs of milk, a woman bumped into her. She turned and realized it was her mother, even though her fiery hair had become a bleached-blonde, frizzy look. The tank top she was wearing had stains on the front of it and the smell emanating from her mother indicated that she hadn't bathed in weeks.

She was so shocked by the appearance of her mother that she stood there speechless, unable to move. Her mother just looked through her as if she wasn't even there. She blinked once and walked away from Harley without even saying a word. Harley wasn't sure if her mother knew she had been standing right in front of her. There was no recognition.

She had never forgiven Harley for leaving her behind. What had she expected her to do? She thought about her mother daily; it wasn't exactly something she could escape from. She saw her mother every time she was forced to drag in a drunken disorderly person off the street or show up to a drunken domestic. She had been dealing with her mother's alcoholism since she was young enough to know what "drunk" meant.

How many times had she undressed her mother at night, pulling off her shoes as she lay passed out on the bed fully clothed? Harley used to be the one that tucked a blanket around her mother at night when all she wished for was to have her mother read her a bedtime story. As far as she could remember, she didn't think her mother had ever tucked her in at night. It was a wonder how Harley had survived as a baby. As far as her grandmother was concerned, she couldn't remember a time that Harley's mother wasn't hammered. That never even included the boyfriends, the parasites that would find her mother's perpetually glazed gaze attractive and then stay for days on end until the money and the booze ran out.

When she was in middle school, Harley had often returned home from school to see her mother passed out on the couch with a lit cigarette. It used to terrify her; she never knew if she was going to come home to the house being burned down. Harley was the one that had to put out her cigarettes and pay the bills, which was, of course, when there was actually money to pay the bills. When her attempts to wake her mother up from her afternoon nap would fail, Harley would go into the kitchen to make a box of Kraft Dinner and watch an episode of *Beverly Hills 90210* alone. She never had many friends, as it was too embarrassing to bring people to hang out at home, and no one really understood what her life was like. She had only her best friend, a boy from down the street. Jordan was the one that eventually convinced her to run away from home. It was after her mother went on a bender and never came home. After three days of waiting and crying and wondering if her only life support was dead in a ditch somewhere, Harley packed up her meager belongings and moved in with her best friend. It was the hardest thing she had ever done in her life, because no matter how screwed up her mother was, she loved her more than anything. She would have done anything for her mother; she just wished that her mother felt the same way about her.

That night as she had sat at the kitchen table with

Jordan and his parents, she had eaten the first real family meal of her life. She hadn't realized that pork chops could taste so good. The mashed potatoes were whipped, and tears streamed down her cheeks as Jordan's father kept telling "dad jokes" at the table. They said that she could stay there as long as she needed to.

It took her mother two weeks before she showed up to get Harley. She was marginally sober and asked Harley to come home; she promised to change and that things would be different. Telling her mother that she was never coming home was the hardest thing she ever had to do besides leaving her. Her mother would never change—she hadn't even come to the home sober or in clean clothes. Harley knew that she wouldn't be able to stay with Jordan forever either, since her mother would just continuously show up and disrupt her life. The next day she had made arrangements to stay with her grandmother in the next town over, she knew it was the only place her mother wouldn't be brave enough to find her.

Harley sighed as she cracked open a fortune cookie. She popped a piece in her mouth. As she crunched on the sweet cookie, she read her fortune. *Love is on the horizon. The stars predict he will be tall, dark and handsome.* "Good God," Harley groaned.

TWO

BUTCHER WALKED THE BEACH FEELING self-assured and relaxed. It had been a while since he was in Thailand—he traveled often and being there made him feel alive. He had been there for over a month and he had a plan. His father had always taught him to have a plan. His father had been a cold man, and he had left their home when Butcher was eleven years old, but he had taught him everything that he knew. He never understood why his father would leave him and his mother behind—maybe he had never really loved them in the first place. His mother had been devastated, and because of that, it had left a deep-seated hatred inside of Butcher.

He often wondered if his father saw something in him while he was teaching him the butchering skills. Was that why he had run away? Was he scared of what he had created and let loose in the world? Now Butcher had all the skills he needed to do whatever he wanted.

He took a deep breath, enjoying the smell of the

ocean air around him. He had no worries about anyone finding him there—he was rarely worried about anything. He had a destiny and it would be fulfilled one way or another. It had been a long time since he had been on Phuket Island. He often traveled a lot, but it took him a while to return to the same place. He liked bouncing from one island to another doing whatever he pleased. He had a special sort of skills and traveling made using those skills ideal. Thailand and Singapore were favorites of his; he often attended classical concerts at the Singapore Symphony Orchestra after a delicious steak dinner.

It wasn't long before he found himself back on the Thai resort island of Phuket. He had done work there before and he was now returning to have a little fun.

The smell of freedom was all around him, and he couldn't wait to get back to work—to get back to what made him truly happy: butchering. He glanced up and down the beach looking for a group that he could hang out with and become familiar with. It was never good to be the odd man out; he needed to blend in so that when he started butchering, no one would suspect him.

There were often bonfire parties that occurred on the beach both during the day and at night. It didn't matter what time of day it was, there were always people around, laughing and having a good time. It was paradise, and no one expected to be in danger in paradise. The best part of being there was to find a victim, to hunt her down—he could practically smell the fear come from them. He loved the thrill of the hunt, and he was the ultimate predator. It was perfect. He scanned the beach, looking at one group after another.

That was the first time that he saw her. She walked by him, her long red hair blowing behind her like it was flames licking in the wind. She was breathtaking. Her body was slender, with toned muscle as if she spent many hours in the gym, her stomach flat, her legs long, and her breasts small but firm. His mother had always been a beautiful woman, and this time was no exception. He was shocked to the core, unable to move, his heart in his throat. How could his mother be there? How had she found him? He stared at her, his mouth dry, his hands shaking. It was hard to miss her with that hair; it had reminded him of the *Little Mermaid* when he was young, and he would run his fingers through her hair, the soft strands tickling his fingers. He had loved her hair as a child—she was a natural redhead and she had seemed magical to him. She had let him brush her hair as she told him stories. His friends had always had crushes on his mother; however, he only saw her as his caretaker. He could never understand why he could not feel anything for her—or anyone, for that matter. He could not love or even care about what happened to the people around him. He understood that he was different from other people from a very young age.

He hadn't seen his mom in 17 years, and there she was on the beach, laughing and drinking beer. He watched as she took a joint from another woman—he had never known her to get high. It was like looking at a stranger.

He had thought about killing his mother for a long time, and he still thought about it. She had betrayed him, banished him from their home. She had seen who he was and didn't want to love him anymore. He never forgave her when she had sent him away. He planned on killing her one day, and he thought about what it would be like to slip a knife in between her ribs and watch the light go out in her eyes. He always planned on going back for her and making her pay for how she made him feel. She didn't deserve to live.

She turned to him and smiled, and he blinked. He saw her eyes and they were ice blue, not green like his mothers. He stared at her a beat longer before she turned back to her friends and continued talking. He let out a huge breath, not realizing he had been holding it the entire time. It had been foolish to think that his mother had been in Phuket, as she had never traveled a day in her life, but the resemblance had been uncanny.

He stared at the girl, and the more he looked at her, the less that she looked like his mother, though they did share the same body type and fiery red hair. The reaction to seeing her walk by him had rocked him, rattled him in a way that he had not expected. He wanted nothing more than to kill his mother, and he had thought she was there, like a gift being handed to him. He stared at the girl; she had a fire in her, he could tell. She was a spirited girl. He wondered if he put his hands around her neck if he could pretend that it was his mother. Would it feel the same?

He may not be able to kill his mother, but this girl with hair the color of flames would do just fine for now.

THREE

HARLEY FINISHED HER STREET MEAT as she stared across the picnic table at her partner of eight months. They hadn't been partners for long, but they had grown close quickly. He looked good today, handsome with a playful look on his face. He had been spinning a tale about some documentary he had seen on the television the night before. Some Netflix original he had watched with some girl. There was always some girl.

Harley wished that she had just as much luck as he did in the dating world. The last time she had a boyfriend was in the academy; he had been a law student at Harvard. She thought that she had landed a real catch until she caught him kissing his law professor. Ever since then, it had been random dates that usually didn't last the week. Guys seemed to dig her, but once they got wind of her late nights working and the fact that she would obsess over files, they were usually gone before it was time to meet the parents.

Not that she had any parents to introduce them to.

She crumpled her napkin and dabbed the side of her mouth. "So, let me get this straight. You're telling me that some guy with a punctured lung was able to release the pressure by cutting into his rib cage?"

Chris chuckled. "It was the craziest thing, Harley, and I'm not kidding you."

"Are you sure this was a real documentary? Maybe you were distracted by your date."

"I assure you, we watched the whole thing. The guy's lung cavity was filling up with blood. He punctured his side just below the rib and inserted a tube, and all the fluid just drained out of him. He would have died for sure if he didn't do it."

"Very MacGyver-like. I'm impressed."

"So was I. It was well worth postponing sex."

She groaned. "Please spare me the details."

Chris smiled, and she couldn't help but smile back. "If I didn't know any better, I would think you wanted to know the details," he said with a wink, "but I'll refrain because you're the best partner a guy could ask for, even if you are a ginger."

Her voice caught and all she could do was croak. She just stared at him. He had never said anything like that to her before, and it was the first time that she ever wished that he wasn't her partner. She had always had a crush on her partner. It was hard not to—handsome and nice, a great combination. She nodded and didn't say a thing.

"All right, I'm heading home. You should too, and get some rest."

"Soon. I'm going back to headquarters first, to finish some paperwork. I don't want it there when I return tomorrow."

"You work too hard, Harley. We aren't even detectives yet."

"Yes, well, I want to make sure I get there."

"C'mon, you are a shoo-in. Your instincts are unparalleled. Sometimes I don't know where your ideas come from. You have great intuition—I still don't know how you do it."

"I don't either. I just get these weird hunches and I have to check them out. They are my own personal Spidey senses."

"I know you're amazing, so stop worrying."

"Okay, I'll see you tomorrow."

She got up from the table and made her way to her car, wondering what it would be like if Chris were more than just her partner. She thought about that during the whole drive and she knew she had to get the thought out of her brain. He wasn't even interested in her so she was obsessed for no reason.

Once she was back at headquarters, she almost wished she hadn't come in for the paperwork—it just seemed endless. She hated it more than anything. As she shuffled through papers, the phone on her desk rang. She picked it up absently as she scanned the sheet in front of her.

"Officer Wolfhart here."

"There is a meeting going on in an hour at the warehouse on the fourth concession. Trust me, you're going to want to be there."

"Who is this?"

"Trust me, be there."

"You should—"

She heard the dial tone, and she slowly placed the receiver down. She considered the paperwork before her and the possibility that the phone call was just some prank—they got so many of them. But something about the voice, the desperation she heard, demanded her trust and got her out of the chair, heading for the door.

She tried calling Chris a few times on her way over to the warehouse, but all she got was his voicemail. He was probably watching another documentary with that girl. She pulled into a long driveway that led to a warehouse. There were two black vehicles parked in front.

The caller had been right. Something was indeed going down at the warehouse. She clicked on the radio and called for backup. "This is Officer Wolfhart. Suspicious vehicles in front of a warehouse on fourth concession, a possible 10-87 in progress. I need backup asap."

"10-4, Officer Wolfhart. No units are available at this

time. We will send as soon as possible. Looking at a time of thirty minutes at the earliest arrival."

"Shit. Are you serious?"

"It's the best that I can do, Officer Wolfhart. Just sit tight."

She stared at the building. She couldn't wait for backup. Whatever was going on in the building may not be there in a half hour. She was going to have to go in alone.

The cold of the cement walls seeped into Harley's back, causing chills to crawl up her spine. Her breathing labored from running up three flights of stairs. She took a deep breath, trying to slow down her heart rate. A drop of sweat trailed down her spine and she shivered as she wondered what the hell she had been thinking, walking into the warehouse alone. Being fearless was one thing; being stupid was quite another, and she was treading on thin ice with the latter.

She leaned up against the wall and listened for any sound that might lead her in the right direction of the action. She stealthily made her way through the building, moving from room to room. The warehouse was large, and she was unsure if she was even going in the right direction. She knew there were individuals in the building, but where?

She could still hear the voice of the caller. "You'll

want to be there," the caller had insisted. "Trust me." She had chuckled at the last part—trust a faceless caller? She wasn't born yesterday. But there was something about the voice that gave Harley an itch she needed to scratch. The caller had specifically called her phone. What had she meant when she said Harley would want to see what was going down at the warehouse? It had sounded so personal, and yet, how could it possibly be?

She had to wonder if this had something to do with the drug case that had blown up in their faces. They needed a break like this. She still wanted vengeance for Sam's death. If she could bring down the man responsible for Sam's death, then maybe she could let go of everything.

Harley moved past the hall and through another doorway. Fear was a normal part of her job, and she thrived on that feeling and the alertness that it offered her as long as she didn't allow herself to succumb to it. Something was different this time—her senses felt it. Something was about to happen. She wished she had some control over her heart as it beat like a jackhammer in her chest. She also wished that she had control over Chris answering his phone. They were off-duty, sure, but usually he answered her call no matter what.

She quickly checked her watch. Her backup was still fifteen minutes away. She hoped that they got there sooner than that. She was not afraid to admit that she was scared shitless.

She took a deep breath. She could feel it in the air—the danger, the very thing that was causing her adrenaline to spike. She crept along the wall toward another doorway that would lead her to the center of the room. Her gun was drawn, and she could hear voices, the mumbled curses of two people arguing.

She rolled her body away from the door. Muffled shouts rang out—an argument on the other side of the door. She grabbed the knob of the door, feeling the cold steel against her sweaty palm. She turned it slowly, trying not to make a sound. When she opened the door, she moved through it quickly, her handgun drawn in front of her. The room was empty.

Scaling the wall, she made her way down another long corridor. The warehouse was a bloody maze. At the end of it, there was a massive open space filled with boxes. It looked like a loading dock. She stopped moving suddenly, as she heard the voices again. She was heading in the right direction. She quickly entered the room, moving behind a tower of boxes. She leaned against the boxes, composing herself. By the sounds of things, the meeting was not going well. There were two men talking, and one of the voices sounded very familiar to her. She cocked her ear to hear better, trying to determine if she knew the guy. She recognized the voice, but she couldn't place whose it was. A smile formed on her face as she realized that one of the men was involved in their drug case. She couldn't quite make out the other man. Every nerve in her body was firing, not allowing her to concentrate on the sound of the voice.

"What the fuck do you think you are trying to pull here? This was not what we agreed on."

"Well, the risk is much too high for me, as you well know. If you want the money, then you will do things my way."

The man laughed, but no joy came from the laughter. "Do you really think you are in any position to make demands? You're lucky I don't kill you right here and take everything."

Harley looked up toward the ceiling, wishing Chris was by her side. She could always count on him in a jam, and they were always able to get through anything together.

"You won't, though; you need me."

She leaned to the right and glanced around her tower of boxes toward the back of the warehouse. The angry man was arguing with his colleague in front of a Mercedes with the truck popped open. She couldn't get a good look at the angry man; he was turned away from her. She also couldn't see what was inside the truck, but what else could it be? Drugs. Sam was murdered over those very drugs. Dressed casually, the other man held a briefcase and he had his back to her. She squinted her eyes trying to get a better look.

She needed to move closer. Doing so, however, would mean announcing her presence, and she wasn't sure if she was ready for that. Could she even get a shot off at that range?

The man was yelling in the face of the man holding the briefcase. He was pissed, his face beet red from anger. She watched as he pointed his finger at the other guy's face.

It was as good a time as any for her to make her move as they had their complete attention on one another. She moved fast toward the men. As she moved closer, she vaguely recognized the man holding the briefcase, but her focus was on the angry man.

The man yelling turned toward her in surprise. He went for his gun.

"Freeze. I *will* shoot. Freeze," Harley screamed. He hesitated, unsure of whether he should shoot her down. He fired and she hit the ground and rolled. She raised up on her forearms and fired back. The man grabbed the briefcase from his colleague and ran to the back of the building.

She launched herself off the floor and ran toward the far end of the building. She fired off a couple of rounds, hoping to get him to pause. "Freeze, you sonofabitch!"

She was so focused on the him that she almost didn't see as the other man turn around and swing a gun toward her. She turned to him and shock coursed through her.

"Jesus Christ, Chris!"

"Harley, I didn't want it to be you," he cried out.

Shaking, she steadied her gun on him. Staring at him was like looking at a ghost. She knew damn well there had been something familiar about him, but she would never have been able to imagine her partner talking to a drug runner. "What the fuck, Chris. You're involved?"

He had a pained looked on his face. "I'm sorry. Fuck, Harley, what are you doing here?"

"I got a call, and someone told me to come here."

Confusion etched his face, and she knew exactly what he was feeling.

She shook her head. "What about Sam? You might as well have killed her yourself. How could you do this? Just tell me why?"

"Harley, I didn't kill her. You have to believe me. It tore me apart that she died."

"You could have stopped it."

"I couldn't. They would have killed me."

"Why didn't you tell me? I could've helped you. We could have got through it together."

"No, I was not involving you in this. Jesus, Harley, don't you get it? I would never risk your life for this, or your chance at the detective's exam. You deserve this. I couldn't get you mixed up in this."

Tears of anger welled up in her eyes. She hated him for leaving her out—for taking away her chance to get him out of the mess. She would have done anything for him.

"We're partners. We protect each other."

"And this is me protecting you. Now shoot me."

"What?"

He brought his gun up and leveled it right at her chest. He wouldn't shoot her. "Shoot me."

"What? Are you crazy? I can't. Lower your gun; I'm taking you in. We will clear this up at the station."

"Shoot me," he screamed, his face contorted angrily. "I swear to God, Harley, if you don't shoot me, I'll shoot you. I can't go down for this."

"I'm not doing it; I won't. We can work this out."

He laughed. "There's nothing to work out, and you know it. Just end this. You know damn well what happens to a cop in prison. I'm not going there. I'll be brutalized, tortured, killed. We have all heard the stories."

"We can protect you."

He laughed and it was filled with bitterness. "You suck at lying, Harley."

"There has to be another way."

"Stop it, Harley. I'm not talking about it. You need to shoot me. I mean it."

"I can't."

He raised his gun and fired a shot that zoomed past her head. Shocked, she fired back twice, shooting Chris point blank in the chest. He dropped to the floor and she rushed to his side. His shirt was turning a bright red. She placed her hand on his wound and applied pressure. She pulled open her phone and dialed the number for her captain.

"Captain, I need a bus. Officer down!" She was trying not to yell as she gave him the address. She quickly hung up the phone.

"Chris, please. I'm sorry. Don't die on me." There was so much blood and the sight of it scared her. She looked down at him and was surprised to find a smile on his face.

"You were too good to me, Harley. I didn't deserve you. I loved you…" He slowly closed his eyes and stopped breathing. He was gone. She stared at him, too shocked to move. No, he couldn't be gone. She was still putting pressure on his wound, looking down at him, willing him just to be sleeping.

She glanced toward where the other man had gone, knowing that she should be chasing him down. She couldn't move. Blood pooled around Chris, and she couldn't help but stare at it. Why did she have to shoot him? She had killed him, and she wished more than anything that she hadn't. She loved him.

A scream tore from her throat as she heard the sirens in the distance.

FOUR

RIPPED OUT OF SLEEP, HARLEY screamed. She clutched her chest, feeling a searing pain that she had thought had long faded. She had been terribly wrong. There was an ache inside her she couldn't quite push out. The dream had been so real, so raw. She shivered involuntarily, wishing she could forget the whole dream. It wasn't just a dream, though; it was her whole life. She wasn't sure she would ever be able to escape that part of her life.

"Harley, are you all right?"

She looked around, unsure of her surroundings. She was on the beach; she must have fallen asleep while she was tanning. Suddenly embarrassed, she blushed as a few people walked by, looking at her strangely. She turned to find Craig staring at her in shock. God, he was gorgeous. The epitome of a surfer boy, with shaggy blonde hair and crystal blue eyes—the kind of eyes that you could stare into all day. His body was lean and muscled, tanned from many days out in the sun. Craig was her lover; she had been sleeping with him since she had arrived on the island.

They had met at a bonfire party on the beach, something that seemed like a regular thing on the island. He had been on the island for months while she was new to the area. He had walked toward her with a purpose, and when he approached her, he said, "I have not been able to take my eyes off you all night." It had been simple and she had smiled back at him. She spent the night in his room at the hotel and they had been inseparable ever since.

He was exactly what she needed at that moment: a distraction from her old life. The sex sure didn't hurt either. They met up from time to time, and she often found comfort with him during the nights she couldn't sleep. He had traveled to Phuket Island alone just like she had, and he made friends with some of the locals.

They had met up that day at the beach, and after spending some time in the sun, she must have dozed off. He was staring at her like she lost her mind. She couldn't blame him; one minute she had been sleeping on the beach, and the next she was screaming wildly like a madwoman. She couldn't seem to run from her past; it kept finding her, no matter how far she ran. She had run pretty far too. She was beginning to think she wouldn't be able to outrun her past any longer.

"I'm sorry, it was just a nightmare. I didn't even know I fell asleep."

"It's my fault. I left for a bit to get us some drinks. That was one hell of a dream; are you sure you're okay?"

"Yes, I think so."

As her heart rate slowed down, she took in her surroundings. She was sitting on a towel on one of the most beautiful beaches in Thailand. Harley wiped at her brow, noting that her skin was red hot. Panicked, she examined her naturally pale skin and noticed it was a tad too pink for her liking. She hadn't meant to fall asleep; she had been sunbathing while reading. Her sun-scorched skin would need a little TLC now. She laid back down on the towel and covered her face with her hands. Groaning, she cursed herself for foolishly falling asleep in the sun. Even with sunscreen on, the hot Thailand sun was no match for her fair complexion.

While her eyes were closed, images of Chris's dead body at her feet flashed across her mind, and it made her want to weep. The dream was still there in her mind, and she wondered if there would come a time when the dreams would just go away. Maybe her friends and family had been right—therapy may have been a better option than fleeing the country.

"Are you sure you're okay?"

"Yes, Craig, just give me a minute."

She had traveled all the way to Thailand on an extended leave from work. She had felt lost, and she had come to Thailand to find herself—is that why everyone came to Thailand?

There had been a police hearing before she left to determine whether she was at fault for the shooting. It was an emotional nightmare and as soon as it was over and she was found innocent, she had packed her bags and fled. She needed the time to decide if she even wanted to be a cop anymore. She was supposed to take her detective exam, but she wasn't sure if she wanted to any longer. The shock of the shooting had taken its toll on her, and she wasn't sure if she wanted to return to the force or if her leave of absence was going to be a permanent one. What happened in that warehouse that night changed her, possibly forever. She believed in a system of right and wrong, and she trusted the people around her. Everything she thought she believed in had been a lie. She didn't know who to trust any longer or what the force even meant to her at that point.

She had since been trying to remove those thoughts from her mind. She couldn't think about the shooting again. She would give anything to have a partial lobotomy to remove that whole night from her mind. At least then she might get a good night's sleep. She couldn't even remember the last time she slept through the night. Things were getting better in Thailand, however; it was like being in another world entirely, and that was what she needed most of all—to disappear. She smiled as she remembered her first few days in Thailand.

She had arrived in Bangkok a few weeks earlier,

and it had been one hell of a ride. As soon as she had walked off the bus, she knew she couldn't stay in Bangkok. The culture shock alone was enough to send her troubled mind reeling: the lights, the noise, and the overwhelming smells that made her think of the color brown. She had arrived in the middle of the night, and the air still held tightly to the humidity of the day. It was easily the hottest place she had ever traveled to. The night was alive, however, and it was as if no one ever slept. It was a mental assault like nothing she ever experienced. She ended up ordering cheap Pad Thai dishes and crashed early. She was nervous that she had just added to her troubles rather than escaping them.

Aside from the great deals, though, the city itself was sensory overload. There were street carts everywhere, with vendors that tried to peddle her anything from sex toys to cooked eel. She couldn't imagine buying eel from a street cart. Just walking through the streets, her nose was assaulted with smells, and she couldn't tell what she was smelling half the time. Was that fish sauce or car fumes? Neither, just the latest cologne. The different smells overloaded her brain causing her nose to tingle; she couldn't take the time to decide if she even liked the smell.

Taxi cabs also came in every color imaginable, which she found confusing especially when one time she had slid into the back of a gentleman's car that wasn't even a cab.

Just before she went searching for a car, she ordered food. The best part about Thailand was the cheap food that you could get right on the street. As an American, you could certainly feel rich there with very little money. Their currency was in baht, and 35 baht—which worked out to about one U.S. dollar—could get you some pretty delicious Pad Thai. On her first night, she ordered three without blinking an eye and devoured them until the last noodle was gone. A t-shirt from a vendor was three dollars, and you could haggle for just about anything.

After she had filled her belly, she went searching for a cab. She saw a bright pink car, an odd color she thought, but it caught her eye and she opened the back door and slid into the backseat. She smiled at the driver as he turned to look at her. Leaning her head against the back of the seat, she exhaled, really looking forward to getting on the beach.

"Ma'am?"

She opened her eyes and faced the driver who had turned around in his seat to face her. The look of confusion on his face caused her to sit up in her seat. She looked around the car for distinguishing marks of a taxi and found none.

"Oh, my."

"Are you lost?"

She blushed deeply. "Oh, this is embarrassing. I'm sorry, I thought this was a cab."

"Who are you?"

Harley looked over to find a young girl peering through the open window. She opened the door and slid into the backseat with Harley.

"I think the lady here thought she was in a cab." The driver laughed. "This is my daughter."

Harley laughed. "Well, it's a pleasure meeting you two."

"Can we offer you a ride somewhere?"

Harley shook her head. "No, thank you. I think I've taken up enough of your time already." She quickly scooted out of the other side of the car, her face burning with embarrassment. When she shut the door behind her, she stood on the sidewalk shaking her head.

"Now what?" She said as she looked around for a cab.

Just one night in Bangkok had made her realize she would need to head to another area of Thailand if she had any hope of truly finding herself, as she wouldn't find it in Bangkok.

She decided to stay one night in the city to figure out her next step. She had stayed in a shitty hotel that had walls as thin as paper, and they barely reached the ceiling. She laid in bed wide awake for most of the night wondering if she would be robbed. The travel agent insisted that she purchase some fancy bag alarms to put on all her luggage. Her entire life for the next few months was in those bags, and she couldn't risk having anything stolen. Not that it mattered, though; she didn't sleep a wink during her first night.

The first thing the next morning, however, she planned on getting on a boat and heading to an island called Costa Mui, which was not far from Bangkok. A boat was the only way to the island, and what an island it was supposed to be. She thought it would just be a matter of hitching a boat ride to the island, but the experience had been laughable at best. There were no taxis that went that far so she had to barter with the locals. It took jumping into the back of a truck with a few backpackers to get on her way. They were all hanging on the back of the truck without a care in the world, legs swaying through the air.

The view was rustic and the breeze tousled her hair as the truck drove through the lush jungle. They rode like that for a half an hour before they reached their destination. There were fishermen who traveled back and forth to the island and tourists would get rides with them. The fishermen often lived in the huts on the beaches and did their fishing early in the morning. Sitting on the boat, she watched the island slowly come into view, thinking to herself that she had never seen anything so beautiful in all her life. God, that was really the life—sitting there taking in the absolute beauty of the world around her. She couldn't have chosen a better place to visit. She had needed to disappear, so the islands were the best place to do so. The island beaches were covered with huts, and the beach itself was the most incredible beach she had ever seen. White sand as far as the eye could see, and the water shimmered like sea glass.

When the boat arrived in Costa Mui, people piled off and immediately made a beeline for the beach. There was a large wooden staircase that led down to the beach; it wasn't the kind of staircase you would want to maneuver down while drunk. Exhausted from her travels, she walked slowly down those stairs, in awe of the stunning scenery that surrounded her. It looked like a peaceful place to relax. The moment she turned her head to the right, her mouth dropped open as she saw thousands of people down on the beach. She did not expect to see so many people and only one word could describe the scene before her: NAKED! There were topless women everywhere. All you saw, for the most part, were bikini bottoms, as far as the eye could see. To avoid being blinded by all the skin, she focused on the lodgings. Judging by all the huts on the beach, she knew there wouldn't be an issue with finding somewhere to stay—they were everywhere. In fact, as soon as her feet hit the sand, there was a group of girls that walked up to her and asked if she needed somewhere to stay. They told her how to get in touch with the man who ran the huts. But the first thing Harley did was step into the cool water. She set her luggage off to the side and sat there, letting the ocean erase the last remaining stress of her past life. Things were going to be different for her—she knew that the moment she arrived in Thailand. She couldn't remember how long she had sat like that before going off to find somewhere to sleep.

She had decided to go to the hotel that resided at the top of the wooden staircase. There were a few people on the beach that were staying there, and it sounded like an amazing place. Sometimes the beach parties could go on all night, the people said, and besides, the hotel had a spa. That was all she had needed to hear to change her mind about the hut life.

It was to the hotel that she needed to go now to nurse her sunburn. She stood up and picked up her towel, shaking the sand out of it. She was finally used to all the naked women that walked the beaches. The Europeans always seemed to be the freest about taking off their tops.

Yes, it had been an experience. Looking up, she smiled. There wasn't a cloud in the sky, which explained the mild burn that she was experiencing. It was probably a good thing that she finally got some color.

"We need to get you out of the sun."

She glanced at Craig, realizing that she had been so lost in thought, she had forgotten that he was there with her.

She folded the towel and stretched lazily. She took a final look around, wondering how on earth her terrible past could haunt her in a place like that.

"What do you say we get something to eat?"

She cringed. "Actually, I think I'd rather just go

back to my room and have a bath." She felt a wave of exhaustion after being in the sun all day, and she yawned unabashedly. It would do her good to soak her sore body in the tub and order in some room service.

"C'mon, we can snuggle up together later. It will be fun."

She stared at him, knowing that things had gone too far. "I thought we were just keeping things casual; I told you in the beginning that it was all I wanted. Ya know, taking it day by day. It's really all I can deal with right now."

His brow furrowed. "Yeah, that was weeks ago, and things have been great. I just thought you might change your mind."

She shrugged, unsure of what else to say. She couldn't offer him anything more at that moment.

He sighed. "A beer and some dinner will make you feel much better, I promise. I'm meeting a couple of friends, and I think you would like them."

"You want me to go out for dinner? Oh, Craig, I'm beat."

"C'mon, I will make it up to you. How about I give you a nice massage after dinner?"

A slow smile spreads across her face. "Well, I guess that wouldn't be so bad. But you have to at least let me shower and change."

"Deal."

He grasped her hand, and they headed down the beach.

FIVE

HARLEY HELD HER BREATH AS she walked with Craig. They approached a group of people surrounding a bonfire, and laughter filled the air. She was a little nervous about meeting new people, even though she had hung out with a few groups since she arrived. The weather was not too hot, which made the bonfire the perfect addition to the day's end. All eyes were on her as they approached the group, and she plastered on an awkward smile.

"Hey guys, I want you to meet Harley. She is a New York City cop. She's here on an extended vacation for a few months."

There were plenty of smiles to make her feel instantly comfortable as she shook hands. Craig introduced her to a couple, Devon and Melissa, who looked like they were together but that was only because of their constant bickering. She felt the tension between them, however, and wondered if they weren't protesting a bit much.

Melissa had a mess of brown, wild curls that seemed to have a mind of their own and beautiful brown eyes. Her skin was the color of molasses, and Harley marveled at her beauty. She was giving puppy dog eyes to Devon, who seemed completely oblivious to them.

Craig pointed at Devon who was looking at her with interest while sitting beside Melissa. Devon looked like he spent a lot of time in the gym—he was possibly even a steroid junkie—but he had a warm smile that matched his warm brown eyes. "These two really should be together," Craig said, "but they just won't listen to us."

"Your hair is kewel, Har-ley," Devon said. "You should join us for dinnah."

"Don't pressure her, Devon, she's just met us." Melissa turned her attention to Harley. "Don't mind him, girl."

Harley smiled. She sensed that Melissa didn't want another pretty girl around. Not that she could blame her. Devon had that bad boy vibe about him, and she could bet his eyes strayed a little more than Melissa would have liked. Earlier, Craig had filled her in on the group. Although Melissa was trying to claim him, the two hadn't been hanging out for more than a month. Devon was from Australia while Melissa was vacationing from Spain. They both had great accents that made Harley want to just sit there and listen to them talk all day long. While Melissa was taking time off from work stress, Devon often traveled and wrote articles on his travel blog. He spent a lot of his time during the year traveling from place to place.

Craig continued the introductions. "And this is Katie and Brian who are here on their honeymoon."

Katie was petite in every sense of the word. She had pretty green eyes and blonde hair that was pulled up into a high ponytail. Her husband, Brian, was bald with a lean physique and eyes so dark that they almost looked black.

Harley waved at them. "Congratulations. It's definitely a great place for a honeymoon. How are you enjoying it?"

"Thank you," Katie said. "We've been having a blast. We almost don't want to go back home."

Brian squeezed her hand. "Now, now Katie, you know you are dying to start unwrapping all those gifts."

The group laughed, and Craig moved on, pointing out a girl that was sitting alone. She was a beautiful girl, lanky with blonde hair cut into a pixie style. She had icy blue eyes that just seemed to pull you in. She looked more like a rock star then someone on a beach hiatus. Harley appreciated her cool look; she would never be brave enough to cut her hair so short, but the girl pulled it off well, and the style made her look hot. She had a sleeve tattoo of water lilies and a few themed pieces from *Alice in Wonderland*. It made Harley smile when she saw the Cheshire cat. Keri had the kind of overall style that might suggest to a guy that she was kinky. "This is Keri," Craig said. "Katie's sister."

"Yes, it's true. I hijacked my sister's honeymoon."

"Well, I knew if I left you at home alone, you would get back together with that idiot," Katie said with a laugh.

Keri stuck out her tongue and said, "Love is blind, what can I say. The guy was an animal in the bedroom, and that's not an easy thing to find."

"Too much information," squealed Katie. The two sisters couldn't be more opposite, and Harley liked Keri immediately. Craig had told her that Keri had a problem with bad boys and always got tangled up with the wrong guy. Her sister was often saving her from those relationships. Harley could totally relate to what she was going through. She was surprised that Keri wasn't going for the bad boy Devon; he seemed like her perfect match.

"Cool. Well, it's great to meet all of you," Harley said as she sat down in front of the fire. She loved the smell of a bonfire. She could sit there all day long, smelling the burning wood and feeling the heat against her skin.

Keri stood up and approached Harley. "We were thinking of doing some surfing before the sun sets. What do you say?"

"I'd say, I'm probably going to end up on my ass. I've never tried it, but I'm certainly willing to," Harley said with a laugh.

Devon stood up and pulled Melissa up with him. "Great. We just need one thing first, mate," he said with a devilish chuckle.

They all stared at a sign that read in bold: *Mushrooms Inside*. Harley looked at Craig with incredulity before laughing. "You guys have got to be kidding me." They were standing on the staircase that led up to the hotel. The sign was pointing to the restaurant that stood beside the hotel. The local authorities typically looked away when it came to the tourists because they brought so much money to the island. She hadn't expected them to post the sign in such a manner; it was so blatantly exposed.

"Oh, but we're not. Nothing beats surfing while on mushrooms. If you haven't tried it before, Harley, then you're in for a ride."

"And they just post the sign out in the open like this?"

"Well, it's just a mushroom, Harley," Craig said with a wink. Harley slapped his ass playfully as they all made their way up to the restaurant. She had no idea what to expect. Aside from doing a little weed in high school, Harley had never done a hallucinogenic before. She was assured that mushrooms were the "friendly" drug, and she need not worry about any stints in rehab.

Keri saddled up to Harley. "Is the cop nervous?"

Harley grinned. "I think I'll survive." She moved

closer to Craig. "So, what should I expect to feel?"

"Like the world is yours for the taking. You will feel so free—that's why surfing is perfect for the buzz."

They wanted to enjoy what was left of the sun, so they all sat out on the patio. Harley wanted to order a beer but thought better of it. She wasn't sure what to expect from the hallucinogenic. When the waiter came, Devon mentioned the mushrooms and a different menu was placed before them. Harley opened the menu, surprised to see so many options before her.

Just then there was a commotion at the hostess table and Harley glanced over. A devilishly handsome man was getting a hug from the owner of the restaurant. The woman gripped the man around his waist tightly, and Harley could hardly blame her. The guy was insanely hot. He was obviously a regular to the area. Harley wondered what circles he partied in.

"Rayland, you're back! How long are you here for?"

"Oh, I'm not leaving anytime soon, so don't you worry, darling."

Harley smirked. The man's charm was certainly compelling; he must wheel the ladies in without a problem.

"Are you staying at the hotel again?"

"Yes, of course, it's like my second home. Do you have my usual table ready?"

"You're in luck, sir; it's open for the evening."

Harley watched as the man was led to a table where he sat down.

"Harley?"

Startled, she turned to see Craig looking at her with his eyebrows raised. "Sorry, sometimes I'm like a squirrel who sees a shiny object."

Devon chuckled, and she winked at him.

"Oh, my God, you can get them in an omelet," Katie said, laughing.

"Seriously? Oh, I'm all over that. This is my lucky daaey," Devon replied.

Harley realized that the gang was looking at the mushroom options on the menu. She glanced at the menu, forgetting about the handsome man at the next table.

"Really?" Harley asked as she perused the tea options.

"Yeah, why not, mate? How bad could it be?"

When the waiter returned, Devon opted for the omelet while everyone else ordered their mushrooms in a tea. She found it odd that Devon would even attempt to add a hallucinogenic to his meal. But maybe he was right—how bad could it be?

"Maaaate, I am hungry," Devon said, rubbing his stomach.

Melissa shook her head. "I think you are going to have some serious regrets, babe." Harley looked up to see the waiter approaching with their order. She hoped that she wasn't going to have regrets herself. When the waiter set down the omelet in front of Devon, all eyes were on it. It wasn't so much an omelet as it was a couple of eggs scrambled with jet-black, soggy, and slimy mushrooms in the middle. Harley's gaze slowly met Devon's, and he gave her a sheepish smile.

The sight brought on Harley's gag reflex; the omelet was the least appetizing thing that she had ever laid eyes on. All eyes looked to Devon with pity as he stared down at his plate. He picked away at it with his fork. The waiter then set down a pot of tea and placed cups before the rest of the group. There was a smell coming from the pot that didn't help the nausea coiling inside Harley's stomach. She took the top off the pot, and it was crammed full of soggy mushrooms. She looked up to find the same sad look on the faces of everyone at the table.

"Geez, this sure doesn't look much better," she said.

"Well, at least we don't have to eat the mushrooms," Devon responded.

Devon groaned. "Why did I follow my stomach into despair?"

The table burst out in laughter.

"I certainly wouldn't want to be eating that—at least ours is only tea," Harley said.

"Come on, Harley, you wouldn't share this omelet with me?" Devon said with a wink.

"No way in hell," she said with a laugh.

"Hey, are you flirting with my girl?" Craig called out, and Harley blushed deeply.

"Crikey! Oh, I would never," Devon said with a chuckle.

Harley took the pot and poured what looked like muddy water into her cup. The smell was worse than vomit. She took a tentative sip; it tasted terrible, but she was thankful it was just broth. She could chug it if it came down to that. Devon, on the other hand, started shoveling the mush into his mouth, following it with gulps of water. She thought he might vomit right there at the table.

"I can't even chew on them; I just have to get them in there."

Craig chuckled. "I don't know how you're doing it, man. That looks so nasty."

"It's like having something alive on your tongue, mate," Devon said as he shoveled another mouthful in. He grabbed his glass of water and chugged a few mouthfuls down. Harley couldn't believe he was finishing the meal. She shuddered and downed her tea as quickly as possible. She was truly grateful that she didn't have to ingest any of the mushrooms. Devon never looked happier than after his plate was clean. He was the first to get up from the table. "Let's head back to the beach, guys, and wait for these babies to kick in."

They all filtered out of the restaurant, Devon looking a little greener than he did when he went in. When they arrived back on the beach, they surrounded the bonfire once again. Harley found the walk to the beach a surreal experience—the hallucinogenic was starting to take effect. A tiny Danish girl approached their group with a football in her hands. All she was wearing was a black bikini bottom. She had long wild blonde hair and a wide smile on her face. She was one of the sexiest girls Harley had seen on the beach that day, and she only had eyes for Devon. Harley slowly shook her head as Devon launched himself off his seat and went off to play catch with her. Harley glanced at Melissa who watched them with a narrowed gaze.

The girl motioned for Devon to throw the ball to her, and when he did, she launched herself at it in an attempt to do a header with the ball. Harley and Craig laughed at the crazy girl who threw herself into the surf to go after the ball. She was totally uninhibited; it was as if she had no idea that she was topless.

"Well, the girl is certainly a free-spirit." Harley laughed. It was then that she started to feel something just behind her vision. She watched as Craig and Brian started putting together surfboards and wetsuits. She hoped she wasn't about to make a fool of herself in front of everyone, but she was pretty excited to try surfing. She slowly got up from her seat and dressed in a wetsuit that Craig handed to her. As she turned around to face the water, her jaw dropped to the ground as she saw a large elephant come walking out of the ocean. She gasped as she took a few steps back in alarm and stumbled into Craig.

"Are you okay, Harley?" he said with a smile.

She pointed to the ocean, but there was nothing there. Harley started to giggle, unable to control the feeling. She could barely contain all the giggles. "Oh,

God. What the hell are we in for here, guys?"

Craig came up behind her and wrapped his arms around her waist. "I see the effects have already hit you. What did you see?"

"An elephant," she whispered.

He chuckled. "Let's go."

With a surfboard under her arm, she ran into the surf with her new friends, feeling more at home with them than she had in some time. It was nice to feel like she belonged somewhere again. When she had first arrived in Thailand, she had thought she just wanted to be alone, to escape her past, but that wasn't what she wanted at all.

She had never been surfing before, but she was strong, and she learned quickly. She paddled her way into the surf and sat on the board while she watched the others try to catch waves. The moves seemed to be more about balance and the movement of the body. She looked over her shoulder and saw the elephant swimming toward them. She broke out into a fit of giggles and took in her scenery. Everything seemed brighter and richer in color.

"Harley, come on!" Craig called out. She paddled her way over to him and hopped up onto the board, feeling shaky at first. She tumbled off the board, hearing laughter as she went down. She broke out of the water, laughing, and got back up on the board. She paddled into the surf again, and just when a wave was about to break, she jumped on the board and caught it.

"I did it!" she screamed. She heard clapping around her, and she couldn't remember the last time she had felt so alive. After riding the wave, she pulled herself up on the board and sat to catch her breath and to watch the others catch their waves. It was possible she found her new passion.

Butcher watched Harley catching her waves; she was such an intriguing person. She sat on the board with a proud look on her face, and she had never looked more beautiful. The people that he hung around with at the beach didn't know him—not the real him—and they called him by a different name. He didn't let just anyone see his true nature.

Harley was different from all the other foolish girls that traipsed around the beach half-naked. Her hair looked electrifying against the blue of the ocean. That red—he hadn't been able to take his eyes off her. From the moment that he first saw her on the island, he knew that he had to get close to her. She was stunning, there was no doubt about that, but that wasn't what drew him to her. There was a vulnerability there that ran deep. He had a feeling that she was just like his mother. He felt that she was running from something like his mother ran from him. He was really getting to know her, but she could be a vault at times. Her soul was damaged, and he wanted to feed on it.

He had been watching her all day, the way she took a swig of her beer or brushed the hair out of her eyes, and he was mesmerized by her bottom as she ran ahead into the surf. He couldn't take his eyes off her, and he knew he had to claim her and watch her bleed. She had a lot of spirit, a magnetism, and he wanted to take that from her. He wanted her to beg for her life like he imagined his mother would beg for hers. Out of the corner of his eye, he saw one of the island guards patrolling the beach. He saw them occasionally, but they were nothing more than glorified mall cops. The real authority was in the city, and police rarely came to the island. They didn't want to disturb the tourists having their fun. He felt safe to do his work here; he had been doing it for months.

He was a much bigger monster than people could even imagine—they thought there were bigger things to fear on the island. He didn't feel, not like normal people did; he didn't experience love, compassion, empathy or shame. He didn't have the ability to bestow kindness upon a person. He had been that way for as long as he could remember, he was born strange. His teachers in grade school had often whispered about him, calling him "odd." He could hear them as he lingered outside of the teacher's lounge. They called him that because he stared too long at people—uncomfortably long. It was just his way of figuring them out, looking for their weak spot. He learned quickly, though, that he needed a mask or he would be found out. He needed to blend in, act like everyone else. It was important to not bring attention to himself. So, he did just that; it was all just an act, a persona. His whole life was just a front, a mask to allow him to do what he really wanted.

As a child about to go through puberty, he had always been fixated on living things, but not in the way that a normal person would. He liked to see things bleed; it was the only thing that relaxed him enough to sleep at night. Sometimes he would get the worst headaches. Blindingly painful. They wouldn't go away until he saw the blood; it brought him peace. Sure, he could go a few days without doing anything, but then the rage and headaches would build up so bad that he would lie awake at night in pain.

It started off with bugs—lighting them on fire or pulling their legs off. But it wasn't enough—it didn't elicit the right excitement and there was no blood. It wasn't long before he moved on to animals to feed his need.

His mother was the one person who got close enough to figure out what he really was.

He remembered a time they had gone fishing together, long after his father was out of the picture. They had sat talking early in the morning, waiting for the fish to bite. A cup of hot coffee in hand, his mother could chat his ear off, as she was used to having a lot of attention. She was a beauty queen stunner and always had a man on her arm. Ever since his father had left, though, she had never been willing to settle down again. She was happy just raising her son and going on the occasional date. He had liked to watch her shower when she had no idea that he was watching her. He would watch her steamy silhouette through the glass doors of the shower and wonder if she ever let random men touch her.

That day fishing, he remembered how she had clapped her hands excitedly when he caught his first fish. He reeled it in and took it off the hook. She was searching around excitedly for her phone to take the traditional fish picture and all he could do was stare down at the fish and think about whether it bled. It was all that consumed his mind, to the point that he forgot his mother was there. He picked up the hook and slowly pushed it into the fish's eye, hearing a satisfying squish. The fish flopped around and he wondered if it felt fear as well as pain. It was then that he realized his mother was standing beside him.

"Honey, what in heaven's name are you doing?"

The question hung in the air as he looked up at her—the question didn't matter, it was the look that she had in her eyes, the uneasiness that crossed her face. The phone dangled at her side, the picture forgotten. It was then that she knew something was a little off with him. He had smiled his sweet smile and stood up, acting as if everything was normal, but there were a few times that he caught her looking at him from the corner of her eye.

After that day, he quickly moved up to animals, but he tried to keep his acts on the down low. When the neighbor's dog went missing, she walked into the living room while he was on the couch reading a book. She asked him if he knew anything about it. When he shook his head, acting shocked to find out the neighbor's precious dog was gone, she had stared at him with a look he didn't recognize.

She had shocked him, however, when she said, "Where is the dog, son? I'm only going to ask you once."

"But, I don't…"

"Just show me where the dog is. We'll bring it back and no one will know."

He had stared at her then for a beat, wondering if she knew him better than he had thought. He got up from the couch and went to put his shoes on at the door. She followed him silently out the door. He made his way to the shed in the backyard. His mother hadn't been in there since his father left, as she had no reason to go there.

He unlocked the shed and looked behind him at his mother, whose eyebrows were raised. It was the smell that hit her first when he opened the door, and her hand flew to her nose in revulsion.

He found it almost humorous that she had believed he had kept the dog alive somewhere, as if he wanted a pet. They walked inside and the light from outside shone on the dismembered corpse of the dog that he had on the workman's table. The blood was the most magnificent part, and it was everywhere. It seeped deep into the table and dripped onto the floor. He had meant to clean it all up, but he had grown too excited by his work. There were limbs in a wheelbarrow, along with what was left of the fur, all matted with blood. The head was severed from its body and laid on the floor. He smiled slightly and turned to face his mother. There were tears in her eyes, and a few had slipped down her cheeks. She still held her hand to her mouth and there was a stunned, foreign look in her eyes that he didn't recognize. He expected her to say something, but she just turned from the massacre and shut the door behind her.

He moved to the dirty shed window and watched her walk away. She hurried back into the house, and he wondered if she was calling the police. He turned back to his prize and made haste in cleaning it up into garbage bags.

He had spent the whole day burying the parts in the forest behind their house and disinfecting the shed as best he could. He kept expecting to hear sirens in the distance, but they never came.

He eventually went back into the house and found his mother in the bedroom with the door closed. He didn't try to go inside; he just returned to his book and waited. After that day, she never hugged him anymore, and if he so much as grazed her with his hand, he got the feeling that she had to fight the urge not to shudder with revulsion. She knew that there was something wrong with her son. He wondered why she had never called the police that day. He knew he scared her now, but what was she going to do about it?

He often wondered if she thought about how her perfect genes could have possibly created such a monster. She was the town beauty queen; everyone had been shocked that she didn't go off to Hollywood. Instead, she has settled down with his father. But that was another lifetime. After the dog incident, they had slowly drifted apart, a certain understanding left between them. She would not tell on him, but he had to go. She had handed him a wad of bills when he was eighteen years old and told him he could never return home. A part of him had wanted to hurt her because of it, but he could always go back for her another time. Sometimes, when he killed women, he imagined it was her. He hadn't seen his mother in seventeen years.

He was startled back to reality by the sound of clapping around him as Harley made her first wave. Harley. He liked her. He licked his lips, thinking of his mother.

Pulling herself from the ocean took more effort than she had the energy for. The mushrooms had worn off, and her body was sore from her surfing experience. The group gathered around the dying fire to drink beer. Devon placed a few more pieces of wood into the fire. Harley stripped out of the bodysuit and felt a chill run through her. She curled into Craig's chest and felt the heat of his body radiate through her. She loved spending time with him, but every time she got close to him, she realized that she still felt empty. She chalked it up to the fact that she was damaged, and maybe she just needed a little time to adjust. He wrapped his arms around her and pulled her in tight.

She looked around the group as they conversed among one another. The day had been just short of perfect. The surfing, the drinks, the beach and even the experience of mushrooms had led to a fun-filled day that even included an elephant. For the first time in a while, she felt like things were going to be okay.

SIX

THAT EVENING HARLEY FOUND HERSELF sitting in a lounger on the balcony of Craig's hotel room. There was nothing more relaxing than sitting there and feeling the wind coming off the ocean. She closed her eyes and let the wind play with her red hair as the exhaustion from the day took its toll on her body. The evening was cool, and she was finally completely down from the mushrooms. It was going to be a long night, and Craig had promised her a backrub. She could use a good hard rub. Her arms felt like lead; she could barely lift them. Surfing was one hell of a workout. She was considering retiring for the evening in a bath instead of waiting for Craig. The day on the beach had left her bones weary, and she was still recovering from the burn she had received that day. She took a sip of wine while she waited for Craig to get out of the shower and join her. She was in pretty great shape for a girl of thirty but a day of surfing had totally kicked her ass.

Her phone buzzed, and she looked down at it and smiled.

Keri: You did so awesome today! Let's catch up on the beach again for drinks.

Keri had helped her a lot while they had been surfing. Without her help, she wouldn't have got much surfing done. She was a bright and complicated girl, and Harley was looking forward to hanging out with her some more. Keri wasn't pretentious or full of herself. She was genuine to the point that she had you laughing at all the cruel parts of life. They got along well, mainly because they had the same sense of humor. She quickly responded to the text and settled back in her chair. She thought about how similar Keri's love life was to hers—she always had man troubles it seemed, and she could never seem to attract the right man into her life.

While she sat there, she found herself in a reflective moment about Chris. Despite what she knew, she couldn't help the smile that crossed her face. He had been such a good man; that had never changed in her mind, and it probably never would. It was incredible what someone was capable of when they felt like they were backed into a corner. She couldn't relate because she would never have made the same decisions in life that Chris had, but she still couldn't fault him his mistakes. She just wished that he would have confided in her, and maybe if he had, things would have been different.

That was what hurt most about the situation—that he hadn't come to her when he felt desperate. She could have turned everything around, and they wouldn't have had the tragic ending that they did. She believed that they had been close—best friends, so much more than partners—and yet he had not come to her when he needed help. It was something that she struggled with daily, not being able to understand why she hadn't been enough for him. She wasn't sure how she was ever going to get past that. There was so much pain involved in her past and so many unanswered questions that would forever remain unanswered.

A smile played on her face as she remembered the huge crush she had on him, almost since the very beginning of working with him. He was completely oblivious to it, of course; she never told him because he was always dating some new girl and she didn't know if he ever thought of her as more than a partner. That was until the day they talked about the Netflix documentary when he had told her how much he appreciated her. She wondered then if he had feelings for her too. She always thought she would tell him eventually, but she just never got around to it. She almost had a chance one time, she remembered.

They had just got their morning coffee when he told her that he had broken things off with his latest girlfriend. Harley smiled as she remembered how happy she had been over the news. She was eager to be the next girl on his arm; she believed, after all, that they would have staying power.

"So, you cut her loose, did you?"

"Well, it wasn't meant to be."

Harley snickered. "Oh, where did you come up with that? You met her at a bachelor party, after all." She playfully touched his knee. She felt reckless like maybe she could finally tell him and they could be together.

He laughed. "Hey, hey that was all completely innocent."

"Yeah, sure it was." She knew this was her moment. She looked over at him and caught his eye. "So, there's this new rom-com out that is supposed to be really good with Sandra Bullock in it. Do you want to go and see it sometime?"

"Oh right. Yes, I heard about that. I'm actually going to it with this girl I met at the grocery store. Sorry, bud, maybe we can catch that movie with the Rock sometime."

"Well, that sure was fast."

He winked at her. "You gotta catch them when you can, Harley. You know me: I don't like to be single for too long."

Her heart sank, but she couldn't help but smile. It was just the way it was, and she had missed her shot. She could tell him how she felt regardless and he could change his mind about the new girl. But she was never entirely sure if he felt anything more for her than the love that came from two partners. She heard the resounding sound of him calling her "bud" in her head.

It was hard not to crush on a man like Chris. He was strong and handsome, and exactly the type of person you thought should be a cop. Chris was honorable and trustworthy and always put his job ahead of everything else, even the latest lady in his life. He believed in right and wrong and the pursuit of justice. He made her believe in the job, more so than before she decided to become a cop. He was the kind of guy you could look up to and believe in. At least, that's what she had thought. Her heart felt heavy. Chris wasn't who she thought he was, and she had a lot of guilt about not picking up on the fact that he was a dirty cop. She hated dirty cops.

Sipping her wine, she drifted into another memory that increased the smile on her face.

"I am not looking forward to talking to the captain; he sounded pissed on the phone," Harley said with a groan. "Like, what is his problem?"

"Harley, the man is always pissed about something. You just have to know how to handle him. Once we take the detective's exam, we will be on a whole new level. We won't be beat cops anymore. Just give it time and be patient."

"Well, it's hard to talk to a man with a perma-scowl. We are working our asses off, and he still has to harass us. It's hard not to take his attitude personal."

Chris was staring out the window at something she couldn't see. "Are you even listening to me?" she said with a chuckle.

"Hold on, Harley," he said as he pulled the squad car over to the side of the road. He turned off the ignition and stared out the window.

"What are you doing?"

"There's an old lady on the bench in the park, and she's crying."

She tried to see where he was looking. "What? Chris, we've been ordered back to headquarters asap. The captain is demanding an update, and he's already in a mood."

"Well, then it can hardly get worse, right?" He opened the driver's side door and closed it behind him. She watched from the cruiser as he made his way across the street toward the park. She couldn't believe her eyes as she watched him approach the woman. Chris sat down on the bench beside the senior woman and started talking to her. She wished she would have followed him just to see what he was saying to the woman. She looked so sad sitting there on the bench, and she hoped that she would be okay. If anyone could make a woman smile, it would be Chris. He could be very charming when he wanted to be. The little old lady had been looking down at the ground, and she suddenly looked up at Chris as he spoke.

She was in awe of Chris as she watched the scene unfold before her. He put an arm around the woman, comforting her as she cried. It was the most beautiful thing she had ever seen, and she had no idea that Chris had it in him. Her brow furrowed as she watched him take out his wallet and pull some money out of it. He handed it to the woman who burst into choking sobs. The senior woman took his hand in hers, and she cradled it, talking to him. He shook her hand slowly and then got up from the bench. He made his way back to the cruiser and opened the driver's side door. When he slid in, he didn't make eye contact with her. He started up the cruiser, and she sat there with her mouth hanging open.

"So? What happened out there? Is she going to be okay?"

"Some asshole took her purse. Snatched it while she was walking through the park. She is on a pension and lost her grocery money. I just gave her a hundred dollars. I swear if I saw the guy I would beat him to a pulp."

"He would deserve it. I can't believe you did that; it was amazing." She smiled as she saw his face go red. "Oh, don't start getting soft on me, Harley, it's just part of the job."

She smiled softly. "No, I think that was above and beyond the call of duty. You probably restored her faith in humanity, if not men."

He laughed. "I don't think anyone can restore faith in men. But hey, you can keep hoping, Harley."

"I won't hold my breath," she said as she stuck her tongue out at him.

The memory was a good one, and it was just more evidence that deep down there had been an extraordinary man in Chris, and she wondered at what point that had changed. What caused him to become a different man, one that she didn't recognize? What was worse, though, was that she hadn't noticed the change at all, and that disturbed her more than anything. It made her wonder if she could trust anything or anyone again. She had loved a man that she never really knew, and that was the worst sin of all. He had never known she had fallen for him, and maybe that had been her own fault. It was more than she could bear, and that was part of the reason why she had fled to Thailand. She was escaping a life that she couldn't bear to look at any longer.

Just then Craig walked out onto the balcony, looking fresh in a pair of cabana shorts and a t-shirt. Craig looked good, with his hair wet and those gorgeous eyes. If she weren't so sore, she would jump him. The thought made her a little sad, though, because she knew that her time with Craig was running out.

"Hey, beautiful, you look relaxed. Did you have a fun day today?"

She nodded. "I had a wonderful day, thank you. You have been really good to me since I have been here, Craig. I can't thank you enough."

"Devon sure liked you. He was all over you in the ocean. 'Helping' you to surf."

She was surprised by his tone. She had totally forgotten about Devon helping her back on the board when she wiped out. She never considered that Craig might get jealous. "He was just playing around. Does that bother you?"

"I think he might have a crush on you."

She laughed. "I think that's pushing it. He likes to

flirt, that's all. He also went after the topless girl on the beach. He's just having fun."

"I guess I don't like seeing other guys close to you."

She frowned. It certainly was a little soon for him to feel so possessive over her. "Well, you have been here longer than I have so you must know the people you are hanging around with."

"I probably met up with Devon and Melissa shortly after I got here. Keri, Katie, and Brian have been here just a few weeks. I think the newlyweds are probably returning home soon though."

"Yeah, the honeymoon can't last forever," she said with a laugh.

He sat down in his own lounger beside her and poured himself a glass of wine. He leaned back, looking completely at ease. His hand found hers in the space between them, and he clasped it tightly. She pulled away from him and sat up. She took a slow sip of the wine, not feeling much like getting close that evening.

"What's wrong?" he said, concern etched on his face.

She turned to him. "I'm actually really tired; I think I'm going to go back to my own room."

"What about the backrub? I can make you feel better."

"Sorry, Craig, it's been a long day and I just want to be alone right now."

His brow furrowed as she turned to walk away. She knew he was probably confused about her reaction to him; it's not like he had done anything wrong. Thinking about Chris had made her feel weird, and she realized that something was missing between her and Craig. She needed to start thinking about what she really wanted, and she wasn't sure if she still wanted to see Craig. She wasn't going to think about it right then, though; all she wanted to do was get some sleep.

SEVEN

HARLEY RETURNED HOME THAT EVENING and practically dropped into bed where she fell into a fitful sleep.

She had been standing in the warehouse facing the man she knew was responsible for the murder of Sam. She had stepped forward and screamed, "Freeze." Both of the men turned to her and fired at her. Moving to the side, she fired shots back. One of the men fled while the other turned to her. It was Chris, her partner, her friend, standing there, screaming at her to shoot him. She couldn't; she knew that she couldn't. He fired his weapon and the bullet went over her head. She shot him in the chest, and he dropped like a stone on the ground. Her heart started racing, and her hands shook. She couldn't believe her eyes. She ran toward Chris, collapsing to the ground and begging him to stay with her. Her gaze went to the body on the floor and she choked back the bile that rose in her throat. She stepped slowly toward the body, finally looking down at the face that she had practically memorized from the moment she had met him. Tears trailed down her cheeks as a sob rose up in her chest.

The man lying at her feet, blood pooling around him, was Chris—the man she had been crazy about, the man who had made her believe in justice more than she ever thought possible. She had trusted him more than anyone, had believed in him. He had betrayed her, betrayed his badge, and she didn't see it coming.

Glued to the spot, she couldn't have moved if she wanted to. She stared at the blood that she had spilled, knowing she had killed him. She wasn't capable of chasing after the other man; all she could do was stare skeptically at her dead friend. She knew now why he didn't answer her call, and she wondered at what point he had decided to be a different man. She looked at the dead eyes and didn't know the man that stared back at her. Her mind was reeling; she couldn't even begin to process her thoughts. From that moment, her life was forever changed. She could hear sirens in the distance—her backup was finally showing up. It was then that she started screaming and didn't know how to stop. Her body shook with the power of her screams, her whole soul pouring out through them. She laid her face on his chest unconcerned about the blood on her.

She could hear the men behind her pouring into the warehouse space.

"Harley!"

Silenced, she lay there shaking. The force had shown up to find her sprawled on the body of her dead partner.

"Harley, drop the gun and put your hands up where we

can see them."

She let the gun fall from her hand and land on the ground with a loud thud. She raised her hands and slowly turned toward them.

Startled from her dream, she lay in bed crying softly into her pillow. The dream was always slightly different, but dreams were like that, weren't they? The result was always the same. Chris was dead. Shooting Chris had almost killed her, even though she didn't have a choice. She was doing her job, and she lost everything because of it. He was her best friend; she had acted on instinct and it had killed him. Losing him had been the hardest thing she ever had to deal with in her life.

She rolled over on her back and sighed as she remembered the hearing that she attended after the shooting. She was taken immediately into custody at the warehouse; the other uniforms had no idea why she was covered in Chris's blood, with a gun in her hand. She was released soon after and had a chance to tell her side of the story. Shock coursed through the department because everyone had the same high opinion of Chris that she did. No one could believe that he would betray them. She still had to attend a hearing where she was officially proven innocent and allowed to hang onto her badge. There were piles of evidence that came out shaming Chris for his involvement in the drug deal that not only killed Sam but had him as a drug informant. He had been leaking information to the dark side in exchange for money for quite some time. The whole time she was in the hearing, her stomach roiled as she listened to the evidence.

Although they had given her back her badge, it looked different to her then. She knew she just couldn't go back to work as if nothing had happened. The department told her she would get a new partner, but the idea of sitting in a car with someone new and building trust again was more than she could stand. She decided to take a leave of absence with no promise of return. She couldn't have got out of town fast enough; she couldn't seem to breathe again until she took the step off the plane in Thailand. The thought of returning to the force just wasn't an option for her, and she needed to figure out if she could ever go back. The need to escape was her only salvation. If she had returned to her job, she would have been a dysfunctional detective, basically useless to her partner—if she could even trust another partner again. She had constant anxiety, moments when she couldn't breathe or think clearly, and escaping that world was the best way for her to get over the trauma of killing her partner.

The most humiliating aspect of the whole ordeal was the department appointed psychiatrist that she had to meet with in order to be allowed to return to work. Meeting with Dr. Kennedy was the main reason she had walked away from her job.

Shielding her eyes with her arm, she drifted back into the memory of the meeting with her doctor.

It was exactly the office you would expect from a psychiatrist. Warm and inviting, to lure you in and make you feel safe. There was a leather couch that she refused to lie down on during her session. She just perched herself on the arm of the couch during the entire session. Her psychiatrist, Dr. Kennedy, had long blonde hair and dressed in linen slacks and a loose turtleneck, even though she couldn't have been much older than Harley herself.

"I think that we've made some progress, Harley. What do you think?"

"I don't know. I think I'm only here because of Chris. I can't return to work until I have been cleared."

"Of course, but that's not the only reason why you are here."

Harley rolled her eyes. She like Dr. Kennedy but the doctor's need to always have Harley explain her feelings was irritating. "I almost shot that kid."

"But you didn't."

"It doesn't matter. I felt out of control. I pulled on him and he wasn't even armed."

"You thought he was."

"Yes. But I could have killed him. I shot him."

"You were experiencing PTSD, Harley. It was too soon for you to be at work again after Chris's death."

Tears filled Harley's eyes. "I didn't even know where I was. It was like I was suddenly back in that warehouse. I felt like I was in danger. My body covered in sweat, my hands shaking. I couldn't even control how I was feeling."

"That's all completely normal considering what you have been through. Returning to work probably wasn't the best idea for you. You have made progress, though. You are more relaxed and the dreams are becoming less frequent."

Harley just nodded.

"What do you think returning to your job will feel like, Harley?"

Harley snorted. "Like a wide-awake nightmare."

"Aren't you happy that the hearing went your way?"

"Obviously, I am, but I knew that I didn't do anything wrong. Not professionally, that is."

"Now what do you mean by that?"

Harley sighed. She hated therapy. "I mean I did my job plain and simple, but do I feel great about killing someone I loved and trusted? No. It's not right up there on my greatest professional achievements."

"You sound bitter, Harley."

"Bitter? No, I'm fucking pissed off, Dr. Kennedy, and sitting here trying to figure out why I am pissed is a waste of time for both of us."

"I'm sorry that you feel this way."

She smiled slowly. "Yeah. Me too."

"If you are unable to deal with your feelings about what happened, Harley, then you will continue to have anxiety, and that can get you killed on the job. You will be a dysfunctional individual who will doubt herself on the job when it's going to really count."

Harley just shrugged.

"It must have made you feel a little better to find out Chris wasn't evil."

"Excuse me?"

"The evidence proved that although Chris had been an informant, he had done it because he was forced to. The man involved had kidnapped his sister and was threatening to kill her unless Chris fed him the information he needed. Chris didn't betray the unit for money or because he was a bad person; he did it because he felt he had no other choice."

"He should have told me. I could have helped him."

"What could you have done?"

"Something," Harley whispered.

"It's not your fault."

"He made me kill him. Why? Why did he have to die?"

"He felt shame. He would have been exposed, his badge would have been taken away, and, there's no doubt about it, he would have gone to prison. He wasn't willing to do that."

"I don't think I can go back," she whispered, looking into her lap.

"Excuse me? I didn't hear you." Dr. Kennedy leaned forward in her chair.

Harley looked up and said, "I don't think that I can go back to the job. Not right now and maybe not ever."

The doctor nodded. "Have you ever considered taking some time off? In this particular case, the department would give you paid leave for a certain period of time. After that, you would have to determine if you wanted to return."

She nodded, knowing that was exactly what she was going to do. She was going to escape somewhere far and try to find herself all over again. She had to do it to save herself from going crazy. She needed to find out if she loved her job any longer and whether she wanted to be a cop or even a detective again.

"Will you put things in motion for me, Doctor?"

"Yes, I will speak with the captain immediately, and you can start planning the next few months of your life. Where will you go?"

Harley thought for a moment. "Thailand. I need to go to a place where no one knows me and be alone for a while."

"I think you are making the right decision."

"I hope so."

It had been the right decision. Being in Thailand made her feel free from her life. She still had no idea what she wanted to do with her life, but she had lots of time. The department gave her a six-month paid leave and whether she used it all or not, she had no intention of returning until she felt like she could do her job properly, and only time would tell. In the meantime, she just needed to relax and mourn her loss. It was not only a reflective time for her but a chance to heal without being constantly reminded of what she lost. The people in her life had tried to talk her out of it; her family worried that traveling to Thailand alone was a huge risk. But Harley knew she could take care of herself, and the freedom was too much to pass up.

She finally rolled out of bed. It was late—the clock said 1 am—but she knew that she wouldn't be able to get back to sleep. She decided to make herself a cup of coffee and head out to her balcony. As the coffee pot in her room was percolating—something that smelled incredible—she dug into her bag looking for a book to read. She pulled out *The Beautiful and the Damned* and threw it on the bed. She made her way to the coffee maker and poured a cup. She added some cream and sugar, thinking about how badass Chris had always seemed because he drank his coffee black. She took her cup and her book and went out onto the balcony. She had a view of the ocean and all the huts below her. Despite the late hour, there were still a few people out on the beach. She watched the people on the beach and wondered what they were doing. She found it weird that people would still be wandering the beach at such a late hour. She was too high above to recognize anyone, and she wondered what Craig was doing and whether she should go and see him. She settled into her lounger, and with coffee in hand, she flipped open to the first chapter.

EIGHT

AS BUTCHER WALKED ALONG THE almost-deserted beach, he sought after something that would soothe a need inside of him. Killing to him felt the same way as opening a hundred-dollar bottle of wine did to others. He took pride in his work, and he savored it like tasting hundred-year-old wine for the first time. Butchering people was hard work—people didn't realize just how much effort it took to dismember a body. It took a lot of time. He was an extremely accomplished murderer.

As he walked, he came across his friends sitting on a blanket; he could smell the weed before he even approached them. He knew as soon as he saw them that they would be perfect. He just needed them to follow him along a dark path, just for a little while. He didn't typically kill men—he had a taste for women—but he had been eyeing the wife for so long that he had to kill her, and since the two were inseparable, there was no way to snatch her without him.

He slowly approached them, a bright smile on his face. "Hey, guys!" Butcher said.

They turned to him and Katie giggled. "Hey! We missed you today! I can't get over how beautiful it is here. I could stay here forever; it's just the best place ever."

"What are you guys doing out here alone?"

"Oh, we were at another party. We've been drinking all day. We are the last survivors."

"I was just taking a break myself. I'm having a party up in my room if you guys want to continue to make the most of your night. You are more than welcome to have some fun."

"Cool, man. Yeah, let's do it. That would be awesome. What do you say, Katie?"

"I think that would be so cool. We are so glad we met you, Devon, and even Harley. Everyone on the island has been so nice to us, so friendly and generous. We have been meeting so many great people."

"I agree! It's been great. Well, let's go." Butcher waited while they gathered their blanket and Katie's purse.

Butcher tossed a few ice cubes into a tumbler and filled it a quarter of the way with whiskey. His party was just about to start, and the two most important guests were there. He enjoyed a nice cocktail before he got to work. His friends would allow him to live a few different lives before he would have to travel on to the next island. He took a sip of the liquid and let it burn its way down his throat. He loved the heat whiskey brought to his body; it burned all the way to his stomach. He made his way back into the main room where his friends were waiting patiently for him.

He had classical music playing in the background to help his friends relax and get in the mood. *Danse Macabre* by *Camille Saint-Saëns* was one of his favorite pieces, and he knew his friends enjoyed it just as much as he did. When he entered the room, he found Brian and Katie sitting in chairs, their arms bound by handcuffs behind them and gags stealing the air from their lungs. He smiled at them sitting there anxiously waiting for his arrival. There was clear plastic beneath the chairs. Tonight was going to be a good night indeed.

Brian was straining against his restraints, his face beet red. He was very angry with Butcher; they had been lied to about the party. Brian was cursing through his gag, which only caused Butcher to smile. Brian had no idea what he was in for—neither of them did. They thought it was their worst nightmares coming true, but in fact, it was so much worse than that. Beautiful Katie had not stopped crying since he had forced them at gunpoint to sit in the chairs while he had restrained them. Her mascara had run down her cheeks, and he remembered how she had begged him not to hurt them. She had asked him how he could do this to them. He had been rough with her when he had shoved the gag in her mouth. She had tried to plead with him, but she had no idea that he couldn't feel sympathy even if he wanted to, which he didn't. He looked at her, searching for similarities with his mother. He wished it were his mother sitting in the chair.

"I would offer you both a drink, but I can't trust that you wouldn't scream."

Katie whimpered into her gag. "Please let us go."

"Now I couldn't very well do that, my dear. You would tell on me, and I can't have you sending me back to prison. I certainly do not want Harley to find out about me either."

"Harley!" Katie struggled against her restraints again.

They both shook their head emphatically, and he almost chuckled. It didn't matter; they weren't there by accident. He needed to kill Katie because of his mother; he would pretend the screams were his mothers. Brian was just a means to an end. He often dreamed of killing his mother—killing other women satisfied him until he could get his hands on his mother. Even in his dreams, he was haunted by bloodlust for the woman who betrayed him. He needed to do this so he would have a peaceful night's sleep.

He sat down across from them and drank his whiskey in small gulps. He swirled the whiskey in the glass as he stared at them. He tried to understand how they must be feeling, the terror, the absolute certainty that was involved in knowing you were about to die. As Katie cried and Brian cursed, Butcher didn't have one emotion about the situation aside from excitement that swirled through his body. He got up from his chair and moved to a side table that sat against the wall. There he found the tools that he had accumulated for such a purpose. There was a three-pound hammer, an electroshock device, and a sharp butcher knife. He picked up the electroshock device and the hammer, and he made his way toward Katie. She screamed against the gag in her mouth, but no one would hear her above the music. He was safe to do as he wished.

He moved toward her and swung the hammer at her kneecap, shattering it instantly. She screamed silently, the pain so bad that she gagged against the cloth in her mouth. He suddenly felt warm all over, a euphoric feeling coursing through his body. She was going to pass out, but he would keep her awake—they were going to be at this for a while. Brian was shaking so badly in his chair, Butcher worried that he would topple over. He didn't need the extra noise, so he stuck the shock device against Brian's stomach and pressed a button. Brian shuddered from head to toe as electric shocks ran through his entire body. Butcher watched until his body stopped shuddering, Brian momentarily unconscious. That was okay; he had work to do on Katie, and he didn't need another interruption. He turned back to her, and tears were streaming down her face. A look of sheer and utter terror was in her eyes—they were large pools, her pupils dilated. She was so scared that she couldn't even register what was happening. She looked from Brian to Butcher and started to shake her head violently. She whimpered the closer he got, her whole body trembling out of control. He couldn't wait to see her bleed.

"It's all going to be over very soon, I promise you." She started sobbing uncontrollably, and there was something about her face that caused Butcher to smile.

Butcher sipped at the glass of whiskey, feeling euphoric. He couldn't remember the last time he felt so good, so alive and free. It had been too long. The whiskey was cool, and it soothed him from all the exertion involved in taking apart bodies. He looked down at his clothing, splattered with blood from the couple. He stood up and stripped out of his clothing, letting them fall on the plastic underneath him. It was time to dispose of the bodies; morning would arrive soon, and he couldn't keep them there. He smiled as he remembered how he had tortured his friends with the electroshock device and the hammer. Brian had died from his wounds while Katie had held on until the very end. When they were both dead, he had dismembered the bodies and wrapped the pieces in the plastic wrapping. The severed pieces were split up and put in duffle bags. He would burn his blood-splattered clothing at a later time. For now, he would worry about disposing of the bodies. He dressed in fresh clothing, put the duffle bags over his shoulders and made his way out of his hotel room. There was no one in the hallway, and the elevator was free as well. He shuddered, the feeling delicious, as he imagined the weight of those bodies against his shoulders. He would need to make a few trips, but it was late and he wasn't worried about anyone becoming suspicious.

He made his way to the beach where he had a boat waiting. He dropped the duffle bags in and headed back to the hotel to collect the rest. Once he had everything in the boat, he pushed it off the shore and headed out to the water. He had the perfect destination in mind, a place that he had used once already, a disused tin mine that awaited him in Phuket's Kathu district. No one would have any reason to look for the bodies there.

Once he was far enough from the shore, he started the boat motor, and the boat shot off toward Phuket. He was growing tired and was looking forward to a solid night's sleep. He needed to make sure the bodies were properly disposed of as he was trying to stay off the radar. He often thought about returning home to see how his mother was faring without him. Did she ever think about him, or regret sending him away? He wondered if she ever thought of him. He planned on returning to her one day and putting his hands around her throat.

This wasn't the first time he had killed someone. He had never been caught, and he had been killing his whole life. The only stint in prison had been for drugs and he learned his lesson, he had no intention of going back. He smiled as he remembered his childhood and the neighborhood animals that constantly would go missing. People looked at him strangely, as if they wondered if he had something to do with the cats and dogs disappearing, but they could never prove it. The whole town had probably breathed a sigh of relief when he left. His mother had once thought of him as something good and wholesome, but that's just what he had allowed her to see. Though she was on to him now, wasn't she?

It was his father who taught him how to butcher animals. Before his father had left them, he had often brought his son to work with him, probably thinking he would follow in his footsteps one day. But Butcher had a larger vision for the skills his father taught him—how to slice through the carcasses skin and take their flesh clean from their bones. Butcher had worn a smile of ecstasy every time he went to work with his father and got to slice right down to the bone. His father was an honest man who worked as a butcher his whole life. He passed on his skills to his son, and those skills had come in handy throughout his life.

Butcher learned quickly how to hide who he was; he could never let anyone else get as close to the truth as his mother had. It was amazing how he could fool the people around him. He made them think he was a good old boy who wanted a mortgage and a family. They were fools, just like Brian and Katie on the beach. They would not be returning home to start their life together. Brian and Katie would forever be immortalized in Thailand.

He saw the tin mine in the distance and his smile grew wider still. Welcome to your new home, newlyweds!

When he left the mines, his head was clear, and he never felt so alive. It was exactly what he needed to clear his head. He would be able to go about the week with a focused mind. It wouldn't be the last time—he always needed more—but for now, his mind was at peace. As he traveled back to the island in the boat, he thought about what he needed to do next. There would be another victim, but there was no rush in choosing one. He liked to take his time to find the perfect girl, the one that reminded him of his mother. It was then that Harley came to mind and the thought of her caused him to smile. He wanted to run his hands through her hair and tug on it.

He dug into his pocket and pulled out a folded piece of paper. He had been doing some research on Harley. He unfolded the paper and examined it. It was a printout of a newspaper article from New York City showing Harley at a police funeral for a partner she killed herself. How humiliating it must have been to go through a hearing over the shooting. Now there she was on the island, running away from all that she had done. Just looking at her, he could tell she wasn't over the guilt of killing her partner. That put her exactly where he wanted her. He knew now that he was going to kill her but not before taking his time with her. They would be together soon enough, and it would be glorious.

NINE

HARLEY SHUDDERED AS THE COOL night air touched her bare skin; she suddenly felt creeped out. She stood up, setting her book down, and leaned against the balcony railing. She looked out at the beach, now bare, it's occupants safely tucked in for the night. She couldn't explain the sense of foreboding that came over her just then. It was late, that was all, and she needed to get some sleep. She turned from the beach and walked into her room, closing the balcony door behind her.

She went straight to bed, hoping that she could get the weird feeling out of her body. She couldn't help but allow her mind to drift to Chris; it seemed to be happening more often. She wondered if she would ever be able to let go of her past. Harley thought back and drifted into a memory of her and Chris at a benefit dinner for the NYPD.

Harley rarely dressed up so going to the benefit had been

a pretty big deal. She and Chris had decided ahead of time to go together because Chris had a brief stint where he was single for at least five minutes. He had picked her up at her apartment and he had never looked more handsome in a suit. She had picked out a deep blue cocktail dress that made her hair look like it was on fire. She loved the way he had looked at her approvingly.

"Wow, Harley, you sure clean up good."

She beamed. "Why, thank you. You don't look so bad yourself."

They had stayed beside each other all night, talking and laughing, drinking the night away. She couldn't remember the last time she had so much fun. The more she drank, the more she started to think that it was finally her shot, her time to be with Chris. They were so comfortable together; it almost seemed like the natural next step. He was certainly flirting with her and at one point he had rested his arm around her waist.

When the night had come to a close, they left the benefit and they took a cab back to her place. It wouldn't be the first time he had crashed on her couch, but that time Harley had a different plan in mind. They laughed as they climbed the stairs to her apartment, and when they got inside, Chris made his way toward the couch. She stopped him and spun him toward her. She planted a kiss on his lips that caught him by surprise, but he pulled her into him, and the kiss lit on fire. It was like two people who had been starved for air had finally found a source for it and weren't willing to let it go. She melted into his kiss, their tongues finding one another. It was exactly as she had imagined it: warm and sweet.

Suddenly he pulled away from her. "Harley, we can't."

Her brain was foggy more from the kiss then from the booze, and she stared at him confused. "What are you talking about?"

"We can't do this. It will ruin everything. I've never dated anyone that I work with, and I don't want to start now. What if it's a disaster? I would lose you as a partner."

She was completely dumbfounded; she couldn't believe what she was hearing. "You can't be serious. This would be perfect."

He bent down and kissed her softly on the lips. "I don't think that it's a good idea. I'm sorry. Trust me, Harley; I'm not at all what you need in your life."

The sting in her heart was like nothing she had felt before; she was transported back to that coffee shop where she saw her ex with his professor. "You, asshole."

She walked away from him toward her bedroom.

"Harley!"

"Just go to bed, idiot," she said as she slammed her bedroom door. She lay in bed that night with a mixture of hurt and fury running through her. She felt stupid for putting herself out there only to be turned away. He would go out with any number of bimbos, but he pushed her away.

When she woke up the next morning, he was gone from the couch. They never spoke about it again, and they eventually got back into their normal routine of banter as if it had never happened.

Shaking off the memory, Harley let her eyes slowly drift closed.

TEN

STARING DOWN AT HER FEET in the sand, Harley was quiet while the group passed joints around as they sat on the beach. The fire was large, and Harley was warming herself by it. She was high and being around her friends made her feel happier than she had felt in a really long time. She was snuggled against Craig's bare chest, feeling warm and buzzed.

"Do you want more, Harley?"

Harley turned to see Melissa holding out the joint. Melissa's crazy afro was pulled back into a headband. Harley took the joint in her fingers and took a few soft puffs, watching the end burn, before handing it back to Melissa.

"Hey, guys!"

Harley turned around to find Keri walking toward the group. They all greeted her, and she hugged each one of the group before settling in beside Harley. Keri had her hair styled in a faux Mohawk, and Harley felt that pang of wishing she had the balls to change her hair. Melissa passed Keri the joint, and she took a few puffs off it before she handed it back. Harley really liked Keri; she was a lot of fun, something she saw when they had all been surfing at the beach the other day.

"How are you guys doing?" Keri asked.

"Crikey, Melissa and I were just bickering again, no big deal."

Melissa smacked Devon on the leg while laughing. "Why don't you just be quiet."

"Okay guys, cool it," Keri said, laughing.

"What were you up to today, Keri?" Harley asked.

It was then that Keri frowned, not responding at first. She leaned over, grabbed a beer out of Devon's cooler and popped the tab. She took a long swig before she met anyone's eyes, and Harley started to get a weird feeling. Something was bothering Keri, and Harley watched her carefully.

"Is everything okay, Keri?"

"I don't know."

Melissa and Devon looked over, suddenly concerned. "What's going on?"

Craig stared at Keri, not saying a word.

Keri looked up from her beer. "Have any of you guys seen Brian and Katie?"

Devon and Melissa shook their heads, and Harley wracked her brain to think about when she saw the happy couple last. She looked up at Craig, and he shook his head. It had to be at least 24 hours since she saw either of them. Harley found it immediately weird because the couple always seemed to be on the beach—it was their favorite pastime while being on vacation.

"We haven't seen them in a while. We thought that maybe they went off the island for one of those excursions. Why what's up?"

Keri took another swig of beer. "No, they didn't go off the island. I can't find them anywhere. I made plans with them for today. After we had left them on the beach last night, I agreed to meet them, and we were going to check out a new restaurant and then blaze on the beach all day. But they never showed up to my room."

"Did you check out their hut?"

Keri nodded. "Yes, of course. I waited around for a while, but when they didn't show up, I went to their hut. They weren't there either, and I sat on their porch for over an hour, but they never came back."

"That's so weird. Where the heck are they?" Melissa asked, her brow scrunched in confusion.

Harley thought about it for a minute before responding—she was high, so it was hard to focus on what Keri was saying. "What did you do after that?"

"Well, I headed up to the restaurant. I thought maybe we were supposed to meet there. I asked the staff if they saw them, and no one had. After that, I hit the beach and nothing. I've honestly looked everywhere. I don't know where they are. It's so bizarre, Harley."

"Oh, Crikey, I hope nothing happened to them,"

Devon said.

"Devon, man, don't talk that way. Maybe they changed their mind and did an excursion. You never know," Melissa said.

"Are you kidding? Even if they changed their mind, they would have told me. They wouldn't leave me wandering around confused."

"She's right. I don't think they would leave without telling Keri. They are too thoughtful to do something like that," Harley stated.

Keri downed the beer, her hands shaking. "You're a cop, aren't you, Harley? What do you think happened?"

Harley looked down into the beer in her lap. People often acted erratically while on vacation. She couldn't say for sure that the couple wouldn't go off on their own—people had fewer inhibitions when they were on vacation. She just didn't think the newlyweds were quite like that. They seemed more than happy to spend time with friends, and during the time they had spent on the island, they had not once gone off and disappeared like that. So, where were they? Was it possible that something happened to them? She knew she had to keep Keri calm; she didn't want to alarm her for no reason.

"I don't know, Keri. It definitely sounds strange to me, but I'm sure they are fine. I don't think they would have ditched you without telling you, but people do get caught up in vacationing. I wonder if we could get inside the hut and take a look around."

"I could probably ask the manager and see what he says. Let him know they are missing."

"No, don't do that. The manager is not going to just let you into a person's hut, and the authorities will say it's too soon to start looking for them. We should notify police, though, even if they won't start looking right away, and contacting the coast guard would be good as well. They could have been in an accident while out on the water."

"Oh, my God, are you guys serious? You really think something bad happened to them?"

"Whoa, Keri, relax. We don't know anything. Like I said, they could have just got into an accident. After you talk to a few people, we'll have a better idea. But there's no need to freak out at this stage."

Harley turned to look at Melissa, who had a terrified look on her face. Devon started rubbing Melissa's shoulder to try and calm her down.

"This is crazy," whispered Melissa.

Harley sighed. "I don't think any of us should get worked up without more information. There is still a chance that they are just off somewhere enjoying some time alone. But maybe we can check a few things out just to see if we can find something out. You never know, they may be due to arrive home any minute."

"What are you suggesting?"

Harley looked down the beach toward the huts. Most of them were dark. "I think we should look inside their hut. I can probably get inside; the locks aren't that complicated on these little huts."

"Are you serious?" Melissa asked, her mouth hanging open.

"Of course, she is. Hell yeah, man, I'm in, Harley. Let's go." Devon grabbed his cooler, showing off his sleeve tattoos as his arms flexed. She caught his eye and he winked at her.

The rest of them stood up, brushing the sand off them. They made their way to the huts and Harley waited while Keri pointed out the couple's hut.

"It's that one."

Harley made her way up the steps with Devon and Craig right behind her. She took a look around to make sure no one was watching her break in. She jiggled the knob a little bit before looking at the lock. It was her childhood friend, Jordan, who had taught her to pick locks long before she ever decided to become a cop. Now those skills acquired during a rebellious youth were going to come in handy. She dug around in her pockets for a bobby pin and smiled when she found two. She bent one at a weird angle and then slid it into the lock. She fiddled around until she heard a click. She turned the knob and pushed the door open. She turned to Devon, who nodded.

"Guys, wait out here and keep an eye out. We will quickly check things out."

The two girls stayed outside while Devon, Craig, and Harley made their way inside the missing couple's hut. It was dark, and there wasn't much light to help them out. Devon went and turned on a lamp to give them a bit of light. With Keri and Melissa on the porch, anyone walking by would assume it was their hut. The only people who would know it wasn't were Brian and Katie, and they were missing. Harley looked around the room but didn't see anything amiss. If the couple was missing, they hadn't been taken from the hut. Their beds were neatly made, and everything seemed to be in place.

Harley went to look at the laundry hamper that stood in the corner of the room. "They probably didn't even come back last night," she whispered.

"What makes you think that?" Craig asked.

"The clothing that they wore yesterday is not in the hamper. There are no towels or wet bathing suits."

"Crikey, that's not good."

"No, no it's not."

Devon walked to the dresser. "What are we looking for here?"

Harley glanced around the room. "A purse or possibly their passports."

"I don't see any of that stuff here."

"She had it with her the night before," Craig added.

Harley called for Keri to come inside. Her friend came in and looked around anxiously.

"Keri, do you see anything else missing?"

The girl scanned the room to see if anything was out of place. "Oddly, yes."

"What is it?"

"The red dress she wore dancing the other night. It's not here." She flipped through pictures on her phone and then showed Harley a shot of Brian and Katie together.

"It's beautiful. But that could be anywhere."

"No, it's her favorite dress. It's always hanging on the back of the door. She takes very good care of it."

Harley glanced at the door where an empty hanger swung on the back of the door. "Weird."

"Shit, man, this is really happening? Our friends are missing?"

"I don't know, Devon; it's too soon to tell. I can start looking around tomorrow once it's daylight. I'll start asking some questions. But let's not freak out quite yet. We may all wake up tomorrow and they will be back."

"I hope you're right."

"Me too," she muttered to herself.

They all made their way out of the hut, and Harley closed the door behind them. They all collected together on the porch, and Keri started crying. Harley sat beside her friend and wrapped her arm around her shoulder.

"It's bad, isn't it?"

"Relax, Keri. They didn't come back to the hut last night, but you never know. They could have crashed somewhere else; you know they still wanted to party after we all left," Harley said.

"Yeah, they were definitely up for partying. Maybe they slept at the hotel. But even if they did, they should have been back by now," Devon added.

"Oh man, I know something happened to them. I just know it. What are we going to do? How will we find them? That's my family," Keri cried out.

"Keri, I know this can be upsetting but try to think positively. Let me look into it tomorrow. There is no point in looking around right now; we have no information and the cops are not about to help at this stage in the game. I don't want you freaking out until there's a reason to freak out. The best thing to do is notify the coast guards and the police."

Keri nodded, and the group returned to the campfire to finish their beers. The mood was more melancholy than it was before the search at the hut. All Harley could think about was how dangerous the island could be if there was a monster on it.

ELEVEN

WHEN HARLEY WOKE THE NEXT morning, the first thought that crossed her mind was about Katie and Brian. It felt like she had a piece of lead in her stomach every time she thought of them. Her gut was telling her that something was really wrong. She didn't want to alarm her friends, but she had been a cop long enough to know that her friends weren't just gallivanting around Thailand without a care in the world. They were gone. So, where were they? She knew that she would need to check on the hut before doing anything further, to make sure they had not, in fact, returned. There was still a chance that they could have had an accident somewhere on the island, and she would want to talk to Keri about what the coast guard had to say.

She hoped that she would find them safely snuggled up in each other's arms on the beach. That was the way they were—a team, two people who wanted to face the world together. They had come to an island in the hope of creating some memories to start their new life; they would never have expected that something terrible would happen. That thought propelled her out of bed.

She stumbled into the bathroom still groggy from the night before. They had all stayed up late talking, enjoying the comfort of being together. When she left them to return to the hotel, she warned them not to go off alone anywhere; she didn't want to lose any more friends. Though everyone was thinking the same thing: Katie and Brian were two people and yet they were missing.

She looked in the mirror and washed her face, rubbing the soap against the freckles that splashed across her cheeks. She had a small nose and full lips—she couldn't complain about her looks, at least no one could say she was plain. She brushed her long red hair and tied it back into a ponytail. She started applying makeup, but then she stopped and stared at her reflection. The green pools that stared back at her showed the fear that she felt for her friends. She had to believe that they were okay or she might lose her cool. She had work to do that day, and she hoped that she would find some answers to where her friends were located.

Once she was finished getting ready and dressed, she made her way to the dining area to grab some coffee. She needed it after being up all night worrying about her friends. She had been trying to figure out where her friends could have gone. Had they met someone else after they had left them on the beach?

She sat at the bar and considered a plan for the day while she sipped on the hot liquid. She knew she would have to ask around the hotel to see if anyone recognized the couple. She pulled a notepad out of her bag and started to make a plan for the day. She jotted down notes on who could have lured the trusting couple away. Had they known the person? She also made notes of areas that could be checked out if the couple just had an accident.

"Harley!"

She looked up from her notepad to see Keri walking into the dining room. Keri pulled up a chair beside Harley and sat down. Harley took a sip of her coffee, grateful for it. Keri had dark circles under her eyes, and it appeared as if she hadn't styled her spiking blonde hair that day.

"Hi, Keri, how's it going?"

"I've been better." She motioned for the waiter to bring her coffee as well. The waiter quickly retrieved the coffee and set it down in front of Keri.

"Did you happen to check the hut to see if they got back?" Harley asked.

"Yes. They aren't there. I checked the beach again too. I think something really bad happened to them, Harley. I didn't sleep a wink last night. The first thing I did this morning was to report them to the Coastal Defence Command and they said they would send some boats out, maybe a helicopter. I also filed a missing person report, but they said it had to be 72 hours before a search party would be out."

"Yeah, that's pretty standard. We'll see what the coast guard comes up with. I'm going to start asking around the hotel to see if anyone remembers seeing them. You wouldn't happen to have a picture of them, would you?"

"Actually I do." Keri flipped through her phone and found a couple of pictures of Brian and Katie and sent them to Harley's phone. "Hope this helps."

Harley clicked on the pictures. They were of the couple laughing at the beach together. They truly were a beautiful couple, and she hoped that they were just off somewhere taking some time to be alone. It was highly unlikely at that point, but she could only hope.

"Well, this is better than nothing. I was really hoping they would have shown up this morning."

"Yeah, me too. Melissa and Devon are surfing today, so they said they would keep an eye out for them if they do show up at the hut."

She plastered on her best fake smile. "That's good. They'll turn up, I'm sure of it. Don't worry about it right now, okay?"

Keri smiled. "You're right. I'm sure everything is okay."

Harley took a sip of her coffee as Keri got a sly look on her face.

"What now?" Harley asked.

"Did you hear that Devon and Craig got into a fight this morning?"

"You're kidding me. About what? They're friends. We were all just together last night."

"They may not be friends for too long; I guess Craig didn't like the fact that Devon wanted to move in on his main squeeze."

Harley stared at her. "Me? I'm not his main squeeze, Keri! We're just hanging out, it's casual."

She laughed. "I know, but it's still pretty funny. I guess Craig brought up the fact that Devon is flirty with you and the two started arguing. Craig totally lost his shit. I wish I would have been there, but Melissa said it was crazy. Devon has that total badass vibe about him. Now that he got into a fight, I almost feel attracted to him."

Harley snickered. Devon was cute, but she tried to avoid the bad boys—she had learned too many times that it was more trouble than it was fun. "Why, what happened?"

"Craig lost it and tackled Devon. It turned into a fistfight pretty quickly."

"What? That's nuts. And so not cool. I will have a word with him, that's for sure."

"I've never known Craig to be violent, but I don't know him that well. He just lost it, and a couple of guys had to pull them apart. Craig was screaming at him to stay away from you."

"Holy shit. Well, that's just great. I sure know how to pick them."

"Hey, don't knock it. I wish I had some guy willing

to fight over me."

Harley laughed. "Yeah, no thanks. Besides heads turn when you walk in the room."

Keri winked. "Just thought you should know that Craig's fire is definitely burning hot for you."

"Wonderful. It sounds like maybe I don't know him as well as I thought I did."

Keri nodded solemnly before she took a drink of her coffee. "Anyway, I gotta run. If you need any help, Harley, just let me know."

"I will. But I think right now I should handle things on my own. It's too early to tell and I'd like to make sure that it's not just an accident first, which is pretty likely. These islands can be dangerous if you slip and fall in the wrong area. If you want, you can show those pictures around the beach to see if anyone recognizes them. But don't go off with anyone."

"Okay, I understand. I'm going to get going then. I'll see you later."

"Sure."

Harley watched her leave and finished her coffee. She ordered another one to go and collected her things. Before she left the bar, she showed the picture to the waiter and asked if he recognized the couple. The man shook his head, and she decided to move on. She approached the front desk and waited until there was a clerk available.

A young woman looked up and smiled warmly at Harley. "Welcome, how can I help you?"

"I'm staying at the hotel right now, and I'm looking for a couple of friends who have seemed to have gone missing. I was wondering if you have seen them around the hotel at all."

The woman suddenly looked nervous as she took the phone from Harley. She stared down at the picture. "Yes, I have seen the couple before."

Harley's heart skipped a beat. "When did you see them?"

"It was a few days ago; they came in to dine in the restaurant."

"You haven't seen them since?"

She shook her head. "No, ma'am."

Frowning, Harley asked her to check with the rest of her staff before she headed out of the hotel. The woman took the phone and brought it to the other two clerks, showing them the pictures. Both shook their heads, causing Harley's stomach to plummet. She was not off to a good start. It wasn't the end of the world, however; the couple was not staying at the hotel, so it wasn't surprising that no one recognized them. She would try another avenue. She decided then that it was time to visit the police department.

It took another trip on the back of a pickup truck to get Harley to the city where she would find the local law enforcement. It gave her a lot of time to think about Brian and Katie. The couple was definitely far too trusting; they often talked about meeting new people and going to parties. Though there was no reason to assume the worst, lots of things could have happened to them that were purely innocent. She thoughts about the boats that often left the island, and she decided to text Keri.

> **Harley: Go down to the beach, ask the men who rent out the boats and see if there were any rented that never came back.**

She thought of another avenue and sent a second message.

> **Harley: Also, ask if surfboards were rented that didn't come back. We'd have a good idea if an accident occurred.**

She had a terrible signal so she was sure it would take some time for the message to be delivered to Keri.

So, if there was no accident, then what? They could have made friends with the wrong person. It could also possibly be someone they already knew. If it were someone they were friends with, they would have had no problem going off without a care in the world. She was going to stick to finding out about the boats first, and then go into something worse.

The truck arrived in the city, and she hopped off the back, thanking the locals for giving her a ride. When she walked up to the building, she was surprised. It was certainly different from the precinct she was used to. The building was small, and it didn't look like there was a lot of upkeep to the structure. She walked inside and made her way to the front desk. She stood there as officers milled past her, not paying her any attention. She raised her eyebrows in annoyance and finally knocked hard on the desk. A male officer looked over at her, clearly surprised that someone was there. and slowly approached the desk.

"Can I speak with Officer Ornlamai?"

The officer gave her a once-over before he barked to another officer with a broken accent. Then he said to Harley, "He will be here in a moment."

Harley sat down on a bench and waited for Officer Ornlamai. The last time she had seen him was at the academy. He had returned to his home country of Thailand when he graduated because he wanted to take care of his parents. She had looked him up after her friend went missing and was looking forward to seeing him after all that time.

Her annoyance level was growing as she waited. She looked down at her phone; the signal was always stronger in the city. On the island the signal was always in and out, and sometimes she didn't get text messages until much later. Her phone buzzed just then and she opened a message from Keri.

Keri: Sounds good. I'm heading there right

now, I'll let you know what they say.

Harley: Great.

Keri: Just saw Craig. He's looking for you. I told him you know about the fight and he's freaking out Lol

Harley: Wtf. The guy just punched his friend out. I'll have to chat with him l8tr.

Keri: Ok lol

Harley couldn't help but chuckle out loud. Keri was awesome. She couldn't imagine why Craig was behaving so erratically, but she didn't like it one bit. How could he have such a strong reaction to her when she felt so little for him? She found it strange. Maybe he was just one of those clingy guys. She was certainly disturbed by the fact that he got into a fight with his friend over her. She had never got the impression that he had a violent side to him. They had been tangled in the sheets for weeks now, and she thought that she had a good grasp on who he was from the time they spent together. She wondered what else she didn't know about her lover.

After a solid twenty minutes passed, she was starting to wonder if they even told her friend that she was here. Finally, he came around the corner with a big smile on his face.

"Harley!"

She got up from the bench and smiled at him. He had thick black hair styled in spiky fashion. His dark eyes looked her over. He was only about five feet eight, but he was muscular all over. "Hey, stranger," she said.

"Sorry, I was in the middle of something. It took you long enough to come and see me."

She blushed, she wasn't even sure if she would have come otherwise, as being in a police station wasn't exactly what she was looking for. "Yeah, well, the beach was calling to me. I would have made it in here eventually."

"It's good to see you, Harley. I'm sorry about what happened in New York."

She sighed. "Me too. How are your parents?"

"Good. They are very proud of their cop son," he said with a laugh.

"Look, Ned, I'm here for a specific reason."

His eyebrows raised. "Really? What's up?"

"A couple of my friends have gone missing, and I'm worried that something happened to them."

Ned cringed, which didn't settle well with her. "Harley, we have a pretty strict policy here about looking for people. You would be surprised how many people disappear around here for days, only to turn up hungover."

She nodded. "Yeah, I understand that, but my instincts are telling me that's not the case."

"I get it. Let me talk to my chief here."

She watched as he went to the hallway and called down it. Less than a minute passed, and an older man walked up to Ned. He had salt and pepper hair and a weathered face. He was short as well but thin as a weed. They both looked over at her, and she watched as they discussed her right before her eyes. She knew right away that she was going to have problems with the chief. The man approached the desk and motioned for her to come over. Ned was just a few steps behind him and was looking at her sheepishly. It wasn't exactly a good sign.

"What can I help you with…Officer?" He had a strong accent, but he spoke English quite well.

"Officer Wolfhart, but you can call me Harley. Are you in charge here?"

"I'm the chief in charge here, yes."

"Two of my friends have gone missing. I believe my friend Keri filed a missing person's report. I have reason to believe something has happened to them. I was hoping your department could look into it."

He snorted. "Yes, we did receive such a report. You have no jurisdiction here, Officer Wolfhart."

She fought the urge to roll her eyes. "Hence the fact that I asked you to look into it. I'm not trying a case here; I'm asking you to. I'd be more than happy to linger on the beach awhile longer."

The disgruntled chief looked her over, causing a small amount of discomfort on Harley's part. It was obvious right from the get-go that he was not going to take her seriously at all.

"What do you think has happened on the island, Officer?"

"It's Harley. My friends are missing, and they've been gone for over a 24-hour period. It could just be an accident for all I know, but they are missing."

He slowly smiled at her as if it was her first day on the job. "People tend to jump from one island to another; it's not unusual for people to leave and then come back a few days later."

"I understand that, Chief, but I don't believe that is the case here. My friends went missing one night and never returned to their hut. It is very unlikely that they are skipping around islands—it's just so unlike them, they wouldn't do that."

"You know these people for a long time?"

"No, I just met them the last couple of weeks."

"So, it's possible you don't know them as well as you think you do?"

Her mouth fell open. She couldn't believe what she was hearing. "You can't be serious. I'm reporting a missing couple, and you need to look into it. It could already be too late for them; time is of the essence. You need to start looking for them immediately."

The chief chuckled, which only caused her blood pressure to rise. She pulled out her phone and put the pictures right in his face. "They are missing. What are you going to do about it?"

"I'm afraid at this point we can't do anything. We need 72 hours before we look for missing people. We have many missing people cases come into the office, and I can't tell you how many times it turns out to be a bunch of kids who just partied too much or people who hopped around the islands. It happens all the time, Harley. If your friends are still missing after 72 hours, then please let me know."

She looked at him with disgust. She couldn't believe he was just going to ignore the situation. "There is much more to this then kids partying. They are here on their honeymoon; they wouldn't have left without telling us where they were going. They are here with their sister."

He put his hand up, which irritated Harley even more. "I can't help you right now, Harley. I don't believe any crime has been committed. I assure you that your friends will turn up."

"You're making a mistake. I could help you look for them."

"I will ask around, Harley, and see what I hear, but I assure you that we don't need a United States police officer to help us solve any cases."She raised her eyebrows in indignation and glanced at Ned. He shrugged, looking completely helpless. She had half a mind to punch the chief in the face, but she knew that wouldn't help. Instead, she snatched her phone out of his hand angrily and stormed out of the building. She couldn't believe the nonchalance of the chief regarding a missing person. How could he blatantly ignore a missing person's case without even getting all the details?

Once outside she sat down on the front steps of the building and held her head in her hands. She considered walking right back in there and telling the chief exactly what she thought of him, but she knew that getting into a fight with the local authorities would not help her if she needed them later. She couldn't wait a few more days either for them to realize her friends were missing. If something had happened to her friends, then time was not on their side.

She startled as a hand rested on her shoulder. She turned around to find Ned there.

"Sorry about that. The chief is a bit of a hard ass, and he has a thing about Americans."

"I gathered that."

"If you can come up with anything more concrete, I could probably talk him into looking into things."

She really didn't want to get involved in the whole thing; she had enough shit going on in her life. God, she wasn't even sure she wanted to be a cop again, never mind getting involved in something of this caliber. She had been hoping that the chief would do all the work and leave her out of it. It didn't look like that would be the case, however, so she needed to do some digging herself to find enough evidence that they were in trouble to light a fire under the chief's ass. That thought brought no small amount of unease to her. She had gone to Thailand to get away from police work, to leave it all behind her. She didn't know that she wanted to get involved in a situation she wasn't ready for. But could she just leave the couple out there with no answers?

She sighed. "Yeah, I guess I will have to. It was nice seeing you again, Ned."

"Yes, hopefully, next time it will be under better circumstances."

She got up from the steps and went to find a ride home. She had a long trip back to the island, and she had work to do.

TWELVE

WHEN SHE ARRIVED BACK ON the island, her limbs felt like jelly, and she was looking forward to a long bubble bath. She didn't think she had the energy to get any work done that evening; she would just try to get some notes together for the next day. She would need to get together a game plan for her own investigation in the hopes that she would be able to find her friends on her own. The likelihood that they would still be alive at that point was not good, but she could still hope for the best. She knew she wasn't in the right headspace for any of it, though; she had been baking in the sun and getting high for weeks. She hadn't even thought about a case in months. To say that she was rusty would be the understatement of the year.

She made her way up to the hotel and headed to the front desk to see if she had any messages from her friends. If Katie and Brian had returned, there would be a note stating that everything was okay. She hoped that there would be a message for her stating just that.

"Hey there, do I have any messages?"

The clerk dug through a pile of messages sitting on the desk. Harley's heart soared at the thought that the couple had been found and everything would be okay. That was all she really wanted. Then they could all return to the beach and get back to relaxing and drinking. Until her friends were found, however, Harley wasn't sure she would ever be able to relax again. The very idea seemed like a betrayal. The clerk shook her head. Just then her phone buzzed with a message from Keri.

Keri: Harley, no news. Hope you found something. Will talk tomorrow.

The message was straight to the point. Harley's stomach plummeted. The news was not good, and if the couple was still missing, it was pretty safe to say that something terrible had happened to them. She didn't want to linger on that thought for too long; she had plenty of work to do and if she allowed herself to wallow, she would get nothing done. She needed to come up with a solid game plan, and if she had to search the entire island on her own, then that's what she would do. They were there somewhere—it was just a matter of searching for them.

She thanked the clerk and made her way up to her room. Her eyelids fluttered closed when she walked into the elevator. She would skip the bath altogether and just flop on the bed and go to sleep. She took an elevator up to the tenth floor and got out of the elevator. As she walked down the hallway, she saw someone standing in front of her room. She groaned inwardly as she realized that it was Craig, waiting for her. She would take just about any punishment at that point rather than have a conversation with him. She hated awkwardness, and she hated confrontations even more. After the day she had, she just wasn't in the mood for a verbal tango, even though she was interested to hear what he had to say for himself.

He spotted her as she was coming down the hallway and sort of waved at her sheepishly. *Yeah, I bet you feel like an idiot,* she thought. He waited until she made her way to the door before he said anything.

"Hi." He smiled softly at her.

"Hey."

She stood outside of the door, not willing to open it as long as he was there. They would talk in the hall all night, if that's what it took—she was going to bed alone that night. The personal comfort would have been tempting because the sex was always very satisfying with him, but she was just too tired to be with another person.

"I hear you had quite a day today. You want to explain to me why you were fighting with Devon at the beach?"

His eyes darkened and he frowned. She had never

seen that look before. "You weren't supposed to hear about that."

"Yeah, well, word travels fast. What the hell were you thinking?"

"Devon was trying to make a move on you the other day. I wasn't about to let him think he could try to take you away. I'd kill him first."

"Who the hell do you think you are? I have no interest in Devon. And you definitely shouldn't be punching people out over me."

"Harley, calm down. Dammit, you act like we haven't spent an amazing few weeks together."

She stared at him; his sandy blonde hair looked good against his tanned skin. He looked just like a beach bum, handsome and lean from his days surfing. Where did the angry streak come from?

She sighed. "What are you doing here, Craig? It's late. I just want to go to bed; can we talk about this tomorrow?"

His shoulders slumped. "Look, I just wanted to apologize in advance. Obviously, Devon and I shouldn't be fighting at all."

"Oh, I'm glad that you see the error of your ways. I was hoping you would acknowledge how ridiculous you behaved."

"Well, I wouldn't go that far."

"Seriously? Craig, you fought with your friend over me. Which is totally unnecessary, by the way. It's not pistols at dawn, you know?"

He laughed. "I know. I'm sorry. I just get a little crazy when I see other guys look at you. I'm crazy about you."

She looked him in the eyes, and he seemed to be genuinely sorry. Not that it mattered at that point. "Well, I appreciate it. But you didn't need to come all the way up here to say that. I'm sure we would have run into each other at the beach tomorrow."

"I know. I just wanted to see you. I didn't get a chance to hang out with you today." He tried to reach for her hand, but she pulled away from him.

"Craig…"

He frowned. "What's wrong?"

"I'm tired. Please, can we do this tomorrow? I've had a long day and I just want to crash."

There was silence between them before she spoke up again.

"Please, Craig."

Her eyelids were growing heavier by the minute as they talked. All she wanted to do was go to her room and sleep, but that would have to wait for the time being until she could get Craig to leave.

"Okay, you're right. We can do this tomorrow."

"Thank you." She leaned over and kissed him lightly on the lips.

He smiled back at her but didn't move from the spot. "I heard about Katie and Brian. They're really gone," he whispered.

She took a deep breath. "I don't know that yet. Did you see them that night?"

"No. I was just chilling alone that night. Do you think you will be able to find them?"

She shrugged. "Again, I don't know. It's too soon to tell. For all I know, they just got into an accident."

"You really believe that?"

She swallowed hard. "No," she whispered.

His gaze grew more serious. "Really?"

"Too much time has passed. They would have been back by now. If they were kidnapped or taken, there's no way they would still be alive. I don't want to think about it or think the worse, but I've been a cop too long. I can feel it in my bones that something is very wrong. I just wish I knew how to find them."

"Don't you?"

"Resources are limited here. I have no contacts. Jesus, I don't even have a gun. Don't say anything, though, Craig, I don't want to upset anyone until I know for sure."

"Well, if anyone can find them, it would be you, Harley."

She smiled. "I appreciate that, Craig. I hope I can do something for them, wherever they may be."

"I'll see you tomorrow, babe."

She nodded. "Sure Craig." She watched him walk away feeling confused about her feelings for him.

THIRTEEN

THE NEXT DAY, HARLEY HEADED downstairs to the lobby of the hotel in search of some Wi-Fi. The night before she had made a list of the things she needed to accomplish, and one of them was looking through the missing person's reports for the area in the past few years. She headed to the dining room to grab a cup of coffee; she hadn't been sleeping well, no thanks to Craig, and she needed some kind of pick-me-up to get her through the day. With coffee in hand, she made her way to the front desk.

"Where can I find the internet café?"

The woman did a double take before a slow smile spread across her face. "Follow me."

"That sounds promising." She followed the clerk to a room and waited while she opened the door. Inside the room, there was one solitary computer sitting against the back wall.

"You have to be kidding me, right?" Harley was

looking at the oldest computer known to man—it didn't even have a flat screen monitor.

"I'm afraid not, miss. If you want something better, you are going to have to go into the city. We don't have Wi-Fi here."

"What do you have?"

The woman just smiled and walked away. Harley turned back to the computer and closed the door behind her. She sat down at the desk and turned the computer on. She couldn't remember the last time she used a desktop computer. She clicked on the internet symbol in the right-hand corner, and the loud screech of dial-up caused her to shake her head slowly.

"What the fuck is this?" she whispered as she closed her eyes. She waited out the screech until it finally died off. Now that she had the slowest internet known to man at her disposal, she could finally get to work. She pulled up Google and started searching for missing persons for Phuket. She sipped her coffee as she waited for the page to load. The little hourglass turning in circles almost drove her crazy while she waited. Finally, the page loaded, and she started scrolling through the list.

It was just as she had suspected. The island had a rash of missing person reports in the past few months, none of which led to any arrests. Without any bodies, however, there was no proof that anyone was being killed. It could just as easily be a sex traffic ring, though typically men weren't the target of such things.

Without any bodies, she couldn't be sure of an MO; in fact, she could only guess that it was one person involved and not just random acts of violence. She continued pulling up the cases to see how many there were; she counted five missing persons in the past two months, and her friends weren't even included in the mix. What the heck was going on in Phuket? There was something unusual going on, and it seemed as if the police were unaware of the connection or they were completely ignoring it. If there was an epidemic going on in the area, why wouldn't they immediately start looking for her friends? Scrolling, she said, "Oh shit."

Her Spidey senses were kicking in as she read a few news clippings. As she read, it was much more serious than she had thought. She leaned back in her seat and sipped at her coffee, thinking. She knew she would have to travel to the city once again to talk to the chief. She had to make him see that there was something wrong. She knew she had to get him to take her plea seriously to start looking for her friends. So much time had already passed, and they needed to start searching the island immediately. She was not looking forward to making the long trip back to the city, but she didn't have a choice—she just wished that there was an easier way.

She turned off the computer and grabbed her cup of coffee. She rushed out of the room and right smack into a tall gentleman. Her coffee covered the front of his shirt, and her mouth dropped open.

"Oh my God, I'm so sorry. I'm such a klutz." She started wiping at his shirt with her hand only making the situation worse. "I need to stop. I'm sorry."

He chuckled. "Hey, it's okay. I hear they have a great dry-cleaning service here."

She looked up to meet his gaze and felt instantly warm all over. She had just spilled her coffee all over one of the most gorgeous men she had ever laid eyes on. She recognized him from the restaurant. He was a businessman and he was well-known in the hotel, and definitely well-liked. He seemed to come to Phuket frequently, and she could see why people liked him—he was hot. She had seen him a few times on the beach as well, talking to the ladies and drinking beers with people. She never had the pleasure of meeting him face-to-face, though she wished she had. He had black hair, short on the side and a little longer on top. He had blue eyes that reminded her of the very ocean she had tried surfing in for the first time. He was smiling down at her, and even his teeth were perfect, not a tooth out of place. God, he was the perfect male specimen, and she had covered him in coffee. Just being near him, she felt a heat radiate off him, and it drew her to him.

"I really am sorry. I was rushing, and I didn't see you."

"I'm not complaining."

She blushed as she smiled up at him. He had to be well over six feet. "I should go."

"I didn't even get your name. Though I think I

recognize the hair."

She couldn't believe that she had the sudden urge to start giggling around him. His gaze was mesmerizing. "I'm Harley."

"Harley, that's beautiful. It's nice to meet you, Harley. I'm Rayland."

She smiled. "It's nice to meet you as well."

"Can I convince you to have a drink with me? It's a little early, but they do serve mimosas."

"But your shirt."

"Oh, it always looks like this. Don't worry about it."

She laughed and glanced at the entrance to the hotel. She really had to go, but when she glanced back at him, she couldn't seem to pull herself away. "I don't know."

"C'mon." He motioned to his shirt with a big grin on his face.

Smiling sheepishly, she shrugged. "Okay, maybe just a quick one, but then I have to go."

"I understand. Let's go before you change your mind." He surprised her by grabbing her hand and pulling her along after him. Her smile widened as she followed him to the dining room where they grabbed a seat at the bar. There was an instant connection between them, and it's like she had known him all along. He was certainly handsome, and the connection she felt toward him intrigued her greatly. She would never have agreed to sit down with anyone for a drink when things were so crazy in her life, but she felt like she would regret it forever if she didn't. He was exactly the kind of guy she could see herself staying in bed all day with. It was only one drink and maybe it would allow her to clear her head for a moment. She settled in her seat as he ordered them both mimosas. When the waiter served them, Rayland handed her a glass, and she took a tentative sip.

"So, what brings you to Thailand, Harley, business or pleasure? By the way you were running out of the office, I would say business."

She smirked. "Yeah you would think, but I was just doing a little research. I'm actually on an extended vacation from work. What about you?"

"All pleasure for me. I'm a businessman who rarely takes vacations, so I like to enjoy them while I can. Thailand is a beautiful place."

She sipped her drink, loving the sound of his voice—it was so deep and throaty. She could get lost in a voice like that.

"This has been my first real vacation in a while as well. I'm sort of a workaholic." Wasn't that the truth—there she was on the island doing detective work all over again while she was on vacation.

"Well, lucky for me you decided to take that vacation."

She smiled. "I agree." She felt good around him; they talked naturally together.

He smiled back at her. "Is there any way that I can talk you into spending the day with me? I was thinking of taking out a catamaran, and you would be a hell of a partner."

She stared at him, wishing that she could go. She wanted nothing more than to shirk responsibility and spend some time with this mystery man. She suddenly felt guilty for the way she felt when she was with Craig. It just did not have the same spark. She couldn't help the gravitational pull she felt toward Rayland—when his hand grazed hers on the table, a spar of electricity went through her. She couldn't believe that her heart was beating hard with a man she met, like, five seconds ago. She felt flushed around him and that made her want to explore what it all meant.

Now was not the time, though. She knew deep down that she needed to go and find some answers for her friends. Something was terribly wrong with the island, and she couldn't just sit there having drinks with a guy while time was running out. There would be another time, a moment where she wasn't so on edge, a time that she could relax and enjoy his company.

"I wish I could, Rayland, I really do. But I was on my way out to take care of some business, and I still need to do that."

"Business while on vacation, that's not the way it's supposed to work."

She finished the rest of her drink while smiling at him. She had time, possibly enough for another drink before she took the exhausting trip back to the city. "I really can't. But maybe I could sit and have another drink before I go."

"Well, I'm going to take what I can get." He motioned for the waiter to bring them another round. Two more drinks were set before them, and she collected hers, taking a drink from the glass. What were the chances that she would meet Rayland when she was already spending time with another man? She hadn't felt this good around someone since Chris. He grazed her hand with one of his fingers, and it felt like the most natural thing in the world.

"I should probably mention that I've been spending time with someone on the island, so running off with another man would probably be inappropriate."

"Oh? And who is this other man? Your soulmate?" There was laughter in his eyes.

She laughed. "No, probably not." "Well, I would hate to lose an opportunity over someone who's not your soulmate."

She nodded. "I should probably talk with him first, though, before we spend any time together. I hope you can respect that."

"Of course, Harley."

She smiled up at him just as she heard her name being called. The connection was broken as her brow furrowed. She turned to see Keri walking into the dining room. It looked like she was crying and had been for some time. She reached Harley and grabbed her hand.

"I'm so glad I found you. I need your help."

"Keri, calm down. What's wrong?" The girl was in hysterics, breathing heavily, unable to catch her breath.

"Please, Harley." She looked anxiously at Rayland.

"Has something happened?"

"No, I just need to talk to you. I'm sorry, I haven't slept."

Harley looked at Rayland. "I'm sorry, my friend needs me. Maybe we can catch up another time."

"Absolutely. You are needed—I completely understand."

He had a warm smile, and she squeezed his hand as she got up from her chair. She grabbed her purse and followed Keri out the door.

"Geez, where do you find these guys? Even upset, I can still appreciate his level of hotness."

Harley burst out laughing as she squeezed her friend around the waist.

"Sorry for being a wet blanket, you seemed to be having fun."

"Oh well, that's a long story. You just gave me a reason to get out of there. He was distracting me, and I need to get back to the city."

The two of them sat on a bench outside of the hotel, and Harley hugged her friend tightly. "Are you okay, Keri? You really didn't seem like it in there."

"I just can't stop thinking about Brian and Katie. Where are they, Harley? It's been days. They must be dead, right? The worst has happened."

Harley sighed deeply. "We don't know that, and although it doesn't look great, we can't lose hope yet. Maybe they are just two crazy lovebirds enjoying some time alone."

"Without a change of clothes, without telling me?"

"I'm trying to stay positive here, Keri, and you're making it difficult."

Keri smiled. "Why are you going into the city? What's there?"

"The police. I was at the station yesterday morning, and it was a disaster. They didn't file a report or anything, but I went digging today, and I think I have enough probable cause to get them to at least start looking around."

"I'm coming with you."

"That's not necessary, Keri. Go enjoy the beach and try to take your mind off things."

"No, I'm coming with you this time. You don't need to do it alone. Besides, maybe they will be more willing to hear you if there is someone else there with the same story."

"Okay, fair enough, but I hope you like tailgating."

FOURTEEN

THE TRIP BACK TO THE city was a little more enjoyable with Keri by her side—time seemed to go by a little faster. Harley discussed what she had found on the internet about the things happening on the island. Keri's hand shook as Harley explained to her about the many people that had gone missing over the past months. Harley wasn't sure that she should have said anything, as she didn't want to scare the girl, but Keri had a lot of questions.

They were almost at the city—Harley could see it coming up in the distance—and Harley said, "Well, let's talk about something else. We don't need to dwell on the evil going on the island."

"Okay, so distract me. Anything to stop me from thinking about Katie and Brian."

"Absolutely. What would you like to talk about?"

"I don't know."

"What do you do back home, Keri?"

"What do you mean?"

"I mean, what is your life like back home? What do you do for a living?"

"I'm an airbrush artist."

Harley's eyebrows raised. "What's that?"

"I do custom body art on vehicles, mostly motorbikes, but I've done cars too. I use old school tools like an airbrush gun. My mother sent me to art school thinking that I was going to come out painting Picassos, and I ended up airbrushing Harley's. She feels like she wasted her money," Keri said with a smirk.

"You're kidding me? That's pretty cool. I've always appreciated people who can be creative. I couldn't draw or paint anything if my life depended on it. In the end, I think you should just do what you love and not worry about what other people think."

"Yeah, but Katie was always the perfect daughter. She's a dental hygienist, you know. No money wasted there, and she met the perfect guy, got married. She did all the things that parents want you to do. I think they just wish I was more normal, more like Katie."

"I think we all feel as if we disappoint our parents at one point or another, though I don't think that my mom ever really cared what I did," Harley smirked. "For the most part, our parents just want us to be happy, Keri, and if we show them that we truly are, then they do come around to our way. It's not like you ran away with the circus."

They both laughed, and Harley liked seeing a smile

on Keri's face. Her goal was to distract the girl, and that meant avoiding conversations that could get them back on the topic of her sister. As the truck rumbled its way through to town, Harley focused on talking about the latest movie, or how much she loved *The Beautiful and Damned*.

The pickup truck rumbled to a stop outside of the police station, and the two girls hopped out of the back. Harley thanked the men once again and gave them a tip; she had gotten to know them during her travels to the city, and although they never asked for payment, she was grateful for the many times they had helped her and asked for nothing. There weren't too many places in the world you could safely hop into the back of a truck without being worried about kidnapping—though, considering they were at the police department to discuss just that, maybe she needed to reconsider what she was doing.

They walked into the police station and made their way to the front desk. The officer standing there didn't look impressed to see her again. "Can I help you?"

"I'm here to see the chief."

"Is he expecting you?"

"That's doubtful."

He turned from them and spoke to an officer in another language. The man walked down the hall, and Harley could hear him yell, "Chief Aat."

A few minutes later, the chief rounded the corner and looked at her with disdain. She held his gaze unwaveringly as he approached the desk. He eyeballed Keri before meeting Harley's eyes again.

"I'm surprised to find you back here again, Harley. What can I do for you?"

"You know exactly why I'm here. My friends are still missing, and I would like you to do something about it." She glanced at Keri before looking back at the detective. "Is there somewhere that we can speak in private? It's important."

He stared at her for a moment before nodding.

"I'll be right back," she said to Keri with a smile. Keri nodded before sitting down in a chair in the waiting room. Harley followed Chief Aat to the back where he led her into an interrogation room. He closed the door behind them.

"What can I do for you?"

She hated the way he looked at her as if she had no business being there. She paused. "Is Ned here?"

"Officer Ornlamai has the day off today."

Shit. Well, she better just get it over with. "There is something wrong on the island. If you don't do something about it, I'm calling a ton of newspapers in the United States and discussing the conduct of the police department in Thailand. You won't get another tourist here again." She paused for effect. "You have a serial killer on the island."

She was pleased to see his mouth drop open; he recovered quickly, though. "Who the fuck do you think you are?" Chief Aat exploded.

"You heard me. I've been digging around and this is a much larger problem than I realized. The fact that you don't know what's going on is shocking, to say the least. It's time to do something, Chief, or I'm blowing this wide open."

"Don't threaten me, Harley. It wouldn't be the first time a couple has joyridden to another island only to come back weeks later."

"Yes, well, that isn't the case this time. We know our friends, and they just don't behave that way. Not to mention, I did a little of my own digging and it appears that there are many unsolved missing persons on the island." She pulled out papers from her searches and passed them to him. "Are you telling me that all these people have been hopping from island to island for months? They are dead, I guarantee it."

Chief Aat stared at Harley before he took the papers and scanned them quickly. He glanced at her momentarily, and Harley couldn't decide if she was getting through to him or not.

"Something is wrong. I understand you deal with crazy tourists all the time, but I have reason to believe that our friends have met a terrible fate. I'm afraid at this point it would only be bodies we would be looking for. That's the girl's sister out there, and she's worried. She knows her sister isn't just galivanting on the island. She hasn't received so much as a text message from her."

He turned from Harley and opened the door. He called for one of his men to come to the room. The man approached them, and the chief handed the papers to him. "I need you to scan these pictures of the couple and get a team together to start scavenging the island."

Harley breathed a sigh of relief as she watched the men collect together to get the pictures scanned. Chief Aat turned back to her, still looking very unhappy to see her. "We will take it from here, and I will let you know what we find out."

"Look, I'm not pumped about being thrown in here either."

He smirked at her, and she once again had the strong urge to punch him. "We can handle this situation. We don't need some American cop putting her nose where it doesn't belong."

Harley tried to hold her temper. She felt like she was going to blow her top, but she knew that would be a mistake. She needed to finesse her way into the situation; if she lost it on him, he would just have her escorted out.

She took a deep breath. "Can I get access to your database as a professional courtesy? I would like to do some digging of my own."

The chief snorted. "What database?" He walked back out of the room to the front where Keri was waiting. "Are you talking about these?" He held up some folders full of files. "Oh yes, we have plenty of these in the basement if you would like to take a look at them."

She stared at him in incredulity. "You don't have a computer database? You must be joking."

"Oh, sure we do. We ordered one—it's just been on back order for the past two years."

His tone dripped with sarcasm, and the look on his face was making it hard for Harley not to strike him. She was starting to understand why no one did anything about the missing people in the area.

"This is ridiculous. How do you get anything done around here?" Her words were just as biting as his, and she heard Keri suck in her breath.

"Let me show you something." Chief Aat motioned for her to come around the side of the desk, and she followed him down the hallway. He stopped at a door and unlocked it with a key. When he pushed the door open, she followed him inside. The room was massive, and it was filled with shelves. On the shelves were boxes and boxes filled with files. Just the sight of it was overwhelming. It would take her months just to find what she was looking for, and that's if she knew where to look.

"Dear God."

"This is just one room. The basement is about four times the size, and it's full. I can point you in a general direction if you want, but you won't solve any crimes in this room, Harley, I can assure you of that."

Harley groaned. "I'll pass, thanks." She could

probably get more done with the dial-up service at the hotel. She didn't really want to be part of the investigation—she was afraid of fucking things up—but the chief wasn't exactly going full steam and she was afraid that he was going to miss something important. She was going to have to start digging on her own; she certainly wasn't getting much help and support from the chief. She planned on doing her own search of the island as well, with or without the chief's permission. Judging by how they had handled things so far, she wasn't about to leave everything in their hands any longer. She was thrilled they were taking things seriously, but she knew she would have to get involved whether she wanted to or not.

"Let us handle it," the chief emphasized. "We will start searching the island within the hour. We have your number—if we find something, I will call you."

All she did was nod as she followed him back to where Keri was waiting for them. Without another word, they left the station as Harley wracked her brain on what she needed to do next.

"Well, that went over rather well," Keri muttered.

"I didn't expect anything more. They don't like foreigners butting into their business. Who cares if I can offer them some real help? They just aren't interested."

"God, how could they be so blind?"

"Let's go back. It's getting late and you must be emotionally exhausted."

Tears welled up in the girl's eyes. "I am."

When Harley made her way back to the hotel, she was looking forward to bed. She was exhausted from traveling all day, and by the time they arrived back on the beach, she had enough sun for the day. It wasn't long before they saw some officials showing up on the beach. They stayed out of the tourist's way and appeared surprisingly discreet. Harley knew the authorities would do anything to protect the tourist trade; it was what kept everyone in business. Harley, on the other hand, didn't care about the tourists, and if she had to make some waves, she certainly wasn't afraid to do so.

She was looking at the map that Keri drew her as she walked into the lobby of the hotel. She parked herself on one of the couches and tried to figure out where to start the next day. It wasn't a small island, and there were plenty of areas that were completely unknown to her. There were only so many places that one could hide a body, however, so she would focus on those areas first. The map was pretty rudimentary, but for the most part, she could figure out where things were and how to get to them. She would start first thing in the morning. Suddenly she had an idea. She got up from the couch and made her way to the front desk.

The woman at the desk smiled and approached her.

"How can I help you?"

Harley slid the map over to her. "Are there any abandoned buildings in the area? I'm thinking about areas that don't have a lot of tourist traffic."

The clerk looked down at the map. "There are tin mines in the area, scattered across the island. There are four of them."

"Are they empty?"

"Three of them are abandoned, one is still in use."

"Which one is the closest to us?"

"The Phuket tin mine." She pointed to a spot where the mine would be on the island.

Harley took the map back and looked at it, thinking about how easy it would be to hide bodies in the tin mine. Was that where her friends were? Would there be others?

Harley checked the time on her phone—it was too late to head to the mines, so she would wait until the next day. She motioned for the clerk to come back over.

"I need directions to the tin mine."

FIFTEEN

BUTCHER HAD HIS EYE ON his next prize: a girl that was sitting at the bar of the hotel that he was staying at. She was perfect. She radiated insecurities as her eyes darted around the bar, hoping to find someone to talk to. It was embarrassing to watch. She didn't have a single shred of confidence, and anyone in the room could see it. She didn't talk amiably with the bartender, nor did she keep to herself. Her eyes darted around from one man to another, her gaze lingering far too long as if she were mentally begging them to come and talk to her, pay attention to her. She was practically breaking into a sweat waiting for someone to buy her a drink. He knew that if he approached her, she would leave with him without a second thought. It was almost unfair how easy it would be.

A shout caught his attention, and he gazed out into the lobby. There was a man at the front desk shouting.

"What do you mean, mate? I just need her room

number."

The front desk clerk shrugged helplessly at the man. Butcher smiled when he realized who it was. The man had been hitting on Harley a few times while on the beach. He had a crush on her, and Butcher didn't like it. He would be an issue when it came time for Butcher to take Harley. He didn't need anyone getting in his way. He glanced quickly back at the woman at the bar and debated his options. He really wanted to feel her desperation in another way, but it looked like it was her lucky night after all. He turned back to the shouting man and watched him. Frustrated, the man turned from the clerk and marched out of the hotel room. Butcher slowly followed him outside to see where he was going. The man stood in front of the hotel as if he wasn't sure where to go. Butcher knew he would have to sneak up on him, as he would recognize him immediately; he didn't want him to see his face. He would have to use the back entrance of the hotel for this one.

Butcher grunted as he walked up the back stairs of the hotel. It was times like this that he wished he wasn't staying on one of the top floors of the hotel. The man was no slouch and carrying him over his shoulder was no easy task. He was taking a big risk, but he liked risks and he was confident that no one would ever catch him. He got to his floor and pushed open the door that led to the hallway. He glanced down the hallway to see if anyone was there, he didn't see anyone and he proceeded to his door. He put his key card in the door and when the green light came on, he pushed on the handle of the door.

He moved through the door quickly and brought the man to the living room and laid his body down on the plastic. He looked down at him and relished the thought of cutting him.

There was just something about *Bach's Toccata and Fugue* that got his blood pumping. The music reverberated throughout his hotel room, masking the sounds of the muffled cries for help. Butcher was staring down at the man as he was tied to a chair, his hands behind his back and cloth taped to his mouth. Butcher didn't like him one bit—this was the man that had been hitting on Harley regularly, and it was that knowledge alone that made Butcher want to end his life. It wasn't jealousy that he felt, because he was incapable of feeling anything. But no one would get in the way of him taking Harley.

The man was struggling in the chair, but Butcher knew he had no shot at getting out of the restraints. He smashed him in the face once, though, just to get him to stop struggling; he expected some decorum from his victims while he enjoyed the music. He closed his eyes as he felt the music. It was his mother that had given him the love of classical music. She would play it as she sat on the porch, a glass of wine in her hand.

When he opened his eyes, he looked at the man sitting there with his eye already starting to turn purple and tears streaming down his cheeks. Butcher went to the side table and poured himself a glass of whiskey. He swirled it around the glass, listening to the ice clink. Tied to a chair, the man sat on top of plastic that covered most of the room. Butcher always went to great measures to ensure that he didn't make a mess and splash DNA all over his room. There was something about blood splatter that was a work of art in of itself.

"I know you don't understand why I'm doing this to you, so let me be frank with you. I don't like you hitting on Harley. I thought I had made that clear already, but here you are at the hotel. I just need to get you out of the way. I'm sure you can understand that."

The man's eyes widened as the realization of his circumstance—and possibly Harley's—occurred to him. He started mumbling things furiously that Butcher couldn't make out.

"If I take off your muzzle, you won't scream, will you? If you do, I will gut you pretty quick."

He pulled the gag out of the man's mouth, and at first, he coughed and took a deep breath. "Crikey, man. How could you do this? Please don't hurt her. I will do anything. Just leave her alone."

Butcher shoved the gag back into the man's mouth as he looked at him with disgust.

"I don't know how Harley could stand even spending a moment with you. You don't even try to scream, do you? You just roll over to be killed, pleading for the sake of some girl. I'm going to enjoy your screams more than you realize."

He started to scream, and Butcher just watched him with a smile. No one would hear him no matter how loud he tried to scream. Killing him seemed more like a mercy killing than anything else. Butcher took a sip of his drink and let the liquid burn down his throat. The killing would be quick this time because he had already tired of the pathetic man. Harley would never have dated such a man, someone who was too weak to get away and save her. The crying man in the chair was just an embarrassment. Butcher set his drink down and picked a tool off the desk in his room. He brought it back and showed it to him.

"Have you ever found objects on the beach and just thought to yourself how lucky you were to find it? Sometimes, it can almost feel like kismet. This is what I found; it's a little rusty, but I think it will do the job well enough."

Butcher held in his hands a hacksaw rusted out from spending time on the beach. The man's eyes widened, and it was as if all the life just suddenly went out of his eyes. Had he given up already? The fun had not even started yet. He slowly set the rusty blade of the hacksaw on his leg, and the man suddenly thrashed and screamed out. Butcher smiled, loving the fact that the guy was finally showing a little life. He couldn't risk too much noise, however; he wasn't that brazen. Thankfully, the man passed out from shock. Butcher picked the hacksaw up and went about sawing off Devon's legs.

Butcher finished his whiskey while he listened to the music. The sound just set the tone for his deed, and he couldn't imagine killing without the melody in the background. Each time he sliced into something, he got the same chill as when the violin bow touched the bow, making magic.

    Butcher had been watching Devon for a while now, and suddenly he saw the man's eyelids flutter open. He didn't look well at all; he had lost a lot of blood, and his skin had become ashen. When he met Butcher's eyes, there was terror in them, and Butcher smiled. He continued to smile until the man looked down into his lap and saw only stumps. Butcher had wrapped them in plastic so he wouldn't bleed all over the place. He wanted him to see his artistry before he killed him, to know he should have stayed away from Harley. When he saw his stumps, tears streamed down his cheeks in a continuous motion. He started to sob silently in his seat which sickened Butcher even more.

He got up from his chair and calmly set down his drink. He picked up a long butcher's knife and walked toward the man. He wanted to make art just like the violin bow did.

"Harley will be mine. I just wanted to keep you alive long enough to fully understand what I'm capable of."

He shoved the blade into the man's stomach and stared into his eyes. He felt a rage building up inside of him, something he rarely felt during his kills, but he hated him. His rage wasn't directed at the right person. That red hair brought images of his mother to him. He would not let this man get in the way of him executing another redhead. He pulled the knife out and lifted it above his head. He plunged it down into Devon's chest, burying it deep. He kept stabbing him over and over again in a sea of red rage until the body hung limply in the chair. All he could see was his mother as the blade was brought down time and again. There was so much blood, much more than usual. But the rage was gone now, and that was all that mattered. Staring at the body, Butcher felt pleased with himself for finally shutting the man up and getting the peace he so rightly deserved. He needed to get to work on taking him apart so that he could bury him.

After Butcher had chopped up the body and sectioned

off his parts, he started placing them in a large suitcase. He would be able to take the body down in one trip because the suitcase had wheels. It was quite a roomy case and he filled the whole thing with the body. He felt better about himself now that Devon was out of the way. He wouldn't have to worry about him going after Harley. Not that he really needed to worry—the guy had been a lot weaker mentally than he had originally thought. He wasn't sure how Harley could even smile at him. She would probably thank him in the end for getting rid of him for her.

Once the body was packed away, Butcher took the handle and pulled the suitcase behind him. He left the hotel and made his way down the hallway toward the elevator. Once inside he breathed a sigh of relief—the demons inside him were settled for the night. He would dispose of the body at another tin mine and finally be able to return to his bed to sleep. His mind had quieted, and he would be able to sleep soundly. Maybe he would dream of Harley and see her again. He couldn't wait to have that red hair in his hands. He would fall asleep with Harley close to his thoughts.

SIXTEEN

THE TIN MINE WAS A creepy, dingy place that looked like it hadn't been used for centuries. Even in the daylight, the sight of it caused shivers to go up Harley's spine. She had learned from the desk clerk that there were a few tin mines in the Phuket and Phang Nga regions of Thailand. It used to be a fairly popular enterprise years ago, but not so much these days. Large amounts of tin were found in Thailand during the 30s and 50s, and a means of extracting it made the cost go through the roof. Corporations came in to do the job, and many committees and councils were set up to control the tin market. Of course, a lot of that changed when the stock market crashed in the 80s leaving the business of tin mining cut practically in half. Over the years, the need for tin decreased significantly, and in 2002, only 30 of the 145 tin mines were still in operation. There were only a handful of mines in Thailand, and very few of them in the area were operational.

Harley stood outside of the mine wondering where she should start. She didn't realize how massive the place was until she had arrived. On the outside of the mine, there were handmade wooden tracks extensively built up to ten stories high. They looked as if they were still in good condition. The tracks had been used to bring the tin out from the mines on carts.

She made her way to the entrance of the mine and turned on her flashlight—despite the fact that it was mid-day, there wasn't much light inside. The flashlight didn't offer her much light as she moved into the cavern. It was cooler in the caverns than it was outside, and as she made her way inside, sweat beaded on her forehead but it felt cool against her skin. The mine that Harley found herself in had been shut down for years. It would be the perfect place to deposit bodies, and she was shocked that no one had thought to look there when people started to go missing. The place was massive, and Harley wasn't sure where to start looking or how safe it would be for her to go deep into the tin mine. The mine looked no different than any other mine; there were caverns deep within the land of Phuket and once inside, it opened up to large spaces where equipment could be brought in.

She followed one of the caverns into an open area where there was abandoned equipment lying around. The smell hit her first, and she knew she came to the right place. Her stomach roiled as the soiled smell hit her nose. She covered her nose and mouth with the sleeve of her sweater and gagged a few times. The smell of decomposing flesh was in the air, and it was made worse by the heat of the room. It was bloody hot outside, and that likely accelerated the decomposition. The air grew hotter as she went deeper into the mines, and she started to feel uncomfortable. The day was growing late, and inside the mines, the air was still humid and damp. The further in the mines she went, the riper the smell became. There was something dead in those mines, and Harley really hoped that it was an animal. She instinctively reached for her gun, though there was nothing to reach for. She closed her eyes and took a deep breath, feeling the old anxiety creeping up inside of her.

She decided to circle her way around the open area to check all possibilities.

As she took each step slowly, her eyes scanned the ground for anything out of place—disturbed earth or rock that had been moved out of place. The mine was so silent that it was unnerving. The stillness in the air still had a life to it, like a breathing, feeding entity. Being in there creeped her out, and the idea that there were dead bodies in there to be discovered was not helping.

Circling the room, she discovered that there was nothing amiss along the walls of the large space—nothing appeared out of place. She made her way into the middle of the room where the equipment was laid. There was a tractor in the center of the room, and Harley climbed on it. She sat in the seat and looked around for keys. She checked under the seat, but they were nowhere to be found. Judging by the amount of dust on the tractor, there hadn't been anyone using the equipment in quite some time. She turned around looking behind the tractor, her eyes settling on a mound of earth that looked to be disturbed. She slowly got down from the tractor and made her way to the freshly disturbed earth. She hid her face in her sleeve as the smell grew worse. She reached down and swiped the area; it was obvious that someone had been in the mines recently. She stood up and surveyed the area, feeling suddenly as if she were being watched. The mines stayed silent, but the feeling stayed with her. Looking around, she spied a rusty shovel. She picked it up and went to work on the mound. As the ground piled up around her, she dug in again and hit something soft. She bent down and moved the remaining dirt to find a couple of garbage bags. She narrowed her gaze and pulled at one of the garbage bags. The bags spilled and she gasped as a foot tumbled out into the hole. She recoiled and let go of the bag.

"Oh shit."

She threw herself out of the grave and went running out of the open area and down the caverns. She raced through the cavern, her heart beating a mile a minute. Once outside, she sucked in the fresh air as she desperately tried to catch her breath. She fished her phone out of her phone and checked the signal. She walked around for a while before she saw the bars show up. She laughed with relief as she made a call to the police department in Thailand.

She barked into the phone. "I need to speak with Chief Aat immediately. It's an emergency."

She waited as she tried to catch her breath, her heart still hammering in her chest.

"Chief Aat here."

"I found a body." She burst out with excitement.

"Who is this?"

"It's Harley, dammit! I found someone in the Phuket tin mine. You need to get here immediately."

The line disconnected and she stared at the phone. *Well, that was rude,* she thought. She shut off her phone and looked around the area, wishing that she wasn't alone. She wasn't sure how long it would take for the police to get there but she returned to the site of the body and waited. She didn't want to disturb the crime scene even more than she had done, but she stared at the garbage bag lying in the grave wondering who was inside of it.

Harley stayed to the side of the commotion as police and the medical examiner's team milled into the mine. She had briefed the chief as soon as he walked in, and then she stepped aside so that they could do their job. She expected there to be more care brought to the crime scene, but there were way too many people walking around in areas that they had no business in. As she watched the crime scene investigators survey the area and look for evidence, she had a sense of foreboding. The team was a lot more lax than it would have been in the States. Harley worried that evidence was going to be disturbed or looked over. She had already tried to get involved in the crime scene, but the chief had sent her away. It wasn't her job to secure a crime scene; she was just anxious to find out who was in the bag. She had no idea how she would be able to break the news to Keri if she discovered that her sister and husband were in those bags. Keri would be inconsolable, and Harley wanted more than anything to save her friend from that kind of pain. Although she no longer believed that the couple was alive, she hoped that she would be wrong about that.

She watched as they extracted the garbage bags and opened them. She watched as her friend Ned approached the team, and she was happy to see him there. The investigator's hand had gone straight to his nose to prevent the smell from affecting him. The examiner looked through the bag and started pulling out a body part. Fear filled Harley's entire body and she wished she could turn away, but her eyes were glued to the body. The chief bent down and spoke with the medical investigator. He then turned and stared at Harley. She steeled herself for the news as he walked over to talk to her. She was glad to see that Ned was following right behind. Ned smiled at her, but the chief wasn't as happy to see her.

"What the hell were you thinking? Do you have any idea how out of bounds this is?"

"It was just a hunch and I decided to follow it. I didn't exactly have time to make another trip into town to inform you."

"You had no business being here in the first place, Harley. You have no jurisdiction here, for Christ's sake, and you have no right involving yourself in this situation. This is not your case, so stay out of it."

She sighed. "Is it them?" she whispered.

He stared at her for a moment before answering. "No. It's a single female. She's been cut up into pieces. Not all the pieces, just the torso—there isn't even a head. Why would he break up the pieces?"

"Maybe he likes keeping souvenirs, or maybe he's trying to make identification harder. How do you know it's not just Katie?" Harley asked.

"She's probably been there for a week longer than your missing friends. It's not her. We will have to look to see if there are any more missing tourists."

She snorted. "Oh there is," she said rolling her eyes.

"How did you find the body? How would you know where to look?" He eyed her suspiciously. The look on his face ruffled her feathers.

"Oh, do you think I'm the killer? It was just a hunch; my friend made me a sketchy map of the island, so I started to look for abandoned places. The hotel clerk told me there were a lot of tin mines in the area, so I decided to take a look."

"Sounds like you got pretty lucky."

She sighed. "Fuck luck, it was brilliant."

Ned was stifling a laugh behind the chief. The chief stared at her, and she couldn't read his expression. She wasn't sure if he was getting the severity of the situation. Did he understand that this was just the beginning? That there could be bodies all over the island? She could bet that he had never experienced anything like that before. He was shocked that she had even come across the body. This was a tourist area. The last thing they would want is for word to get out that someone was dismembering the tourists.

"You have a serial killer on your island."

"I think you may be right, Harley."

"My friends are still out there."

"I will do everything in my power to find them. You have my word. We will do an extensive search of the mine and then start checking other areas on the island."

Harley breathed a sigh of relief knowing that she had finally lit a fire under the chief's ass so he would go out and help find her missing friends. She knew that whatever happened now that they would treat her with respect because she found a body when no one else had. In their eyes, she was a hero—the only person that had found a body and discovered a deranged killer on the loose. She was going to get involved whether they liked it or not.

"Look, I don't mean to be harsh with you," the chief

said. "What you did was reckless and dangerous. I can't just let you run loose around here. But I also can't ignore the fact that you made a huge discovery, one that I have to admit we probably wouldn't have found on our own. You did a great job, Harley. We may never have found the body, and you should be proud of yourself."

She slowly smiled. "Now are you going to let me help?"

A sheepish look came across the chief's face, and Harley felt a small moment of satisfaction. He would have to listen to her now. He surprised her, though, when he sighed. "I can't have you here in any official capacity. I can't hand you a badge like the old west. I can keep you informed, and that's all."

He turned and walked back to the crime scene.

"That was pretty awesome," Ned said with a pleased look on his face. "Seriously, it would have taken us a while to get to this point. I'm glad you're here."

"Then help me. Get me what I need."

He stared at her for a moment. "I'll see what I can do."

Seeing the body being processed and bagged, Harley felt a chill go up her spine.

SEVENTEEN

HARLEY STOOD OUTSIDE OF THE tin mine as she watched the medical examiners bring out the body of the woman they found. Just the thought of that body, with all its pieces missing, would keep her up at night for sure. It could hardly be considered a body, of course, being only the torso, after all, but it was all they had. She wondered where the other pieces had ended up and why the killer had decided to leave them somewhere else. Was it just a means of distraction or was he keeping the heads for souvenirs? The killer would need some serious storage space if he were going to keep multiple heads. She shuddered at the thought that there may be a room somewhere on the island with a bunch of heads lined up.

The chief came out of one of the caverns with a few of his men, and they were talking animatedly. She couldn't help but smile knowing that she finally got them moving on the case of the missing people on the island. They had no choice but to search everywhere for her friends. She knew that the chief was in the process of getting a search of the caverns done immediately, and she wondered if there were any more bodies in the tin mine or if the killer would have scattered them all over the island. It would be her job to help use all her resources to find the killer, hopefully before something happened to her friends. Every part of her cop instinct was telling her that they died the night that they went missing, especially after she found the torso. It was just unlikely at that point that they would still be alive.

Her heart hurt for Keri, and she was not looking forward to the day that she would have to tell her that there was no longer any hope. Keri had become her closest friend, and it hurt her to think that there would be nothing she could do to help her friend. She could only offer her some measure of peace once they found the bodies. But she would be returning home alone to grieve with her family. Katie and Brian would never unwrap their wedding gifts or move into their new home. It was almost too much to bear, but she knew she had to keep her shit together because she would be useless if she started to fall apart now. It was pretty clear, though, that they were dealing with a sick serial killer—it was unlikely that he was keeping anyone alive. There was no telling at that point how many people had been killed; they could be looking at a real problem. How dangerous was this person and how long had he been allowed to roam free, killing anyone he wanted to?

The body was being lifted onto a boat; it was the only option to get back to the island from the tin mines. The killer would have had to come in the same way; she would have to check to see if any boats had been rented out recently to tourists. The idea of someone floating over with a bag full of body parts was cringe-worthy.

She couldn't help but think about Chris and the day that she watched him be buried. The day of his funeral was surreal, and there were parts she couldn't clearly remember. She barely connected at the moment because she had to be on Valium just to get there. She had great friends on the force, and she almost considered not going to the funeral. She had been hysterical the day the funeral arrived. She couldn't imagine attending an event where she was supposed to pay respects to the dead, but he was only dead because of her. She had killed him, and now she would have to face his family and friends, and she didn't think that she could do it.

She remembered sitting on her bed, tears streaming down her cheeks. She had been sitting there knowing that there was no way that she could go to the funeral when the captain and a few of the officers from the precinct showed up. They had found her in the bedroom, and the captain had bent down in front of her. The team had been through so much together, good and bad. She hated crying in front of them because she had always been so tough before and now she just felt weak.

"I can't do this."

He nodded his head slowly. "Harley, you know you will regret not going for the rest of your life. He was your partner, and you need to say goodbye."

"He's dead because of me, Cap, because of me."

"No one blames you, we all would have done the same thing. This is not your fault. He would have killed you, to keep his secret and to save his own life. He shot at you—what were you supposed to do? He didn't exactly leave you much choice."

Tears were streaming down her cheeks. What he was saying was true, but she still couldn't go—she couldn't stand there among those people and not have every bone in her body ache to bring back the man she had loved in more than one way. She could barely live with the fact that she had killed him. She shook her head.

"The captain's right," Kevin, one of the officers, said. "We respect what you have gone through, but you need to be there."

She stood up suddenly, feeling her blood boiling beneath the surface. "What the fuck would you know about anything?" she screamed. She was feeling hysterical and a little out of control. Her hands were shaking as she stood in Kevin's face.

"Harley!" the captain warned.

"What?" She turned on the captain. "I'm sick to fucking death of everyone pretending they know how I feel. You don't have a fucking clue."

She had marched away from them before she lost complete control and was tempted to hurt one of them, and she went into the bathroom, slamming the door behind her. She sat down on the cold tile floor, willing her hands to stop shaking. There was a soft knock on the door.

"*Stay the fuck away from me!*" *she screamed at the door. She might kill one of them if they came through the door. Just like that, she was sobbing, tears streaming down her cheeks.*

"*Harley, are you alright?*"

She put her hands over her ears and started to scream. She screamed so loudly that her throat felt raw. Someone grabbed her shoulders and shook her.

"*Harley, stop it. Stop it!*"

She stopped screaming and looked up, her eyes wild, to see her captain bent over her, concern etched on his face.

"*I'm fucking losing it, aren't I?*"

"*Well, you've definitely had better days.*" *Kevin and the other officer, Phil, were standing outside of the bathroom looking awkward. It probably wasn't every day that they saw someone unravel right before their eyes. The two had been partners and comrades with her and Chris for years. She loved them—they were all really great friends.*

"*Breathe.*"

She started taking deep breaths until she felt a little more stable.

The captain held out his hand. "Take this; it will help you get through today. If you don't go, you will regret it for the rest of your life."

She looked down at the pill in his hand and nodded. She took it from the captain, and Phil passed her a glass of water. She placed the pill on her tongue and drank the remaining water in the glass.

"Now get up and do something with yourself, because you look like hell," Kevin remarked with a laugh.

She laughed as well, feeling much better about her circumstances. "Sorry for being such a pussy, guys."

Phil chuckled. "Pussy? I was scared to go to the bathroom a moment ago. You're holding your own, Harley; I couldn't even imagine being in your position right now. We know you're a badass."

She sighed deeply and got up from the floor. She made her way to the sink to get ready for the funeral. She knew she would be able to do it with her squad behind her. They had her back, and she knew it would give her the strength she needed to get through the day.

As she washed her face, applied her makeup, and brushed out her crimson hair, she felt her mood shifting, and a calmness settled over her. The Valium had kicked in; it would save her from that day.

She had stood at the gravesite feeling numb as she watched the casket get lowered into the grave. She was thankful that she couldn't feel anything.

When Chris's mother approached her, Harley wasn't sure whether she should shrink away. Her husband had his arm around her and neither of them looked very happy to see her.

"I don't know whether I should slap you or hug you. Whether I should hate you or understand that you are feeling the same pain we are."

Harley's eyes welled up with tears. "I'm so sorry. I realize that I'm the cause of your pain."

His mother nodded. "I know how much he meant to you, Harley; I saw it on your face every time that he brought you by the house. I also know how much you meant to him. I understand you did what you had to do and that it wasn't what you wanted to do. But I can't exactly be happy with what's been done either."

"I know," she whispered. Tears trailed down her cheeks. They were in so much pain and whether she liked it or not, it was her fault. They had lost a son because she pulled the trigger.

His mother leaned in and pulled her into a hug. The two women cried together for the boy they loved.

"I don't blame you, Harley, I just wish my boy was not dead."

Harley nodded into her shoulder. "Me too."

She hoped one day she could get beyond the guilt of losing her partner.

As people started to leave the cemetery to head back to Chris's mother's place, Harley stood in front of the gravestone, looking down, thankful for the fact that the Valium calmed her so that she didn't have to feel the extreme emotions she felt when she was at home. Her best friend, and partner—she couldn't understand how she didn't know that he had gone bad. At what point had he decided to turn his back on the badge? She felt lost when she thought about it because she felt that she should have known. Why had he decided to go to the dark side? If it was all about the money he was getting, why couldn't he have come to her first? She didn't have millions of dollars, but she would have done anything to help him. They could have gotten through anything together—that was the whole point of friendship, after all. How could she have not known? Could she even trust her own judgment anymore? She had fallen in love with a man that had turned his back on everything he believed in, and he had not come to her for help.

She felt crushed that she had been betrayed by the one person that she had complete trust in. She couldn't control the sobs that built up from her chest. She fell to her knees in front of the grave and broke down. She stayed in that spot until the captain came to find her and pull her up from the ground.

"It's time to go, Harley."

She nodded, wiping her tears. He had grasped her hand and pulled her away from the gravesite.

"Harley? Harley! Are you okay?"

She snapped out of the memory realizing that someone was trying to talk to her. She turned to find Ned behind her, looking at her with concern.

"Sorry, I'm fine. Just lost in thought."

"You did great in there. You were right, and I want you to know that. I just don't want you to get your hopes up about your friends. It's not looking good."

"I know the reality of the situation. I get it. I just want to give her family some peace at least. I don't want Keri to have to go home never knowing what happened to them."

"We'll get the person who did this."

"I sure as hell hope so."

EIGHTEEN

A FEW DAYS LATER, HARLEY was sitting on the balcony of her hotel. She was still trying to process the events of the previous few evenings. She had a lot on her mind, and things had been crazy.

She had a glass of wine in her hand as she stared out at the ocean. God, it was just so beautiful there, it was hard to believe that so much could go wrong in a place like that.

Her phone buzzed and she looked down at it, seeing a text message from Craig pop up. She sighed. Setting her glass down, she went back into her hotel room, sliding the balcony door closed. She left her hotel room and made her way to a higher floor and knocked on Craig's door.

He answered the door and there was a look of surprise that came over his face.

"Harley, wow, it's so good to see you."

"Are you busy? Can we talk for a bit?"

"Of course, come in."

She walked into his hotel room which was very much like her own. "Do you want a drink? I was just having a whiskey myself."

"No, thank you."

They walked out to the balcony and she took one of the chairs.

He smiled down at her and the moment she met his eyes, she felt sad.

"Craig, we need to talk. Things have been off with us a little lately, and I don't think that I want to continue this anymore."

"What? What are you talking about?"

"This isn't what I was looking for when I came to Thailand."

"Well, neither was I. I came here to party and chase topless Danish girls down the beach. It was supposed to be a guys' vacation of fun for me. I didn't mean to get attached to someone, but these things happen, and I'm not sorry they did."

"Craig, please."

"What? I don't understand." He sat up, looking exasperated.

"I don't feel the same way."

"You can't be serious? We've spent so much time together. You know that we always have a wonderful time together. So, what's the problem?" "The problem is, you're not the one for me. I came here for some freedom, not to settle down with someone. I don't want strings attached to me while I'm trying to figure out my life. Yes, we got close, and we've had some fun together, but I just don't feel it. We can still be friends and hang out. I just don't want to continue sleeping together; I don't want to lead you on."

"I can't believe what I'm hearing. Are you throwing the friends card at me? I thought something real was happening between us. This should make it really easy for Devon to swoop right in."

She closed her eyes to avoid rolling them. She hated these talks—they were so awkward, and there was always one person who loved more than the other, and that's what made falling in love so brutal. You never knew where it was going to lead and who would be more damaged when it finally ended. That was her experience—it always ended with someone falling out of love while the other wondered what the hell happened. She had never been lucky in love, and she had always believed that she would one day win Chris's heart, so she never really dated much. Her last boyfriend had cheated on her, ruining any hope she had that there were any decent men left out there. She thought maybe they could work things out, but he told her he didn't love her anymore, and that knowledge had crushed her more than his betrayal. Now she was hurting someone else, and she wished she didn't have to.

"I'm sorry that I gave you the wrong impression—it certainly was the last thing that I intended to do."

"Oh, give me a break. Don't treat me like a charity

case."

She shook her head. "I'm not." She got up from the chair.

"You're crazy; that's what your problem is. You don't see something amazing right before your eyes. You're just willing to throw it away."

She sighed. "I think this conversation is over. I'm not crazy just because I don't have feelings for you. This behavior certainly doesn't have me feeling the warm and fuzzies toward you either."

He picked up the glass of whiskey and threw it against the balcony floor, causing her to jump.

"What the fuck is wrong with you?"

"Just go, Harley, you ran from your other life, go ahead and run from this one too."

She stared at him in disgust and then walked off his balcony without another word. She started walking through his hotel room toward the door when she heard him call out to her.

"Harley, wait!"

Without turning around, she flipped him the bird and kept on walking, slamming the door behind her.

He was out in the hallway in seconds. "Harley!"

She turned, glaring at him.

"The way that I just behaved wasn't right, and I just wanted to say that I'm sorry. I'm upset that you want to end things and I really don't understand why. We seemed so hot together, you know? So, I didn't know why it has to end. We can fix this."

"Really? Because you didn't seem to think anything was wrong to begin with. So, what exactly would you fix? There wasn't anything wrong; we're just not meant to be together."

The last thing that she wanted to do was discuss all the reasons why she didn't want to stay with him. Why couldn't he just accept that things were over and move on? He was a handsome man—he could probably have one of those topless Danish girls after him by the end of the day.

"I can be the kind of man that you are looking for. Please, Harley, just give me a chance."

He looked desperately at her, and all she felt was pity for him. He was a great guy; he just wasn't the one for her.

"I don't want you to change, Craig. That's not what I want at all. You're a great guy; I'm just not looking for anything serious. I have a lot going on in my life these days, and when I came to Thailand, I never intended on looking for love. I needed to get my life together, and I just don't want you to get hurt."

"Please, I can take things slow. I've never met anyone like you before. I don't want to lose the connection that we have."

"That connection only existed in the bedroom, Craig. The sex is great—I'm not going to lie—but it's not enough. Again, it's…"

"It's not you; it's me," he said bitterly.

"I'm sorry. I really am."

"Can you come back inside and talk?"

"Absolutely not. I'm stressed and, no offense, but I don't need to get sucked back into the bedroom with you. It would be far too tempting."

"Would that really be so bad?"

"No, it wouldn't be so bad, but that's not what either of us wants. You want more, and I just can't give you that."

He slid down the wall and sat on the floor. She fought the urge to roll her eyes. She was clearly not getting rid of him anytime soon. She looked down at him on the floor and wished she could just go back to her room. She wasn't a complete bitch, however, so she sat down on the floor beside him and hoped that they were at least able to sit in silence. She didn't want to talk any longer. He was just looking into his lap, and she decided to wait him out. There was nothing more that she could say to him that would make him feel better about the situation. She would not go backward and try again. She knew what she wanted, and it wasn't Craig. She needed to feel a strong connection, the same thing that she used to feel when she was around Chris. He always had a magnetism that was addicting in every aspect. Without it, she always felt like something was missing. When she looked at Craig, all she could see was a weak-minded man who lacked confidence. She didn't want a man that was willing to change everything about himself just to please her. She wanted a man that was strong to complement who she was, and Craig was not the kind of person that she saw herself spending the rest of her life with. She felt bad for him, and that wasn't what you wanted from a lover or a soulmate.

Every time she thought of the perfect man, Chris's face came to her. That was the saddest part of all, the idea that she had already met the love of her life and he was now gone from her life forever. By her own hands, nonetheless. She wasn't sure what her future held or who would be by her side, but she knew it wasn't going to be Craig.

"Craig."

He looked up at her. "I'm sorry."

"You don't need to apologize, but it's getting late. I'm exhausted."

Harley made her way to her hotel room. Her thoughts were clouded and the more she thought about some of the things Craig had said to her, the angrier she got. He had behaved like a dick all the while she was just trying to be honest. She wasn't nuts. It wasn't like she was unraveling at the seams. She just didn't want to linger in his bed any longer. Hell, maybe that did make her nuts. They were having fun, and he sure was handsome, but there was no spark, no intensity to their bond. There were even times that she forgot he was even on the island unless they were together, and that couldn't be good.

Her eyes were growing heavy, and all she wanted to do after her altercation with Craig was to crawl into bed and drift off into a dreamless sleep. But she still had a lot of work to do. She walked into her room and settled on her own balcony, determined not to think about Craig any longer.

She couldn't believe that her extended vacation away had landed her in a situation where she would be hunting down a serial killer. Maybe it was fate's way of telling her that she would be crazy to give up being a cop. That was why she had come, after all, to figure out what she wanted for her life now that Chris was gone. There she was back in the mix of things and she felt useful again. She did not doubt in her mind that she could do the job effectively and find who was dismembering people on the island. She just wished she could have done more to help her friends—though, she had certainly tried. No thanks to the chief, but she knew he had his hands full now. The last thing he would want is bad press from the U.S. Once word got out that there was a killer in Thailand, tourism would take a hit.

She yawned as she looked out at the ocean. It was such a soothing sight and yet there was something menacing out there, stalking prey like a game. She hadn't been sleeping well since they found the body at the tin mine. She had been playing in her mind over and over again what had happened at the tin mine.

The search of the mine had come up with more body parts that belonged to the torso. The head was still missing, but they were able to at least identify the body from the fingerprints.

Ned had sent her a copy of the file without the chief's knowledge, and she flipped through it while she sipped her wine. She wasn't supposed to have the file; he was sending her things under the radar. There were pictures of the autopsy conducted on the torso. There were no fingerprints, hair samples, or any other form of DNA that they could have traced back to the killer. The killer was meticulous with his work. There was no indication of where he killed the woman, and the body had obviously been wrapped in plastic before it was dumped in the mine. It was completely clean. The headless woman had been a tourist from Texas, in Thailand on the first vacation she had in years. The only identifying mark on her was a tattoo she had on her back. They could use that tattoo to scout to see if anyone knew her. It was by sheer luck that she had been seeing a guy on the island who immediately recognized her tattoo. He said she had been missing for weeks; he thought she had just picked up and left without saying goodbye. The family had already been contacted and the body would be transported back to the United States. A search was being conducted in her hotel room, but Harley knew that she wasn't killed there—the killer was taking them somewhere. She flipped through the autopsy photos trying to see if there was a message. The girl had been beautiful with flowing red hair that almost reached her behind. Harley looked for something that the killer was leaving behind.

Serial killers were a tricky bunch. They didn't think the same way as normal people did. Studies had been done on psychopath's brains. Common words such as "rape" and "murder" triggered a response in a normal person's brain. But not a psychopath—when they heard the same words, they felt nothing. They felt the same about those words as they did about sitting down to drink a coffee. To cut a person's body open would be nothing more than opening up a package of lunch meat.

She was frustrated that they had found no fingerprints, nothing that would tell them who the killer was. What was the killer trying to say with the missing head? Was it a souvenir, and where was he keeping these heads? They wouldn't know if there was a pattern until another body was found, and she dreaded the thought that there were more bodies out there. She remembered all the missing person reports—there were definitely more bodies out there. Where were her friends? The tin mine had been searched thoroughly for days and there were no other bodies but the tourist.

The killer they were looking for was sick and dangerous. The things that he did to his victims was monstrous. How long had he been doing this? He could have been killing people for months, years even. They would never have known about the body had she not done some digging and went looking on her own. So, the killer probably felt pretty safe at that point, maybe even confident that he wouldn't ever be caught. The fact that his work was not sloppy indicated that he had experience. A serial killer, possibly another Ted Bundy when it came to numbers. She shuddered involuntarily.

She planned on scouring the island for clues, something that could lead them in the right direction because, currently, they had nothing to go on. The killer was meticulous in every aspect. There was nothing that led them toward who was responsible for the murders. If they didn't get any leads soon, they would be waiting around for him to kill again, and that wasn't ideal. She was certain that the killer had to be a man, as there was just too much heavy lifting involved for it to be a woman. The victim's body parts had been carted from one island to another, so that made her believe that there was a strong man behind it all. How was he choosing his victims? Why go after a couple, instead of just one person? Did he choose his victims for specific reasons or was it all random? She needed to understand the mindset of the killer, and they just didn't know enough about him yet. She had to consider the fact that the victims knew the killer. It's one thing to sneak up behind one person and knock them out, but not two.

When it came to Brian and Katie, it would have been hard to kidnap them without making a scene. Had the couple known the killer and felt safe enough to leave with him? It was certainly possible. It couldn't be anyone within their direct group however, as that would be nuts. Or could it? She really didn't know any of them that well. Devon would have to be the only option unless he was working with someone. Though, there was Craig. He did have violent tendencies, something that had just come to her attention. He wasn't who she had thought he was. Could she have slept beside a serial killer and not known it? She shook her head. No, it couldn't be him. Melissa? She shook her head vehemently. No, she couldn't go there. She stopped herself. Maybe she didn't know them that well. She had only met them and maybe she didn't know them as well as she thought. The idea that any of them could be part of something so horrifying was too much to process. She wouldn't rule anyone out, but she needed to think broader.

She hadn't seen anyone new in the group or anyone her friends talking to that would have drawn her attention. Someone who acted slick, however, probably did his best work behind the scenes. Katie and Brian may have just met the guy the night that they were killed—they were certainly very trusting people. Her heart hurt when she thought about the newlyweds. They were on vacation during one of the happiest times of their lives. It saddened her to think that they died during a time when they were supposed to be celebrating their love for one another. The thought of them buried somewhere, their body parts torn apart and scattered around was not something that left her mind easily. The fear that must have gone through them would be chilling. She wanted to find them alive, but it just wasn't realistic at that point. There would be no reason for the killer to keep anyone alive.

Staring down at the file, tears welled up in her eyes. She couldn't imagine her friends in that condition. Her shoulders shook softly with the sobs as she felt helpless to save her friends. She just knew she had to do whatever it took to keep the rest of her friends alive. She couldn't lose anyone else. The only way to be sure would be to bring down the killer herself. Could she do it? She didn't have the experience, just her instincts. She was just so scared that her past failures would come back to haunt her. She didn't want to fuck up again.

She jumped as there was a knock on the door. She walked in from the balcony and glanced at the clock—it was ten o'clock at night. She hoped to God that it wasn't Craig, as she wasn't interested in going round two with him. She couldn't imagine who else would be visiting her at that hour, but considering all the new developments, she thought it was best to answer it. She paused, though, as she got to the door and thought about the killer. She leaned her head against it and said, "Who's there?"

"It's Rayland. I apologize if it's late."

Surprised, she smiled immediately. She hadn't

seen him since she ran into him in the lobby. She had thought about him, but things had gotten too crazy for her to think about anything else but Keri and the case.

She unlocked the door and swung it open. Rayland was standing there in jeans and a simple black t-shirt that hugged his muscles. He looked fantastic as he smiled sheepishly at her.

"I might be completely presumptuous here but I've been thinking about you and I hoped that we would bump into each other again, but I haven't seen you around much."

"Yeah, I've been busy. How did you find my room?"

He blushed slightly and she gazed at his mouth before meeting his eyes.

"I asked the front desk; I told them you were expecting me. I can be pretty charming when I want to be. Plus, they kind of know me."

She laughed. "I bet."

"Anyway, I have wine. Care to invite me in for a glass?"

She stared at the bottle of wine as a chill ran up her spine. Just a few days ago she had discovered a dead body on the island. She thought about the file on her desk and wondered if there was anyone that she could trust on the island. She stared at him. Was it safe to allow him in her room? She really didn't know anything about him. She thought about how quickly she had got involved with Craig and how he had thrown the glass against the wall. With a killer loose, she should be avoiding everyone.

She watched as the smile left his face. "I'm sorry, Harley, I probably should have called first. Maybe we can grab a coffee one day." He smiled awkwardly as he turned to move down the hallway. She suddenly felt bad. She doubted he brought up a bottle of wine so that he could kill her after. Plus, people knew him on the island.

"Rayland, wait."

He stopped with a surprised look on his face. "I would love to have a glass of wine. Thank you. I don't normally have visitors show up at my hotel room is all."

"That's my fault, of course. I'll try to be more low-key in the future."

He stepped into her room with a smile on his face. She had forgotten how good she felt just being in his presence. He was definitely the kind of guy she could see herself falling in love with.

She moved out of the way to let him in and closed the door behind him. Her suite had a sitting area with a couch in it, and Rayland moved toward it. Harley glanced at the balcony where the files still sat on the chair she had vacated. She moved quickly to the door as she said, "There are wine glasses on the mini bar. Please help yourself."

He got up from the couch and moved toward the mini bar while she stepped out onto the balcony and set her book on top of the files so they wouldn't blow away. She didn't want Rayland to see them and question her about them. She was far too on edge to discuss them. Plus, it probably wasn't something she should be discussing in the first place. She closed the door behind her as she entered the room again.

"If you prefer the balcony, we can sit out there," Rayland said. "It's not too cool tonight."

"Oh no. I'm fine in here; I think I got a little too much fresh air today anyway."

He handed her a glass as they sat down on the couch together. She was surprised by how comfortable she was with him being in her room.

"So, what has been keeping you so busy this past week?"

She searched her brain for a plausible excuse for her absence. "Have you really been looking for me?"

"Well, not to sound like a stalker but I did keep my eye out for you on the beach. You said you and your friends hang out there."

"Yes, we do. Actually, I was seeing someone for a bit and we broke up, so I've been avoiding the usual hangout. I went to Bangkok for a few days; it was fun."

"Well, it's his loss that's for sure…and my gain?"

"We'll see."

He laughed and moved in close beside her. She could smell his cologne and it caused something to stir inside her. She missed having a man around for all the obvious reasons.

"What do you do for a living?"

"I'm a security consultant for a marketing firm in

LA. My job is to advise the CEO and the managers on matters of security."

"Oh, that sounds exciting."

"Sometimes it is. The company deals with a lot of famous people, so there are a lot of events."

"That's really interesting. What about your family. Are they in LA too?"

"No. They are in New Orleans."

She smiled. "What are they like?"

"Oh, pretty normal, maybe even boring. Both my parents are still married and they made lots of babies, so I have a ton of brothers and sisters."

"Wow, really? You certainly are lucky."

He spoke about his large family in jest, the fights they had and how they all got together at Christmas in one house that seemed to burst at the seams when they were all inside. She couldn't help but smile as he talked about hay rides over Christmas while his mother made homemade hot chocolate in the kitchen for when they returned. He loved them all very much, that was obvious.

"It's crazy because now everybody has started having kids and the family is as big as ever. The holidays can be quite the adventure, that's for sure. But it's important for us all to get together because we lead such busy lives."

"Rayland, that's wonderful. God, I couldn't even imagine that. Sometimes I feel as if I've spent my whole life alone."

"What happened to your family?"

"I never really knew my dad—he left when I was young. He wasn't that great of a guy anyway. My mother was all I had, no siblings or anything, and she was a very destructive person to be around. She drank and sometimes it was like I had to take care of her, which was tough because I was so young."

"I'm sorry. You seemed to have turned out just fine, though, didn't you?"

She laughed. "I'm not sure I would go that far, but I survived. I can't imagine experiencing the memories that you have. There were a few Christmases that I didn't have because my mom either disappeared or was too drunk to get up. It's surprising that I never ended up in the foster care system."

"What happened to her?"

"I was seventeen and she just left, went on a binge. One of the neighbors said she was with some guy. I packed my things and went to stay at a friend's house before she got back. She showed up to get me a week later, but I refused to go home. I don't think she ever forgave me for leaving her."

She took a sip of her wine and lingered in the memory of the bitter look her mother had on her face when she walked away from the house. She just couldn't take it anymore. The drinking, the men, not knowing whether she was ever going to come home, or if she was out dead in a ditch somewhere. Sometimes it was better not knowing. It was why she wanted to get into police work; she wanted to try to make a difference in someone's life because she was never able to help her mom. She hadn't been worth enough or good enough for her mother to want to get better and make a good life for them.

She looked up at Rayland, and he was watching her, with a soft smile on his face.

"She didn't deserve a daughter like you."

"That's sweet of you to say."

"Well, it's true. What a bitch."

Harley almost spit out her wine. They laughed together as he refilled their glasses.

"Did you get that shock of red hair from your mother?" he said, looking at her over his shoulder.

"Yes, we look very much alike, and my father doesn't have the ginger genes," she said with a laugh.

"Well, it's beautiful."

"Thank you."

She loved talking to him; they talked easily about their families and what it was like growing up. She found she wasn't embarrassed at all to talk to him about her upbringing, despite the fact that his was so different from hers. The hours passed quickly as they talked. and when she yawned, she couldn't help but laugh.

"Whoa, I think it's way past my bedtime."

He smiled. "Sorry, it feels like I just got here."

"I know. I love that," she said with a wink.

He leaned in then and kissed her. His lips were warm against hers and she melted into him. Her lips parted and his tongue slid into her mouth where it was gratefully accepted. Her heart started beating faster as the kiss grew in intensity, with all the passion she was feeling toward Rayland all coming out in one kiss. A moan escaped her, and he pulled her in closer. There was an urgency in the way that he kissed her, and it sparked something inside of her. She could have kissed him all night long and more.

She pulled away from him. His eyes opened and met hers. "It's late Rayland," she whispered.

"Are you sure?" He looked at her and she wanted to change her mind, but she felt it was too soon. She had so many things going on in her brain at the moment.

"I think so."

"Can I see you again?"

"You bet your ass you can."

He laughed as he pulled away from her. She glanced at the empty wine bottle on the table and got up to follow him to the door.

"Thank you for the wine. It was a nice surprise."

"It was my pleasure. I would have come for that kiss alone."

She grinned at him as she shut the door. Leaning against it, she felt her heart still racing in her chest. "Oh boy."

NINETEEN

WHEN HARLEY OPENED HER EYES the next morning, a smile slowly crept across her face. She stretched lazily in bed and the smile only grew bigger. She threw aside the sheets and practically leaped out of bed.

She snapped up the case files and kept them under her arm until she got to the coffee pot, where she set them down on the table. She started humming *Happy* by Pharrell Williams as she added a packet of coffee into the machine. She flipped the switch and welcomed the scent of percolating coffee into the room. Her whole body was humming with newfound energy.

While she waited for her cup of coffee, she opened the files and flipped through the photos to see if something clicked. After a few minutes, she closed the file and poured herself a cup of coffee. Her mind drifted to Rayland while she added cream and sugar to her cup. She stirred the coffee lazily as she smiled. She continued to mouth the words to the song as she remembered the kiss that they shared. Her face suddenly burned as she thought about his mouth on hers.

Rayland's kiss had certainly awakened something inside of her. A feeling of hope, perhaps, that everything was going to be okay. That she could move on with her life and be happy with a man. In the same way that she had once envisioned being happy with Chris. Was it possible? That was what that kiss had brought her, a feeling of hope. It was rare to find a man that you had instant chemistry with and forgetting that kiss would be impossible. She wondered when she would be able to see him again. She now had responsibilities, and just gallivanting on the beach with a new man was not her first priority any longer.

As she was lost in her thoughts, her phone buzzed and she looked around to see where it was. She saw it still on the nightstand. She picked it up to see a text message from the Ned. *Oh, aren't we just cozy now.*

She clicked on the message.

> **Ned: Everyone's impressed with you, Harley. You did well. Remember to keep things on the down low, though. The chief still has a perma-scowl. Talk soon.**

She started typing:

> **Harley: No worries, your secret is safe with me. I won't mention I'm digging around.**

She smiled as she set her phone back down. She picked up her coffee and took a sip. *Damn, that was good.* She was reveling in the newfound respect the officers had for her at the headquarters. Since she had found the bodies, they developed respect for her that wasn't there before. They all knew they had pushed her around and behaved in an unprofessional manner. She knew she had to keep her involvement a secret; otherwise Ned could get in a lot of trouble for allowing an outsider into the case. He knew how much it meant to her to help her friends.

Harley was in a fantastic mood and she needed to start planning her day. She needed to continue the search for bodies and start questioning people on the island about suspicious behavior. They didn't have any leads to go on at that point and the last thing she wanted was the case to go cold. Nor did she want to wait for more bodies to pile up—she wanted to get the guy before he hurt anyone else.

She made her way to the bathroom to get ready. She had a full day to look forward to and one of the tasks would be to find her friends and update them on the progress. She wasn't looking forward to seeing Keri, but she knew her friend deserved the truth.

With her makeup on, she was dressed in cargo pants and a tank top for a long day of walking, Harley left the hotel room and made her way downstairs. She had a lot of experience tracking down leads from her days as a police officer, and she had notified Ned that she would be asking around. He was digging out all the files of the most recent missing persons so they would have some idea what they were dealing with. They were trying to keep things as quiet as possible and out of the papers so that the killer would not know they were on to him.

She approached the desk and the clerk was all smiles. "How can I help you?"

"I'm interested in the mines in the general area. Can I get a list of them and how they can be accessed?"

"Certainly."

Harley watched as the woman went to the computer and typed. It wasn't long before she was printing out a list of the locations. Not knowing if she would have much access to the internet once she left the hotel, Harley typed a quick text to Keri to see how she was.

Harley: hey, how are u?

Harley reached out and took the papers from the clerk. "Have you seen anyone behaving oddly over the past week? Any type of suspicious behavior?"

The woman looked alarmed. "No, not at all. Why do you ask?"

"Just curious. I'm not trying to worry you. Would you mind asking the rest of your staff if they remember seeing anything weird? And please keep your eyes out for the future."

The clerk only nodded before returning to her

duties. Harley's phone buzzed and she looked down at a message from Keri.

> **Keri: Was starting to worry about u. Is everything okay? Any news?**

Harley typed a message back, wording it carefully so as not to freak her friend out.

> **Harley: I will explain later. Can u get everyone together for burgers and beer for dinner at the bonfire? Let's say 5? I will explain everything then.**

> **Keri: No problem. See you then.**

Harley put her phone away and set out toward the beach. She wanted to sit down for a moment and figure out a plan for the day. She plopped her bottom in the sand and took a sip of her still hot coffee. There were four other mines in the area of the island, two of which were quite large. If the killer was only using the mines, he could still manage to hide a lot of bodies there before anyone got suspicious. She wanted to check out all the mines that day, but she wasn't sure that she would have the time before she had to meet her friends for dinner. She studied the locations to see which mine would be the closest to examine when her phone started ringing. She stared at the local number, confused as to who would be ringing her.

"Hello?"

"Harley, is this you?"

"Ned?"

"Yes. We found another body. Can you meet me?"

"Shit. Yes, of course, where am I going?"

He named off a location of one of the mines that she had on her list. It was confirmed that the killer was burying the bodies in the mines. How long had he been doing it? There could be so many bodies.

"Is there only the one body?"

"Yes. How soon can you be here?"

"Twenty minutes. I'm on my way."

She nodded at a few of the officers as she passed them on her way to the entrance of the tin mine. She was told that the chief was still inside, and she made her way inside one of the caverns. She was dreading seeing the body as she feared it would be one of her friends. Ned said there was only one body, so was it Katie or Brian? It could, of course, be another unknown victim, but her pulse raced just the same. The cavern opened up into a wide space just like the other tin mine did, and she saw the chief standing around a team of medical examiners. Ned was with them, so she hurried over and the chief turned as she made her way over.

"What the hell are you doing here?"

Ned stepped forward. "I called her, Chief, I thought it was only fair."

The chief nodded and then pointed to the body. "He has not been here long, possibly just a few days."

"Really? The body can't be one of my friends. Where are they?" She felt a building anxiety at how helpless she felt at being unable to find them.

"Do you mind taking a look? There's something new this time. He left the head; it might be a message. The body has been dismembered, but all the parts were buried together this time," the chief asked.

"Really? That's very interesting."

"Follow me."

She nodded and he brought her over to where the medical examiners were getting it ready to move. She looked down at the torso and then her gaze traveled to the head. She gasped. The body was most definitely not Brian's. There was a tattoo on the chest to the right of the torso. She had seen that tattoo before and she knew exactly whose body she was looking at. Even without the tattoo, she would have known—she recognized him right away.

"Oh. My. God. It's Devon."

"You know this guy?" the chief sputtered.

She felt bile rise in her throat and she spun away from the body, vomiting on the ground. She choked up fluids, as she had only had coffee that morning and no breakfast. She couldn't seem to catch her breath, and the chief was at her side instantly.

"Harley, are you alright?" He barked orders at his men to bring a bottle of water.

She gasped for air and the chief handed her a bottle of water. She stood up and took the bottle from him, tears streaming down her cheeks. She gulped the water, letting it ease her sore throat. Her mind was racing and she couldn't seem to collect herself. She took a few deep breaths until her breathing slowed and she didn't feel like she was going to have a heart attack.

"I'm sorry. I didn't expect that at all," she said as she wiped away the tears. She tried to rein in her emotions so she could help the chief.

"That must have come as quite a shock to you. Who is he?"

"His name is Devon Jones. He's been staying in a hut on the beach with some friends. He's Australian. I know him, we're friends." Harley tried to wrack her brain for the last time she saw Devon; it wasn't that long ago. At what point did he fall into the clutches of a serial killer? She couldn't help but feel responsible; he was just flirting with her a few days ago.

"It's probably been two days since I saw him, maybe more. We were all hanging out. I should have warned him."

"This isn't your fault, Harley; it could have happened at any point. You can't protect everyone. Your friends are already aware that people are going missing."

She sighed. It felt like she wasn't protecting anyone. Her friends were dropping like flies and she was powerless to stop it. Who was this guy? How had he got the best of Devon? He was a young, athletic guy, how had the killer got him away to a secluded place to cut him up? It made her wonder again if it was someone that they knew, someone that Devon would trust enough to leave with. That would only leave a handful of options, and she couldn't even comprehend any of her friends doing something so brutal.

"Is he targeting my friends?"

The chief shook his head. "It could just be a weird coincidence, Harley. The Texas tourist wasn't part of your group and there could be so many others. The missing person's reports are worse than we originally thought. This guy has been at it for a while. I think we can rule out a female killer here. The killer has to have a strong build to be carting these bodies around to these mines."

She stared at him as she felt a flash of red flash before her eyes. "Yes, it has been going on for a while, thanks to you," she hissed. She walked away from him, feeling a rage build up inside of her. She needed to be away from him, or she was going to lash out far worse than she did. He and his team had been so inept to what was going on across the islands that the killer had been allowed way too much freedom. If he would have looked into things earlier, her friends might not be dead right now. She heard him coming up behind her, but she just kept moving.

"Harley, that is not fair."

She spun around. "Fuck being fair, Chief. Body parts are all over the island and you guys had no idea that this was going on. It's bullshit. Did you really think people were partying from island to island or did you turn a blind eye to save your tourism? Because things aren't looking too great from my angle. There is a fucking serial killer loose and you guys didn't have a clue."

They stared at each other while Harley tried to rein in her temper. She knew that lashing out at the chief was not going to help them find the killer. They needed to work together despite the mistakes that were made.

"Look, we fucked up. I fully admit to that, but we aren't hiding anything. I'm just as determined as you are to find the killer."

She sighed. "I'm sorry. I just spent time with him and now look at him, and we still haven't found the bodies of my friends. Where are they?"

"Well, we have a whole island to search. It's going to be harder to keep this out of the press if we keep digging up bodies."

"Hopefully we can hold it off as long as we can. But we have no idea if the killer is aware of our movements. Once he becomes aware, everything will change."

"Which means he will start looking for a new place to hide his trophies."

"I've had enough for today. I have to break the news to my friends about Devon, and that's not going to be easy."

"Look, I don't want to say anything to upset you. I

know finding your friend here is quite upsetting, but you might want to consider that this is an inside job."

She stared at him. "What are you saying?"

"I'm saying, have you considered that it's one of your friends? I mean, how well do you actually know these people."

"I can't believe you are even suggesting such a thing. Granted, I don't know them very well but they are friends with each other. They know each other. I'm the outsider."

"Well, aside from the tourist, the other body is your friend and you also have two other friends that are missing. I'm just saying, keep your eyes open."

"I know, the thought has crossed my mind, I'll be honest. It's just hard to imagine that any of my new friends would hurt anyone. They have been devastated over Katie and Brian, and now Devon? It's the last thing that I would want to consider, but it's true—there is now more than one missing person from the group."

"Is there anyone in the group that you think would hurt Devon?"

Craig flashed into her head immediately as she remembered the fight they had. "I don't know. Like I said, we're all friends, what was done to him…that's just savage."

He nodded. "We'll find him, Harley."

"I hope so." She turned away from the two men and walked away from the caverns. She felt dazed as she made her way back to the beach. She couldn't believe what was happening all around her. First Brian and Katie, and now Devon? What was Melissa going to say? It was madness. She couldn't help but feel like she should have been able to do something. Now Devon was dead.

It felt like she had been sitting on the beach forever, dazed and exhausted. When she had first arrived back to the beach, it had been almost lunchtime. She had gone to grab a bowl of rice and vegetables and ate it on the beach. She had been there ever since. Since then she had just been lying on one of the shaded lounge chairs, staring off into the ocean. Hours had passed in that daze. She had planned on searching the caverns that day, but her morning gave her a little more than she had bargained for. In fact, she was surprised that she could even hold down food. All she kept picturing was Devon dismembered, no longer looking much like Devon at all. He had been good to her and she was thankful for his place in her life. He had been fun and playful, always making sure that she was having a good time. She checked her phone and realized it was almost time to meet her friends, and she was not looking forward to it. Things were becoming scary for her small group of friends, and she had to wonder if they were being targeted. But, why? As a group, they didn't know too many people and generally kept to themselves. But their small group had been almost cut in half by the killer. Could that really be a coincidence?

She got up from her spot on the beach and made her way toward the huts to meet her friends. As she walked, she could see her friends in the distance and there was laughter in the air. Keri looked up and saw her and waved at her frantically. Their laughter wouldn't last long. Harley trotted to the campfire and smelled burgers over an open fire. It smelled delicious. She noticed that Craig had also been invited, and he was sitting with the two girls. It was a little awkward since last night, but he needed to hear the news as well.

"Hi guys, already cooking?"

"Well, Melissa got us stoned, so we needed to get some food," Keri said with a smile on her face.

"I got everyone together as you asked, but I couldn't find Devon," Keri stated. Keri had dark rings under her eyes and Harley wondered how she had been sleeping lately. She looked completely rung out.

"He's probably off with some girl," Craig added.

Melissa sent him a dirty look and he just shrugged.

She hadn't seen Craig since the episode at his hotel room, and seeing him again was just inevitable. She would at least stay cordial around everyone else, even if he did call her crazy. The last thing she wanted was to lose her newfound friends.

Harley looked at Melissa who was holding out a beer for her; the weed explained why they were all in good spirits. She took the beer from her and continued to stare at her while she turned back to the others. She was going to be destroyed by the news.

She looked and found that Craig was staring at her, an unusual look on his face. "Hi, Harley."

There was an awkward silence as everyone stared at him.

"Hi, how are you?"

"I've been better."

She nodded her head slowly.

"Are you hungry?" Melissa asked her.

She turned back to the group and took a seat in the sand. She took a pull from the beer bottle and the cold liquid slid down her throat most satisfyingly. She was most likely going to stay on the liquid diet for the rest of the night; she wasn't sure if she could handle a burger when there was bad news to come. She shuddered when she thought about Devon's head separated from his body.

"Maybe in a bit, this is good for now." She motioned toward her beer.

Keri laughed, but her face sobered quickly. "You said you had something to tell us, Harley. Is it about my sister and Brian? Did you find them?"

She sighed heavily—well, she might as well get it over with. "There were two bodies found in the caverns over the past week. But neither of them was Katie or Brian. The police still have places to search, but there is no news of them yet."

"Is that good news, the fact that they haven't been found yet?" Melissa asked.

Harley frowned. "I don't know. I wouldn't get your hopes up; they've been gone for a while, but you never know. It's hard to say right now."

Harley took another swig of beer, steeling herself. "Like I said two bodies were found, one was a tourist and the other was…well, it was Devon."

There was a stunned silence around the group as they stared at her, eyes wide and mouths hanging open.

"Oh, my God," shrieked Melissa. "Devon? No, it can't be." Melissa burst into tears and Keri was instantly by her side, pulling her in close. Harley could imagine how the girl felt; she had a feeling Melissa had been in love with Devon.

"I'm afraid so. I'm sorry, Melissa, it's all terribly upsetting. There is someone on the island doing horrible things to people. If I were any of you, I would head back home because three members of our group have already been affected."

Melissa looked frantically to Keri who just stared back in stunned silence.

"When was the last time you guys remembering seeing Devon?"

"Not for a few days. He said he was going to look for you one night and I haven't seen him since. To be honest, I thought you guys were hooking up because I haven't seen you either," Melissa said.

"What?" Harley couldn't believe what she was hearing. "I've been working." She glanced quickly at Craig, feeling embarrassed.

"Oh, Devon wouldn't have a chance with her," Craig spat out, and Harley stared at him, her gaze narrowing. His face was red with rage and she was suddenly glad she broke up with him when she had the chance. He had anger issues and his possessiveness toward her was a tad bit alarming.

Melissa looked sheepishly at Craig. "Sorry." He glared back at her.

Craig had always thought Devon had a crush on Harley—the last thing Harley needed was for him to think that they slept together as well. Craig downed the rest of his beer, looking pissed. Harley continued to stare at him until Keri addressed her.

"I haven't seen him either," Keri added sadly. "We should have gone looking for him," she said to Melissa. "Everyone is just so free here that I wouldn't have imagined he would go missing too."

"This isn't anyone's fault. We couldn't possibly have known something like this would happen, we all knew the risks after Brian and Katie went missing. Devon knew the risks just like we all did," Harley said.

"We need to leave," Melissa said, looking at Keri. Harley was relieved to hear that they would be leaving and going somewhere safe.

"I'm not going anywhere," Keri said. "Not until I know what happened to my sister."

"Keri, it's not safe here," Harley insisted. "I can let you know what we find out. I'm staying here until I see this through."

"No, I'm not going. I have to be here. I need to see for myself what happened to them."

Harley nodded. She knew she would not be able to talk Keri out of staying. She would have done the same thing in Keri's position. "Fine. But don't you dare go off alone or leave with anyone. Don't make yourself a target."

"I won't, I promise. Something really bad happened to them, didn't it?"

Harley pulled her over and embraced her tightly. She would not give her the gory details just yet, not until she had to. Keri pulled away and the group sat there quietly for a moment.

"How soon can you two leave?" Harley asked Melissa and Craig.

"First thing in the morning," Melissa said.

"I'm not leaving," Craig muttered.

"Why not?" Harley asked.

"I'm not being chased off. I came to the island for a reason. I've been here for almost two months and nothing has happened to me. I think I'll be fine."

"That's ridiculous. Look at what's happening to the people around us."

"I'm staying. You made it perfectly clear to me that

we aren't together any longer, Harley, so you don't get a say."

She blushed deeply as she stared at him. Why did he look so angry? "Fine. Do what you want."

She took another drink of her beer. She had completely lost her appetite and she wondered if the rest of them felt the same way. She hoped they would all be safe now that they knew what they were up against. She needed to stay and make things right; the case had become personal for her and she needed to see it put to rest. She needed to prove that the deaths were not for nothing; she just hoped that she could be a detective again without hurting those she loved.

TWENTY

BUTCHER FELT DESPONDENT AS HE made his way to the hotel bar. People were messing with his business and he didn't like it. The police had found a few of his treasures, disturbing them from their sleep, and it angered him. He had been there for months, killing without fear of discovery, and all of a sudden, these cops were sniffing around in business they didn't belong in. They had better watch what they were doing, or he would have to start removing them. He couldn't help but feel like Harley was to blame for rattling the cages. He couldn't fault her for being more intelligent than the rest—that's why she was destined to be his last kill before he left the island. She stumbled upon his crimes in no time at all; it was like she knew what he was thinking. He could barely wait until he could touch her skin and hear her speak to him. She had been avoiding him lately, but he would connect with her again. The more he saw her, the more he knew that he wanted her. Not in a romantic way but to give him a final release before he left.

When he thought about Harley, he just wanted her dead in the same way that he wanted his mother dead. There was something about Harley that reminded him of his mother and it went way beyond the color of her hair. They were the kind of women that would be his undoing if he allowed them to get too close to him. He knew that he would one day return to kill his mother, as she had lived far longer than she deserved to. He would only feel free when these two women were extinguished. They drew him in and that wasn't what he wanted. He wanted no attachments, and Harley would only turn on him if he gave her a chance. She already proved how easily she could turn on someone. He needed to be free of her and his mother—only then would the headaches be gone from his life forever.

The discovery of the bodies irritated him, but it didn't worry him. It would not stop him from executing the things he was born to do. They couldn't stop him; he was a God among men. He had been killing for six years and no one had ever come close to catching him. These bodies they were digging up were just a few among hundreds he had laid to rest. He had been doing this for a long time and a bunch of ambitious cops wasn't about to bring him down. In fact, he was walking into the bar to find someone to entertain him for the evening and put him in better spirits. He had no fear of killing again even with the cops sniffing around.

He saddled up to the bar and sat down, subtly looking around the room. He ordered a whiskey on the rocks and took in his surroundings. He was looking for a woman, someone vulnerable and insecure. Devon had distracted him and he wanted to hear a woman scream again—he wanted that more than anything. He wanted someone that reminded him of his beauty queen mother. Someone he could silence in the same way that he had wanted to silence her so many years ago. He had always regretted leaving her alive. The way she had turned on him, unwilling to love him for the monster that he was. Wasn't a mother's love supposed to be unconditional? She had turned her back on him and sent him away, sickened by him, and she would pay for that. He had just wanted her love and she had turned him away. She would pay for that with her life. He wanted her head cut clean from her body.

In the meantime, he wanted to take out his fantasies with another girl. It was not yet time for Harley or his mother—someone else would have to do for now. He had killed men throughout his life, but it was women that he sought out. He usually only killed a man if he got in the way and needed to be removed. It was a woman's scream that he cherished the most. He chose women that reminded him of his mother, whether it be because of her beauty or confidence or the fact that she believed in all the good things of the world.

It wasn't long before he found a girl. She couldn't

have been much older than twenty and she was giggling uncontrollably with her friends. She was beautiful despite all the makeup she had on. She exuded confidence and flirted with the men at her table mercilessly. She had that beauty queen look and all the confidence that went along with it. She reminded him of his mother, which made her the perfect target. It was obvious that she was trashed, and it wouldn't be long before she was kicked out of the bar due to the volume of her voice. Butcher settled into his seat, waiting for his opportunity to strike. He sipped his whiskey and smiled. She was perfect and she had no idea she was about to fulfill some of his most disturbing fantasies. It was then that he thought of Harley. The time was closing in on her—they would be reunited soon enough and then he would be one step closer to being complete, until he saw his mother again. But Harley first. He would share his fantasies with her right before he killed her.

His thoughts were disturbed when he saw the girl get up from the table she sat at with her friends and stumble toward the bathroom. It was located by the back entrance down a hallway. He waited a moment, finishing his drink, and then made his way toward the back, slowly walking down the hallway. He waited outside of the bathroom door for the girl and when the door opened, she practically fell into his arms.

"Whoa there, are you okay?"

She giggled. "Yes, sorry about that. I think I had

one too many." She looked up at him and her smiled widened. Girls had always liked the Butcher. "Where have you been all night?"

He laughed. "Well, I'm about to leave, actually. It's been a long night."

"Noooo. You can't leave yet. I just met you. Gosh, you sure are handsome."

He shrugged. "Sorry. Unless you would like to come with me, have a nightcap," he said with a wink.

Smiling, she nodded. She thought she was going to get lucky that night. She couldn't have been more right; she was about to be one of his treasures. He grasped her hand in his and pulled her along toward the back exit. She followed willingly, unconcerned that she hadn't said goodbye to her friends or that she was heading to the hotel room of a complete stranger. Sometimes they just made it too easy for him.

He pulled her around to the back of the hotel, to a door he frequently used to get in and out of the hotel. They didn't have any exterior cameras on the hotel, as it was a tourist community and the hotel believed that nothing bad ever happened in the area. The hotel was an old one and they never opted for an upgrade of any kind. That was why he had chosen the hotel in the first place; they would never catch him on camera with his victims. The girl didn't stop smiling from the time they got to the hotel until they got up to his room. She kept trying to give him the seductress look, but her level of intoxication made it more than impossible. He wasn't interested in sleeping with the girl; she wasn't worthy of him. He unlocked his hotel door and ushered the girl in—there would be no escape for her now.

Taking her hand once again, he immediately pulled her to the room where the chair and plastic were already set up. He wouldn't even need to knock this one out first.

"Ohhhh, this is kinky." She laughed as she plopped awkwardly down into the chair.

"You have no idea."

"Is this really where you want to do it?"

"Yes. Hold still while I restrain you."

Confused she watched as he tied her arms and legs to the chair. "But how am I going to please you like this."

"I'm going to do things to you that are going to bring me a great amount of pleasure, don't you worry."

Her smile removed the confusion from her face. "I like the sound of that."

He went to the desk and removed the duct tape and brought it over.

"You're not going to put that on me, are you?" she asked.

He backhanded her hard across the face, snapping her head to the side. Butcher pictured his mother when he looked down at the girl. Dazed, she shook her head and blinked up at him as he applied the tape to her mouth. In those few seconds, it registered with the girl that her life had changed, forever. Tears rolled down her face and she whimpered beneath the tape on her mouth.

"I need a drink, excuse me for one moment. I'll put on some music for you." He went to the MP3 player and picked *Tchaikovsky's 1812 Overture*. As the music filled the room, she started screaming, though the tape muffled it. He smiled and turned to her, wishing he could turn off the music and just take in the sound of her voice. Maybe during his next destination, he could find a place that was more secluded.

He moved from the room and prepared himself a drink. He poured a shot of whiskey into a glass filled with ice. He brought the glass with him back to the room where the girl sat. He was disappointed to find that the girl had stopped screaming—though that wouldn't last for long. The girl's eyes had cleared. There was nothing like pain to sober someone up, and he had hit her hard enough to break her neck. He sat down across from her as she stared back at him. Mascara had run down her cheeks and she went back to whimpering. She looked like a hot mess and he was once again thankful that he was not someone who had been looking for a night of passion.

He looked over toward the desk where he had laid out his butcher's tools. He finished off his drink and stared down at his knives. He pulled out a 14-inch straight knife and tested its sharpness, smiling as he did so. He walked over to her and placed the knife against her wrist, just below the ropes, and sliced vertically. That was the moment in which the screams started up again.

Blood pooled out of the wound and dripped down her arm. He moved to the other arm and did the exact same thing. He wanted her to bleed out while he tortured her. She started struggling hard in her chair, harder than he would have imagined from the girl. He thought of his mother then, and the looks of confusion when she saw him with the dog. She had no idea what he was capable of. He moved quickly to the desk and picked up the shock device. He returned to her and shoved it into her rib cage before he pressed the button. Her body shook until he pulled the device away. Her body slumped limply in the chair; she had passed out. She wouldn't be out for long, not when the pain started.

Butcher cleaned off his blade and set it back in the pouch that held all his important butcher knives. He took very good care of them just like his father taught him. Tools were essential to any profession and Butcher had been taught to care for his things. He had already packed away the girl's body parts in a suitcase, ready for transport. The plastic, rope, and tape had been disposed of, and all he needed to do now was get rid of her body. She had caused quite a mess when she bled out onto the floor. There had been a lot more blood to clean up that time. Not that he minded—the sight and smell of it thrilled him more than anything else could. When she had become too weak to scream any longer, he had pulled the tape off and listened to her softly ask to go home; she wanted to see her mother. He liked the soft undertones of her voice, the sound of life slipping away. It was a different kind of music to his ears, it didn't please him as much as her screams had, but instead, it relaxed him and put him in the mood to end it for good. She was as good as dead when he took the knife and slid it into her throat, silencing her forever. He no longer had a use for her—the moment her screams were silenced, she had become boring to him. Her death had taken away the blood-pounding headache he had and the desires he felt about killing his mother. He could no longer bury bodies at the tin mines now that the cops were crawling all over it. He had wanted all his people to be placed in the same area, but that was impossible now.

He knew of a five-star hotel in Phuket that had been abandoned after the Tsunami hit in 2004. It had been partially destroyed and never came back after the disaster. He had been watching it for a few weeks, considering it an option if he needed a new place to hide bodies. In the two weeks that he had watched the place, no one had gone in or around the establishment. It had already been somewhat secluded, but after it was abandoned, it stood there like a relic after a war. It was exactly the kind of place that he could feel safe to hide the bodies from the police. They would never think to look there, and besides, they were too busy with the mines. The abandoned hotel was only a few short miles from his hotel, and once she was buried, he could come back to a restful sleep.

Nothing scared him—not even the police sniffing around so close to him. He had moved among people, traveling through his life without a care in the world. Cops couldn't touch him, as they didn't even know that evil such as him moved in the world. He lived a very comfortable existence in the real world, though he did use funds that he acquired from his victims as he traveled from place to place. He never worried about money—over the years he had made a lot of it and now traveling was his desire. Turning from the desk, he lifted the suitcase and moved toward the door, feeling better than he had in a while.

TWENTY ONE

HARLEY HAD SPENT MOST OF the morning surrounded by files and coffee. She had the file of Devon, and as much as she hated the sight of it, she studied it looking for markings on the body, looking for some hopeful clue.

She had photos and file notes taped to her hotel wall, and she often stared at them for hours, looking for a connection. Aside from the fact that some of the victims knew each other, she couldn't see what the motive was. Why was the killer choosing these people? There were a lot of unanswered questions.

Why did the killer dismember the bodies and why did he separate the parts? The medical examiner had said that the body parts had been removed with expert precision, so this guy knew how to make clean cuts through flesh and bone. So, what did that make him? A doctor, a butcher? The crime scenes were so clean, it was possible it was someone who knew forensics. She thought of Chris. Perhaps it was another crooked cop?

Did anyone in her group have these skills?

She had put together a pretty good profile on their killer and had to fax it over to Ned so they could have a better idea of who they were looking for. It was all they had at that point because the killer wasn't leaving them any clues. He was definitely not the kind of serial killer who wanted to be caught, so notoriety was not his goal. Ned would start canvassing the area based on her profile and hopefully come up with some leads. She believed the killer to be a male in his thirties, handsome and very charismatic. Someone that people had a fun time with and would have no problem hanging out with. Someone who could speak easily to strangers, possibly the life of the party or a ladies' man. He was someone that people trusted—otherwise why would they leave with him?

She stood over the fax machine as it beeped the progress of the profile going through. She waited for the confirmation sheet to make sure it actually got to the police station. The paper eventually creaked out of the machine and she was confident the chief got it. She walked out of the computer room and went into the lobby of the hotel. She considered going down to the beach to see if Keri was around when her phone rang.

"Hello?"

"Harley, it's Ned."

"Ned? What's up? Did you get the fax?"

"Yes, I found it very interesting actually."

"Yeah? Why's that?"

"I think we have a solid lead and it matches the profile that you sent us."

"What? Who is it?"

"I've sent a deputy to collect you; he should be there in an hour. We can discuss it when you get here."

"You can't leave me hanging like that. How did you find this guy?"

"He's been under our nose the whole time. I'll see you soon, Harley."

The phone disconnected and Harley was staring blankly out the front doors. Who had Ned tracked down? Was there something she had missed? He couldn't have pulled someone out at random; he didn't even have her profile. She was happy to know that they had been doing their own digging as well. She was going to die of curiosity before she got there. Why wouldn't Ned just tell her who it was over the phone? She walked into the dining area to grab a cup of coffee while she waited for the deputy to arrive.

She decided to text Keri to see how she was doing and to make sure she was staying safe.

Harley: Hey, how ya doing? Staying safe, I hope.

She poured herself a cup of coffee and added cream and sugar while she waited for a response from Keri. Her phone vibrated and she looked down.

Keri: I'm okay. Getting lit at the beach you

should come down

Harley smiled as she typed a message back.

Harley: I may come down later, I have to go to the city.

Keri: Anything I should know?!?

Harley: Not yet. Ttyl

She took her coffee out to the front steps to wait for her ride.

The trip back to the city was excruciating, mainly because the deputy that Ned had sent was a little enamored with her. She was a local celebrity in the office now that she had opened the case by finding the body. He couldn't stop asking her questions about being a New York City police officer. He thought her job was like the *Law and Order* episodes he watched on TV. She sometimes supposed it was, but other times it was like seeing an old lady on the bench and giving her money. She normally wouldn't have minded answering all his questions, but currently, she found it annoying because all she could think about was who Ned had in mind as the killer. How could he leave her hanging like that while she was losing her mind?

When they arrived at the police headquarters, she was out of the car before it fully came to a stop. The deputy shouted out at her, but she didn't even look back. She rushed inside and headed straight for the front desk.

"Ned, what the fuck? I'm losing my mind here."

He sat at his desk and looked up when she walked into the room. "Harley, it's always great to see you," he said with a smile.

"Yeah. Yeah. Let's hear it."

The deputy finally came in behind her. "She lost me in the parking lot, sorry. She slipped away from me."

Ned chuckled. "It's okay, Deputy. I'm going to take Harley into the interrogation room to brief her on everything. You can go back to your regular duties."

Harley watched as the deputy left looking like a lost puppy.

"Follow me."

She followed Ned down the hall toward one of the interrogation rooms. He opened the door and she went in ahead of him. The chief was in the room waiting for them. She was dying to know what they had found out. If they had a lead, it could change everything. They would be able to focus on someone and hopefully bring the killer down before anyone else got hurt. The chief sat down at the desk in the middle of the room and Ned just stood off to the side. There was a file open in front of the chief and he slid it across the desk to her.

"Have a seat."

She wasn't ready to sit, as she was already frustrated and her nerves were on edge. She picked up the file and looked down at it. She saw the picture, but it wasn't registering. She knew the person in the file, but she just couldn't believe what she was looking at. She started to read the file, feeling a numbness crawl along her skin. The picture jumped right out at her. She flipped a page and read through an alarming criminal history that involved barroom brawls, assault on a teacher, and a few DUIs. She looked back up at the chief.

"What is this?"

"You know him?"

"Of course I do, and you damn well know it. I was sleeping with him up until a week ago. Is this some kind of joke? Because I don't find it funny."

"It's no joke, Harley. He has a record. Not murders or anything but enough to raise an eyebrow, and then for a few years he completely disappears. There's a good chance that it's not even his real name. We are looking into that right now."

Harley was staring down at a police file on Craig—the man that had helped her when she first arrived on the island, the one she had slept beside and made love to under the stars. It couldn't be true. He couldn't have done these things. Then her brain flickered to his assault on Devon and his attitude at the bonfire last night.

"I don't understand. How did you even zero in on

him?"

"I told you at the mines that I wondered if it could be one of your friends. You were too close to it. I decided to run the names of all your friends and Craig popped up. He has a lot of priors with theft and even spent some time in jail, never mind all the disappearances. He also fits your profile to a tee: handsome male, age 30-40, charismatic, makes friends easily…"

"Well, he's a traveler. He's going to have some holes."

"It's him, Harley, and he's been here for months. Or at the very least, it looks really bad, and we need to have him checked out. We are looking into a search warrant right now to see what's inside his hotel."

She stared at him in disbelief. This was not possible. She couldn't believe that the man that she laid beside in bed for numerous evenings had done these heinous things. She flung the file at the chief, the contents spilling out on the table and sliding down to the floor. The chief got up from the desk in surprise. Craig's handsome face stared up at them from the floor.

"Harley."

"No, I am not doing this. It can't be him; it just can't be. I just had a fucking beer with him last night. He was sitting right fucking there when I told him about Devon, and he didn't even flinch."

"Serial killers are good at hiding who they are. How well do you really know this guy? You just met him."

"Of course, I did," she screamed. "It's called being

on vacation. What the fuck am I supposed to do, run a background check on every guy that I date? This is bullshit. It can't be him."

"Calm down."

She was pacing like a wild animal; her brain was going a mile a minute. Ned was staring at her wide-eyed and he made sure to stay out of her way. "I can't calm down. It's not him."

"Why can't it be him? You said yourself that he's been gone for a few days and that he disappears sometimes."

"Because I can't fucking be attached to every crazy person on the planet. This goes way beyond attracting the wrong kind of guys," she said as she threw her hands up in frustration.

"What the hell are you talking about? You're taking this personal."

"Personal? Yeah, of course, because Chief Aat would never find himself in bed with a serial killer. Leave that to the redheads of the world."

Chief Aat shrugged. "Some of the most famous serial killers had wives and children. This is your job. We did a background check on you as well. You were minutes away from taking a detective's exam. You were known to have great instincts, the instincts of a detective. You know that these monsters are the masters of disguise. Now just calm down."

"Calm down? You have to be shitting me."

She started pacing the room, feeling like she was

going to snap. Her adrenaline was through the roof as she tried to make sense of everything in her head. Her hands were shaking and all she wanted to do was start screaming and never stop. The chief must have sensed that she was on the edge because he backed away from the desk and crossed his arms in front of himself, waiting.

What was happening to her? Was her judgment just completely fried? Just when she thought things were becoming aligned in her life again, something like this had to pop up. She was right back where she started. First Chris and now Craig? Did she just not know the men in her life? They were constantly pulling the wool over her eyes and she was powerless to stop it. Did she have terrible judgment when it came to men? She had always been good at her job, but her personal life seemed to be unraveling. She must be too trusting. Was it going to end the same way? Her life repeating these awful lessons for her?

"Harley?"

"I can't keep doing this," she muttered.

"Doing what?"

"It can't be him!" she shouted as she slammed her fist down on the table. Her whole body started to shake as sobs rolled through her. "Jesus, I laid beside him, I let him close to me. He can't be capable of these things." She was crying now and she couldn't seem to stop it. Ned walked toward her and she put her hands out. "Don't. Don't touch me."

She backed away from him until her back hit the wall and she slid down it, curling her knees up to her chest. Tears streamed down her cheeks as she sobbed, feeling once again the intense betrayal of Chris and now Craig. What the hell was wrong with her?

Ned approached her slowly and bent down in front of her. She looked up at him through tear-streaked eyes.

"How could I be so wrong about him?"

"Harley, how could you know he was a killer? His own mother and friends don't know that he's a killer. Hell, if it were that easy to pick a killer out of a crowd, we would never have an unsolved case again. You are way too hard on yourself."

"It's my job," she whispered.

"You must have been one hell of a cop back home, considering the way you carry the weight of the world on your shoulders. That is probably how you found yourself here. You can't carry that burden without breaking."

She wiped the tears from her cheeks and ran her hands through her long hair. Her hands had stopped shaking and she could finally look Ned in the eyes. He looked so concerned for her. He must think she was nuts. Maybe she was—she was definitely feeling off kilter. He was right. She was carrying this way too close to home. She thought about how things never felt right with Craig. She still couldn't believe he would be so calculated and hurt the people closest to him. Is that what he did when he traveled from place to place? Meeting new people, befriending them, and then killing them? Of course, he was the killer. Had she sat inches from the man that was dismembering bodies at his leisure? She shuddered at the thought.

"Let's bring him down, Ned."

Ned looked back at the chief and he smiled for the first time since they entered the room. "That's exactly what we're going to do."

Ned pulled her up from the floor and she walked around the desk. She started to pick up the contents of the file, arranging it back in order. She picked up a picture of Craig and stared at it. He looked so normal in the picture—how could she have missed the monster underneath?

TWENTY TWO

HARLEY SAT ON THE BEACH drinking her morning coffee and thinking about Craig. It was a miracle she was even drinking coffee after the day she had yesterday. All she could think of was how great it would be to go somewhere else far away from there and totally forget the whole case. She laughed at that thought. *Running away again, Harley?* Craig was right. She had the urge to bolt when things fell apart. She needed to stop running away because this was just life. The one thing that her job did teach her was there were scary people and scary things that happened everywhere every day. She had to stop running away from her problems. She had come there to be on vacation and now she was involved in something that she had no business being involved in. But there was also a reason that she was there, she truly believed that. Things were getting too close and a lot was at stake.

Yesterday, she didn't even meet Keri on the beach

after she got back from the police station. She had been in a daze and hadn't slept the entire night. How could she? She basically analyzed every moment that she had been with Craig, trying to see the flaw, the thing she had missed the whole time. He had seemed like a good man, albeit a little boring, but still genuinely a good human being. She wanted more than anything to approach Craig and confront him, but the last thing they wanted to do was spook him. They were waiting for the search warrant to see what he had in his hotel; things took a lot more time in Thailand.

In the meantime, Chief Aat had agreed to let her follow Craig one night to see what he was up to. "Agreed" would probably be a loose way of saying it. He had adamantly refused her request at first, worrying about her safety. But it's not like *he* could do it without Craig getting suspicious. She knew where Craig frequented because she had spent so much time with him. She might be able to figure out how he was choosing his victims. In the end, Aat had reluctantly agreed, telling her not to get too close.

She would pick a particular evening that he did his disappearing acts and see what he did. Hopefully, he would lead her somewhere that would implicate him. But if he really was the killer, he was highly intelligent and had been doing it long enough that he wouldn't make it easy on them. The chief had sent his men to the last remaining tin mine to search for more bodies. She offered to go with them, but the chief asked her to focus on Craig so that she could follow him. Ned had sent over the file of Craig and she had begun to review it. In fact, she had stayed up all night looking at all the files. It had been hard to look at the medical examiner's report. Seeing Devon's body like that wasn't easy for her, especially since she had to wonder if Craig killed Devon because of her. He had been annoyed and a little jealous about the way Devon flirted with her. Had he killed him to get him out of the way? She wanted to remember him as the funny guy that ordered the mushroom omelet. She still couldn't believe that he was dead, gone from them forever and at the hands of a friend.

She hadn't wanted to date him, but she had been very fond of him and she never imagined that something so horrific could happen to him. It definitely explained how he was getting his victims, if they all knew and trusted him. Of course, they would go somewhere with him willingly. Maybe he had known the tourist as well—or that could have been a random kill. But Craig was easy to talk to—that was how she had got involved with him—so maybe it was just a matter of Craig striking up a conversation with someone. It was the only thing that made sense to her. Phuket Island was certainly a friendly one, but not that friendly. What was it that made a strange girl go off with a serial killer? She wasn't sure that it would have been a simple act of overpowering her. Craig would have had to drag the tourist's body around the island, and that wouldn't exactly be easy without being noticed. No, he would have had to take them somewhere before killing them, and how did he do that? That was what she had to figure out.

"Harley?"

She looked up in surprise and saw Rayland standing above her. She couldn't help but smile as he stood there in board shorts and a t-shirt that hugged his body in all the right ways. She had almost forgotten how handsome he was; she had almost forgotten him entirely since the case had blown up. He must have thought she was a real jerk because she never contacted him again after she had gone to the station with Keri that day.

"Rayland, hi. Enjoying the beach today?"

"Almost every day. Though I haven't seen you around lately—have you forsaken the beach?"

She laughed. "Yes, a little bit, I guess. I've been a little busy."

"Doing what? Aren't you supposed to be on vacation?"

"Oh, I went off the island with some friends for a few days, sightseeing, that sort of thing."

He sat down in the sand with her and her heart started beating fast. Her body instantly responded to him. "Sounds like fun," he said. "I took up surfing and it's been a blast."

"Yeah, I can tell by your tan." She smiled and he smiled back.

He looked at her cup. "I could use some coffee; I've

been surfing since 5 am. I'm beat. What do you say we grab a cup and go for a drive?"

She considered his offer; there would really be no harm in going. She was planning on following Craig that night but in the meantime, there was nothing she could do on the case until she heard from Ned on the last search of the mines. He would call her cell and she could leave as soon as she got the call. She could use a break from thinking about Devon's death and the fact that her ex-lover was likely a serial killer. It's not like Rayland was a stranger, as they had talked numerous times for hours on end. Maybe an excursion would give her mind a break so that she would be fresh when she was needed.

"You know what…that sounds great. What do you have in mind?"

What Rayland had in mind was four-wheeling through the jungle. She hadn't expected that when she had agreed to go for a drive with him, but there they were side by side on four-wheelers, ready to go into the jungle.

"What have I gotten myself into?"

He laughed. "C'mon, beautiful, you must have ridden one of these before."

"Actually, no. I'm a city girl."

"Well, then you are in for an adventure. Are you

ready?"

She nodded as Rayland turned the throttle and burst ahead of her. She followed suit and raced after Rayland. They whipped through the trails in the jungle as if they were a couple of school kids. Before she knew it, she was laughing out loud as she raced after Rayland. She felt amazing and she couldn't remember the last time that she had so much fun. It reminded her of the day she tried surfing for the first time with Craig. The thought threatened to dim her happiness, so she tried to push it to the side. She hoped that Ned wasn't trying to get a hold of her as she doubted that she had much mobile service in the jungle.

"C'mon, Harley!" Rayland shouted behind him.

She pushed the throttle further and it kicked into a higher gear. She moved toward Rayland and felt excitement fill her. She got up right beside him and smiled across at him.

"Welcome. Hey, you look good on a four-wheeler."

She grinned at him and couldn't help but think about what he looked like naked. His body looked strong and tanned and she considered telling him to pull over.

She turned from him and gasped as she saw a small ravine ahead of her. "Oh shit."

"Harley, watch out."

But it was too late; she didn't have a chance to stop. The four-wheeler went headfirst into the ravine and she was tossed off the front of it. Thankfully it wasn't a large ravine or a long fall. She hit the ground and rolled. She stared up at the sky and mentally checked her pain points. Nothing was broken, and she was grateful that it wasn't a bad fall. She would have some serious bruises, however, but it wasn't anything she wasn't used to. It could have been a lot worse, especially since she was in a foreign country and very far from any type of hospital.

"Harley, are you okay?"

He hopped into the ravine and she saw him suddenly appear above her. She started laughing uncontrollably—she couldn't help herself. It had been so much fun and then it stopped abruptly, but the fall hadn't even bothered her. He looked beautiful above her. She reached up and pulled him to her by his neck. A look of surprise came across him as he realized what she was doing. When she felt the warmth of his lips against her, she lit up inside. She fell into the moment, allowing passion to take over as she tasted his mouth. When she came up for air, he was smiling down at her.

"Wow, what was that for?"

She laughed. "I think I broke the jeep."

He laughed with her. "Thank God for insurance."

She started giggling as he held out his hand for her. She grabbed it and he pulled her up. She brushed herself off and looked over at the four-wheeler. She looked sheepishly back at him. "Oops." She didn't even want to think about how they were going to get that four-wheeler out of the ravine; she felt bad for the person that would be in charge of that job.

"You don't look too bad; do you feel okay?"

"A little sore but I'm fine."

"Let's get you back so you can have a stiff drink."

"Sounds great."

They climbed out of the ravine and walked over to the remaining four-wheeler. Rayland climbed on and she climbed on the back behind him. She was thrilled to wrap her arms around his waist casually as he turned the vehicle on and got them moving. They drove through the jungle at moderate speed, and she leaned against his back and smiled. He was probably worried about driving too fast since she was already hurt. He seemed like a really sweet guy and she could still taste that kiss on her lips.

When they got back to return Rayland's rental and deal with the crashed four-wheeler still in the forest, they made sure to stop and grab some coffee for the drive to the beach. She sipped at it gingerly, being careful not to burn her mouth. Her body would be terribly sore the next day and she tried to stretch it out a bit in the car.

"I think I'm going to need a hot bath later."

"That's probably a good idea. I hope you still had a good time despite the tumble."

She chuckled. "I had an amazing time, Rayland. It

was exactly what I needed, thank you. The coffee isn't bad either."

He smiled. "I'm glad you had fun." He reached over and took her hand in his and squeezed.

When they arrived back at the beach, Harley got out of the car and stretched, feeling every bruise on her body cry out. It had been worth it, however, especially since she got to kiss Rayland. Nothing had made her day better than that kiss. She would be dreaming about that kiss; she just knew it.

Her phone buzzed and she pulled it out of her pocket, thinking it was Ned finally calling. She had been expecting his call and wondered why it had taken so long. The mines should have been searched hours ago. It wasn't, however; it was a text message from Keri. She clicked on it to see what her friend wanted. She was probably just informing Harley that Melissa had officially left. Nothing pleased her more than to know that her friends made it safely out of Thailand.

> **Keri: Meet me in the dining room. I have something to tell you. There's another girl missing!!!**

Shit.

Harley wasn't sure what that meant, exactly, but it

didn't sound good. She needed to get to Keri and find out what she was talking about.

> **Harley: Sounds ominous. Just got back 2 the island. I will be there as soon as I can.**

She shoved her phone back into her pocket as Rayland came around the side of the car to meet her. She hated having to tell him she had to go, and she didn't want to inform him about the case just yet. It was all a little much for a first date. She didn't need to scare him off. But she planned on filling him in sooner than later. The last thing she wanted was for someone else she cared about to get hurt. She may have just met Rayland, but she felt more connected to him than anyone else and she didn't want to be responsible for another death.

"Hey, I thought maybe we could have something to eat before you head up for that bubble bath."

She smiled. "Rayland, I wish I could, but I really think I should just go and rest. I hope that's okay."

"Oh, Harley, of course it is. Sorry for hogging your time. I just had such an awesome time with you today."

"I did too. Trust me; I would love to see you again. I just need to chill out for the evening."

"No problem. I will catch up with you another time then."

She blushed. "Yeah, again, I'm sorry."

"No need to apologize."

She leaned up toward him and kissed him on the mouth, hoping he would feel that she truly did have a good time with him. He smiled when they parted, and then she turned and ran toward the hotel, ignoring all the pain that she felt in her body.

TWENTY THREE

HARLEY WALKED INTO THE DINING room and found Keri eating lunch by herself. She sat down at the table across from her.

Keri looked up at her in surprise. "What the heck happened to you?"

"I was four-wheeling and toppled off. Don't ask—it's embarrassing enough."

Keri smirked. "Are you okay?"

"Aside from some bumps and scratches, yes I am. What's up? Your message was a little weird. How do you know about a missing person?"

"I had a few drinks this morning on the beach with some people and they mentioned that their friend was missing. Apparently, they were hanging out at the hotel bar last night and their friend got up from the table to go to the bathroom and never returned."

"No shit. That's not a good sign. Did they see anyone with her, anyone that followed her to the bathroom?"

"They don't remember seeing anyone. But they were all hammered, so who knows."

"How long before they realized she was missing?"

"Almost a half hour."

"Wonderful. Is she a guest here?"

"No, they just came into the bar to party. They are staying in one of the huts. They checked to see if she just stumbled home, but she's not there either."

The killer had a set of balls, that was for sure. She wondered where Craig had been last night. The killer couldn't have cared less that they were searching the mines—he was still out doing what he did best. He couldn't be still burying the bodies at the mines; it would be too dangerous now. If he was still killing people, he must have found another burial ground.

"I don't suppose you asked for a picture of the girl?"

Keri smiled. "You bet your ass I did. They sent one to my phone. I told them about my sister and so they are really worried now."

"They should be."

Keri passed her the phone and Harley stared down at the picture of the girl. She was on the beach laughing with her friends in a barely-there, purple bikini.

"She's so young." Harley's heart went out to the girl. If she was taken, she would have had a night of terror, nothing that a young girl should ever experience.

"They said she came here for her twentieth birthday. Happy Birthday, right?"

"Yeah, right. Poor thing."

The waiter stopped by their table and asked if they needed anything. "Can I have a coffee, and a bowl of what she has, to go." He nodded and walked away. "Wait!" Harley called.

He turned back to the table. "Do you remember seeing this girl at the hotel last night?"

The waiter stared at the photo on the phone and shook his head.

"That's always the response. No one remembers anyone. There are just too many tourists coming and going."

"Who is doing this, Harley?"

Harley shifted uncomfortably in her seat. Keri raised her eyebrows.

"What is it, Harley?"

"Chief Aat pulled a file yesterday on Craig. It didn't look good; they are focusing their attention on him at the moment."

Keri went slack-jawed. "Are you out of your mind? There is no way that it's Craig. We're friends. My God, Harley, you slept with him."

"Don't remind me. Look, I felt the same way, but there is damning evidence, and at the very least, they are investigating him."

"What the hell, Harley?" Keri stood up from the table. "How could you turn on him like that?"

"I'm not turning on anyone. Sit down...please?"

Keri stared at her for a moment before sitting down.

"Trust me, Keri; I don't want it to be him either. But

he has a criminal record."

"What?"

"It's true, and you know he disappears all the time. Never mind the fact that he's been showing violent signs lately, the way he's been with Devon. Where is he right now—do you know? Where was he last night when the girl went missing?"

"I don't know. I haven't seen him since the bonfire. He likes investigating the island and he has a few different groups of people that he hangs out with, especially after you guys broke up."

"I'm sorry that this pisses you off, but this is our first solid lead since people have gone missing, and we at least have to rule him out. Anyway, I'm going to go see the chief and fill him in on the missing girl."

"I'm coming with you."

"That's really not necessary, Keri."

"Please, I promise I won't be in the way. Everyone is gone now and it's weird."

"Okay fine. But you better eat up. I'm leaving when my food gets here."

Keri stuck out her tongue and Harley went back to looking at the picture. "Craig is slick."

"Harley…"

She smiled. "Sorry, the guy is slick. I don't know how he's moving around with these bodies without anyone taking notice. But you're right, with a number of people going in and out, some only staying for a day, it would be hard for staff to remember anyone."

"I talked to my mom today."

Harley looked up at Keri. "How did that go?"

"Not good. I told her about Katie and Brian and I think I almost gave her a heart attack. I wasn't going to say anything until I knew, but let's be honest, they're not coming back, are they?"

Harley frowned. "It's not looking good, Keri, I'm sorry."

"It's not your fault, Harley. Hell, we all left them alone that night. No one could have foreseen what happened. I just want to find them so that I can bring them home with me. I don't want to leave them here with him."

"We won't. I promise you that we'll find them. We are definitely on the right track."

The waiter brought out her food and Harley and Keri left money on the table for their lunch. As they walked out into the lobby, Harley decided to stop at the front desk.

"Do you recognize this girl?" she asked the clerk. "She would have come into the bar last night." It was the same clerk that she had talked to previously.

"Possibly, she looks familiar."

"Did you see her leave with anyone?"

"No, I'm sorry. What's this about? You've been asking a lot of questions around here lately. We don't want our guests to be upset."

Harley stared at her. "Yes, God forbid. People are going missing here on the island and that should certainly be something the hotel should be concerned about. Have you seen any men carrying around strange packages? Rather large ones?"

The clerk shrugged. "People come in and out carrying all sorts of bags. I haven't seen anything unusual. The worst complaint we have had lately is a guest who plays classical music too loudly."

Harley nodded. "Right." She was beginning to think that questioning the staff was pointless. She would request that Ned send in a uniform—maybe that might shake things up a bit. She turned from the desk and Keri followed her out the door.

After they had tailgated their way back to the station, Harley briefed the chief and his staff about the missing girl. "So, we could have another body on our hands. If we don't move fast, it may already be too late. We don't know at this point how long he keeps them alive, because so far, we haven't been able to determine how long individuals go missing for. In the case of Keri's sister, it was less than a 24-hour period. So, it's pretty likely that he murders them when he takes them."

She then explained to the chief about having an officer sent to the hotel to start questioning the staff; she hoped someone with authority on the island might get more answers than she did. The chief mentioned that there was a team at the last mine, and Harley hoped that news of the search would come in while they were there. No one seemed to mind that Keri had come to the station, as they assumed she was with Harley and they had a whole new respect for Harley at that point.

"Have you looked into Craig's whereabouts at this point?" the chief asked.

"It's not him," Keri piped in.

"You told her?" The chief looked at Harley incredulously. "And that mantra is starting to sound like a broken record."

"What do you expect me to do? She bloody well hangs out with the guy! I can't just let my friends continue to hang out with him and hope for the best. There are bodies everywhere."

"Stop saying that," Keri protested. "You guys are crazy if you think it's him."

"Keri, stop! We get it. You don't believe it's him. Now let us do our job, and if it's not him, we'll know soon enough." She turned back to the chief while Keri sulked. "How is the search warrant coming along?"

"We are still waiting."

"You know, in New York, I probably would have had it in about twenty minutes."

Chief Aat looked at her sternly. "Okay, at this point we are looking at Craig. I set up your profile of the killer. Let's go through it again and maybe we can ring some more bells."

Harley nodded. "I think we are probably dealing

with someone who blends into the crowd. This isn't some weirdo that people are going to take notice of. He's probably friendly and personable, the kind of person you don't mind going to have a drink with. That may be exactly how he gets his victims; people like him, so they leave with him. We know he was at the bar last night drinking, and at some point, he probably met up with the missing girl."

"Her friends don't remember her talking to anyone?"

"No, they were all drunk and barely noticed she was gone until they were getting ready to leave. There's a back exit by the bathroom, so they probably left out through there. There are no cameras—I looked, and it's a joke really."

The chief nodded. "We've never seen anything like this before. It's one of the grisliest murder cases we have ever seen. The way he handles the victims—what he's done to the bodies—he's a madman." His eyes flickered to Keri, and Harley hoped she wasn't listening too keenly to their conversation.

"Yes, me too, to be honest with you. We don't get too many serial killers in New York City—not lately anyway."

"Where do you think he's taking the bodies?"

"Maybe he's killing them in the mines; it would certainly be secluded enough."

"It would be a long way to travel with a victim who's struggling." "Yes, I thought about that too. If he has their trust, then he could really take them anywhere that he wanted to. We don't even know if they are conscious when he kills them."

"The medical examiner thinks that they were tortured for hours."

Harley nodded, it was hard to think of these things happening to her friends, but it was the reality they were facing. "We need a lead. Someone who saw or heard something."

He nodded. "I'll send an officer out tomorrow to start questioning people; maybe we will get lucky. We have Craig's picture, and maybe someone saw them together."

"I hope so."

Ned walked over. "Can I get you girls a coffee?"

"That would be great, Ned, thanks."

"I have to say, Harley, you are looking rougher than normal."

She laughed. "You're not much for compliments, are you?"

He smiled, "I guess I'm not."

"I was joyriding in the jungle today, trying to have some fun, when I took a tumble. I'm sure that I will have plenty of bruises tomorrow. But it was fun."

"You have to be careful in our jungles; some people never come out." He walked away to retrieve coffee.

She frowned as she wondered if that might be a place the killer decided to hide bodies. She would need to look into abandoned buildings or caverns within the forest area. Her mind was constantly spinning about theories and avenues that she hadn't considered before. She needed to get into the killer's mind and figure out what his next step was and how he was choosing his victims. Was it all random? It rarely was when it came to serial killers. What was his purpose? She felt useful again being at the station, among people who understood crime and wanted justice. She no longer needed to hold on to the past—her mistakes were behind her and she didn't need to allow them to define her. She was strong and she would get through the things that happened to her. This was a redeeming moment for her and she would not leave the island until the killer had been stopped. She owed that to herself and Keri. She was going to rebuild her life and return home a different person than the one that left.

Ned returned with coffee in hand and passed one to Harley while Keri walked over to grab the other.

"There was no identification on the bodies at all? No clothing, or pieces—not a purse or wallet?" Harley asked.

Ned shook his head. "Nothing. We are assuming at this point that the killer is taking the passports and any cash and credit cards."

"It could be how he's traveling. Robbing his victims and traveling from island to island on their money. You should check to see if the Texas tourist had her account drained. There may not be cameras, but we would at least know if someone had used her card," she said.

"That's a good idea, Harley. Keri, when you have

THE DISMEMBERER'S HANDBOOK

the opportunity, we would like to go to your sister's cabin with you to see if you recognize anything missing aside from her passport and purse."

"We kind of already did that," Harley said sheepishly.

"Really? Without my permission?" He looked unimpressed with Harley's rogue cop skills.

She shrugged. "You weren't exactly helpful at first."

"Right."

They all turned when an officer called out to the chief. "Chief, you have a phone call."

He left the two of them, and Harley sipped at her coffee. She should probably lay off the coffee before she developed the caffeine shakes, but she wanted to keep sharp. Her body was growing weary from the pain and she longed to go back to the hotel and have that bath and then crawl into bed. She thought about Rayland and what it might be like to crawl into bed with him, curling up against his warm body. Ever since their outing, he had not been far from her thoughts, and she was looking forward to seeing him again.

"Harley!"

Both Harley and Keri turned to the chief. They approached the desk just as the chief was getting off the phone. "What is it?"

"The last mine has been searched and they found two bodies."

Keri grasped Harley's hand and Harley looked over at her. The chief walked over to Keri, looking saddened.

"Judging by the description you gave us, the officers believe they found your family members. I'm very sorry."

Keri crumpled into Harley's arms and her body shook with sobs.

The chief cleared his throat. "There is something I have to mention. We were not able to locate your sister's head."

Keri looked up; the tears frozen on her face. "What?"

"I'm sorry, I know this is all coming as a shock to you. Her head is missing. The body does have the birth mark you described on her inner thigh but of course, we will need a family member to confirm it when the body is viewed."

Keri broke down again and placed her head once again on Harley's shoulder.

Harley held her as tightly as possible, wishing that she could take away her pain. There was nothing she could do, however, and she was thankful that Keri would be able to take her family home and bury them properly.

Harley looked up at the chief and knew what he was thinking. They had one hell of a shit storm on their hands.

TWENTY FOUR

HARLEY WAS SITTING IN THE dining room, enjoying some lunch and thinking about Keri. Keri had been asked to identify the bodies of her family members, and the scene had crushed both of them. She had grown very close to Keri over the past few weeks and always hoped that she could have been able to give her a happier ending to the situation. She had known from the beginning though that in situations like that it was unlikely the person was still alive after 24 hours. Harley had stayed with her long enough to be there for her when she called her parents. She had walked her back to her hut and tucked her in; she had been numb from seeing the bodies. Harley advised her to stay off the beach until her flight home.

She was about to be alone on the island and she wasn't sure how she felt about it. There would be no more beer and burgers on the beach by the campfire. Keri was making arrangements to travel home with the bodies of her brother-in-law and sister, and her mother was making funeral arrangements. Harley would have loved to have gone to the funeral with her, but she had unfinished business in Thailand and she wouldn't be able to live with herself if she walked away from the case. She needed to see it through. She wished that she wasn't going to be on her own, but it was more important that her friends were safely away from Thailand.

The news stations back home had got wind of their situation now that bodies were being transported back to the States. There were currently four going back to the United States and there was no keeping things a secret now. The world was about to find out that there was a serial killer loose in Thailand. The news was slower to spread on the islands, however, as everyone seemed to stay in their vacation bubbles.

The plan had been to follow Craig around but she had been highly unsuccessful at it. She hadn't been able to track him down. She knew that he used to like to island jump before they met so she assumed maybe that was what he was doing. It left her unsettled because she wondered what he was doing when he was away. Following him around proved to be difficult. He always popped back up so she didn't think that it would be long before he was showing up in the group again. The fact that he had disappeared caused doubts to build up in her. Could Craig really be the killer?

"Harley!"

She looked up from her lunch and saw Rayland walking toward her with a big grin on his face. She smiled when she saw him, even though it was a sad one—maybe she wouldn't be alone after all.

"Hi, Rayland."

"I was hoping I would run into you again. How's lunch?"

"Delicious, actually, you should order some."

"I might just do that. Can I join you?"

"Of course."

He sat down across from her and she could smell the beach on him. She had an ache inside of her to get close to him; she could use some companionship after all the horror. The waiter approached the table and Harley watched Rayland order lunch, and she imagined kissing along his chiseled jaw.

He thanked the waiter and looked at her. "What?"

She blushed deeply. "Oh nothing. Look, I wanted to talk to you about something. It might be a little alarming, but I thought you should know."

His smile disappeared. "It sounds serious. What's up?"

"I never told you this before, but I'm a police officer in New York City. I came to Thailand because I needed a break."

He raised his eyebrow. "No kidding? I would never have guessed; you seem so chill."

She laughed. "Well, that's the effect the islands have had on me, along with meeting new people. I was wound pretty tight at home."

The waiter came to the table to deliver the two beer Rayland had ordered. Harley took a satisfying swig of the beer.

"You know, you should probably work on your driving skills if you're gonna brag about being a cop."

She stuck her tongue out. "Watch it."

He laughed. "So, that can't be the news you wanted to tell me. Yeah, I'm a little surprised, but it's hardly alarming."

She looked down at her plate, suddenly losing her appetite. "No. I actually got involved in a case here because some of my friends went missing. Their bodies have recently turned up."

His mouth hung open. "What? I haven't heard anything about it. I can't believe something like that could happen here; it's so peaceful. There's been nothing on the news."

"There will be—there's no hiding it now. It was originally kept out of the news because we didn't want the killer to bolt, but it hasn't even fazed him. There are officers on the island questioning people; I wouldn't be surprised if it were on the nightly news this evening. My friend is taking her family home to bury them today, so that's going to spark national attention. I just hope the killer doesn't leave the island before we can get to him."

Rayland took two long swigs of his beer and set it back down on the table. "Shit. Well, if your goal was to blow my mind, Harley, you've done your job. Are you saying there's a crazy person on the island killing people? Fuck, I definitely picked the wrong place for a vacation."

She chuckled. "You and me both. I just wanted you to know to stay safe. He's taken down two able-bodied men already."

"I appreciate the heads up. Maybe I should think about getting off the island."

A sting of disappointment hit her, but she knew it would probably be for the best. "That's probably a safe idea."

"What about you? It's not safe here for you either. Why don't you come with me? We can take our vacation somewhere else, get away from this dangerous place."

She smiled sadly. "I can't. I need to see this through." He frowned. "Well, I can't exactly leave you here alone and in danger."

"Rayland, you don't have to worry about me."

"If you're staying, then so am I. I promise I will watch my back. I couldn't imagine leaving without getting to know you better. My mother always taught me not to talk to strangers anyway." The waiter came with his food and he started eating.

She smiled as she took another drink. "Fair enough. So, have you seen anything questionable, something you may have thought was weird but disregarded it?"

He thought for a moment. "Truthfully, no, or at

least nothing I remember. To be honest, everyone has been so friendly, and I've been here more than once. I haven't got any weird vibes from anyone. Lately, I've been at the beach early and for most of the day. The surfing bug got me. I've gotten pretty good—you should come sometime and try it out."

"I love surfing, actually, and maybe I will one of these days."

"So, do they have any leads?"

She groaned. "Yes, actually. It just so happens that they have zeroed in on a guy that used to be my lover on the island." She blushed deeply. "It turns out his past is a little shady and I didn't do a thorough background check before we got naked."

He laughed. "You can't be serious. Let me get this straight: you were dating a serial killer?"

She glared at him. God, could it get any worse?

He smiled. "Sorry."

"Don't worry about it. I was just as surprised as you were. In fact, my next mission is to follow the guy around and see what he's up to."

"Really? That's some serious detective work. Want some company?"

She cringed. "I don't know if that's the best idea."

"C'mon, it would be fun, and I could keep you safe. Is it really the best idea to follow a potential serial killer all by yourself?"

"I don't know, Rayland."

He smiled, and then looked at his watch. "Well,

I hate to eat and run, but I'm supposed to meet someone to go spearfishing. What do you say I take you for dinner tonight? Meet me here tonight? We'll talk about our plan to stalk your friend."

She laughed. "Sure that would be great. Maybe having you around wouldn't be so bad." He bent down and kissed her on the forehead. "See you then, Harley."

She watched him leave, feeling a pang of jealousy. She hoped he wasn't meeting another girl. She felt great every time she was around Rayland, and they had a natural chemistry, something she hadn't experienced when she spent time with Craig. Maybe now she knew why. She shuddered again, thinking about the possibility that he was a cold-blooded killer. She found it odd that Rayland hadn't been more eager to leave the island after he found out that people were dying. But maybe chivalry wasn't dead after all. It would be interesting having him on the stakeout, but at the end of the day, she was grateful not to have to go it alone.

TWENTY FIVE

HARLEY SAT ACROSS FROM RAYLAND, laughing and enjoying the wine they ordered with their dinner. The entrée had been seafood and she had just about gorged herself on the delicious meal. She didn't think that she even had room for dessert, but he wouldn't take no for an answer. She was feeling all kinds of good around Rayland and she couldn't remember the last time she felt that good around another man. Was it with Chris? Yes, that would have been the last time. In a lot of ways, Rayland reminded her of Chris—he was good-natured and always seemed to be in a good mood. Never mind the fact that he looked good enough to eat. Though, as it turned out, she had not known Chris as well as she thought she did. She liked to think that she did and that maybe he just got in trouble over money and couldn't find a way out. She was probably giving him too much credit. In the end, for whatever reason, he was no longer one of the good guys—he was no longer her guy.

"Are you okay, Harley?"

She didn't realize that she had gone into her own little world. "Oh God, yes, I'm sorry. I think I just have too much on my mind. I'm having a wonderful time, thank you." She smiled sheepishly at him. She hadn't thought about Chris in a while and she wasn't sure if that was a good thing or a bad thing. Maybe it meant she was finally getting over the things that happened to her. That certainly would be refreshing.

"Great. You need to allow yourself to relax, Harley, even if you are technically back to work."

"Yes, of course. How was fishing?"

"It was great; I just love experiencing the nature here. I'll have to return to my busy life again soon, and I'm not looking forward to it."

"Yes, being away from the hustle and bustle has been pretty great. But at some point, we all have to go back to reality."

"That's the unfortunate part, isn't it? How is your friend doing?"

"I saw her at lunch. She's leaving tomorrow night. It was a little heartbreaking, really. But she will be okay now that she's on her way home. I really feel for their whole family. That couple was on their honeymoon when they were murdered; it's just terrible. They were supposed to be returning home and unwrapping all their gifts and starting their new life together. What a waste." Keri had cried her eyes out on the beach when she said goodbye to Harley. They had hugged for what felt like forever. Harley wasn't sure if she would get a chance to see Keri tomorrow with everything that was going on, so they said their goodbyes early. They would keep in touch, though, and she was safe now. That was all that mattered to Harley. One day she would go out and visit Keri when all this craziness was behind her. In the meantime, they would keep in touch via text, especially with the ongoing case. She would be keeping her updated as they went along.

Rayland nodded and took a sip of his wine. "Tragic, but they do have their memories, and they died in a beautiful place. We should all hope for that."

She sipped her wine, watching him, and wondered if Keri was going to be able to come back to Thailand without thinking about her dead family. Fuck memories.

"So, what do you say we make a plan to hunt down this killer together. I'm ready to go after this guy."

She looked at him and smiled. "You really think you are up for this? Worst case scenario, it could be a very boring night."

"Sure. Why not? Plus, it's an excuse to spend more time with you. A night with you could never be boring. It would be pretty nuts if we caught him. Wouldn't it? Imagine the story we could tell our grandchildren."

"Grandchildren?" she said laughing, "Don't you think you're getting a little ahead of yourself there?"

He winked at her. "Maybe. So where do we start?"

"Well, I've scoped out Craig's hotel room. I wanted to see if he was back from…wherever, yet."

"He's staying at the hotel? That's convenient." He took a drink from his wine, watching her closely.

"Yeah well, he's been missing in action for a few days, but he seems to be back and drinking on the beach. That usually means he will be around for a few days. The chief told me to hold off, to wait for now until he can get a search warrant. But I'll give it until tomorrow and then I'm going to do it anyway. So, I say we start following him tomorrow evening. In the evening is usually when people go missing on the island. Let's see what he's up to and maybe we'll get lucky. Hopefully we will get the search warrant on the room, quickly, so we'll be able to get in there in the next few days."

"A search warrant? Interesting."

"Yes, just a matter of getting through to Thailand officials. Apparently, it's not very easy."

He nodded, thinking. "What do you say we get out of here?" he asked with a twinkle in his eye.

"Sure, why don't we have a nightcap in my room. I have a wonderful view."

"That sounds great, I will get the bill."

She opened the door to her hotel room and they walked inside. She went immediately to the fridge and pulled out a bottle of white wine. She uncorked it and poured them both a glass. White wine was her favorite and it had just the right chill to it. She already had a buzz on from dinner and she liked the idea of having Rayland in her room, close to her bed. They could finish the bottle on the balcony and then who knew what might happen. Whatever it was, she was ready for it.

When she turned around, she saw Rayland standing at her desk, staring at the files she had left open. He was staring, mesmerized at the photos. She had been looking at the files again before she had left for dinner, and she had left them scattered about. She waited for a look of revulsion to come over his face and it never came.

"Sorry, I should have cleaned those up. They aren't very pretty."

He looked up from the files and she handed him a glass. "Thanks. Yeah, these are gruesome. I don't know how you do this, Harley. I think I will stick to business. What happened to them?"

"Things that will haunt your dreams, I assure you of that much. It's not a job for anyone with a weak stomach, that's for sure."

She took a sip of her wine and stared down at the pictures herself. She was used to them by now, but they must have been shocking for Rayland to see. Just limbs and torsos. The pictures were disgusting.

"So, you really think it's Craig?" Rayland asked. "I mean, someone capable of all that, he's got to be really nuts, right?"

"Well, he probably wasn't hugged much as a child, if that's what you mean. But he's also really smart. I honestly hope it's not Craig for obvious reasons, but things are certainly pointing in that direction. This isn't random, and the fact that we have very little to go on at this point means that he's smart enough not to leave any clues. He's not doing this for show or attention. I'm not sure what his reasons are but if I had to guess I would say he simply likes it."

"Likes what? Killing people?"

"Yes, essentially. The victims weren't just dismembered; they were tortured. You don't do that unless you take some joy in it. It's not like he was trying to get information. He kills people because he wants to. This is not a game to him and he has no intention of getting caught."

He took a big gulp of wine. "You have really good insight, Harley. You're incredibly smart, and that's very attractive."

She smiled. "Why, thank you. You just get used to these things, and I learn to read the motives behind a serial killer."

"A serial killer?"

She nodded. "That's what I have on my hands, yes."

"The way you talk about him, you seem kind of attracted to him, to his brain and how it works."

She was sipping her wine when he said it and she almost choked on it. Taken aback she just stared at him. "Are you insane?"

He laughed. "Sorry, you just seem a little obsessed. I don't know anything about being a cop…I mean, how many times have you looked at those files?"

"Maybe I am a little obsessed, but it's only because I want to bring him down."

"I'm sorry, I didn't mean anything by it." He bent down to kiss her on the lips and she welcomed the kiss, tasting the wine on his lips. She melted into his kiss, feeling a passion build up inside of her. She wanted him—she had been wanting him for a while. He pulled her up against him and their bodies aligned. He lifted her up, catching her by surprise, and placed her on top of the desk among the files. Some fell to the floor while others lay open. His lips found hers again and their kisses grew more passionate as she pulled at his shirt, pulling it over his head. His kisses left her mouth and went to her neck, making their impression on her skin. He pushed up her dress and started undoing his pants. She was devouring his lips and nipped at his lower lip as he entered her. She gasped and felt totally complete at that moment, her eyelids fluttering closed.

They lay there in bed together, Harley resting her head on Rayland's chest. She no longer wanted to be apart from him; he made her feel like she had known him her whole life. It was a crazy feeling since they just met but that's how he made her feel. Could she be falling for the guy already? It was impossible and yet she couldn't imagine a day without him. She was grateful that he was staying on the island for a little while now that all her friends were gone.

"Where did you get your name from? It's unusual," she said as she nuzzled against his bare chest.

He chuckled. "My mother was from the South. She liked it and the rest is history. I've gotten a lot of flack for it, but I like it."

"So do I. It's sexy," she said with a giggle.

"No, Harley, you're the sexy one." He hugged her tightly. "Hey, I got an idea, let's go swimming."

"Now?"

"Yeah, why not. No one will be out there now and the water is gonna be warm, just like a bath."

She smiled, feeling suddenly reckless with him. "Sure, let's go."

They hurried out of bed and Harley slipped into her clothes as quickly as possible. Her files were strewn all over the place from their passionate frolicking. She gathered them up and placed them back on the desk, a little embarrassed that they had sex on them. She turned and he was right beside her again, grasping her hand in his. They raced out of the hotel like a couple of high school kids, laughing as they ran down the hallway toward the elevator. Once inside the elevator, she threw herself into his arms and planted her lips against his. They kissed until the elevator reached the ground floor and then they raced again into the lobby. She had never felt more alive in all her life and she wondered if being with Rayland was the beginning of a whole new life for her.

When they got to the beach, they stripped down to their underwear. Rayland had a pair of boxers on. She found herself standing in her underwear, thrilled to be there at that moment with him. He ran into the surf and she laughed while watching. For the first time since she got to Thailand, she felt comfortable and free, and it was all because of Rayland. Just before she ran into the surf, she took off her bra and ran into the water after him.

She was in the warehouse once again, her back against the boxes that lined the warehouse in rows. She could hear the men arguing, but she wasn't sure what it was all about. She peered around the box and saw two men standing across from each other and one was holding a briefcase.

"Shit."

Something was definitely going down—was it drugs, guns? She couldn't tell what was in the opened trunk of the car, but the two men didn't seem very fond of one another. She needed to get closer, but she was at the end of the row, and if she moved, she would be exposed. Judging by how heated things were getting between the two men, she could tell something was going to happen. She needed to move fast.

She stepped out from the boxes and held her gun steady in front of her.

"Freeze. Don't you move or I will shoot you dead."

The men turned in surprise and one of the men raised his gun to shoot her. She moved to the side as she fired, missing the guy but also avoiding getting shot in the head. To her surprise, the man turned and ran while the man with the briefcase lifted his gun toward her.

"Freeze," she shouted. Don't these fuckers listen? When she saw the guy, her mouth dropped open.

"Chris! No."

"Harley, I'm sorry."

"What are you doing?"

"It's over, Harley, shoot me."

"No. I'm arresting you, you're coming with me."

"That's not going to happen. If you don't shoot me, I will kill you."

She just shook her head. He fired at her and she practically felt the breeze from it, the bullet was so close to her head. She fired back and Chris dropped like a stone, the gun dropping to the floor along with the briefcase. She ran to him and fell to the floor around his body.

Her mind couldn't even begin to process the face staring back at her. Rayland stared back at her with dead eyes, his face expressionless. She didn't understand; it was Chris, it was supposed to be Chris. What was Rayland doing there? He would never do something like this. He would never try to harm her. She completely forgot about the man that was escaping. She had just got to know Rayland; he was someone she wanted to fall in love with. He couldn't be gone. Her body was wracked with sobs as she looked down at the lips she has kissed and the body she had lain against.

She was ripped out of sleep drenched in sweat, gasping for air. Her heart beat against her chest and she felt a dull ache. She had shot Rayland; she was so grateful that it was just a dream. She wasn't in love with the guy, but she could see a time when she could be. They had grown so close over a short amount of time; she didn't want it to be over. She wanted to see what the future held for them.

She fell back onto her pillow and thought about Rayland. She couldn't understand why she would have such a horrible dream about him. Was it an omen? Was she destined to lose another man in her life? She couldn't imagine anything happening to Rayland and she hoped that she wasn't putting him in any danger by allowing him to come along with her. She tried to go back to sleep, but she spent most of the night analyzing her dream.

TWENTY SIX

HARLEY STOOD OUT ON HER balcony the next evening with a heavy heart. The chief had warned her not to follow Craig around but they were waiting for the search warrant and she didn't want to risk Craig leaving the island again. She heard a knock on the door and went back inside the room.

When Harley opened the door to her hotel room, she couldn't help but laugh when she saw Rayland standing there with coffee and a bag of pastries in his hand. He was wearing jeans and a tight t-shirt that hugged him in ways that made her remember the night they shared together. She blushed slightly when she remembered the way their bodies had fallen together on the bed, all limbs and passion. She hadn't been able to get enough of him, the way he moved within her, the taste of his skin, the way their kisses went everywhere. Seeing him in her room again brought up every last detail of their encounter, and she couldn't help but smile. He walked into the room and shut the door behind her.

"What are you doing?" she asked as he leaned in for a kiss. "Mmm, you almost make me want to stay in the room." Maybe they could take a few minutes to explore all over again.

"Hey, I've watched enough police shows to know that this is exactly the kind of stuff we need for a stakeout."

"Such a cliché." She rolled her eyes. But she found it sweet how he prepared for their meeting, thinking about her before he even saw her. When was the last time a guy had done that for her? She couldn't even remember.

"Well, shall we go? Because I can't wait for this to start."

She looked at him sternly, hoping that she wasn't making a mistake by taking a civilian with her. "Promise me you're going to take this seriously. I'm technically working tonight and this is no joke."

"Of course. I'm sorry, Harley, I wasn't trying to make light of things. I just know this is heavy business, and to be honest, the thought of you being out there with some killer running loose makes me a little crazy. I guess I'm just glad that I'm going to be with you. I would never want anything bad to happen to you."

He pulled her close to him and she smiled up at him. "You're forgiven." He bent down and kissed her on the lips. She loved the way he tasted, and the warm way their mouths united made her wish that they could just spend the night in her room, in her bed—to forget the craziness that was awaiting them outside and pretend she was on vacation again. Would that be so terrible? "We better get going or I'm never going to want to leave."

"You're so damn sexy. So, what's the plan, officer?"

She grabbed him by the hand and pulled him out of the hotel room. She snickered as she glanced at the bag of pastries again. He was so cute she could hardly stand it. "We are going to check out where he is and then see where he goes. Last time I checked, he was on the beach."

"Yeah, let's go and see where the serial killer goes," he said with a laugh.

They sat under a tree a few yards from the hotel and drank their coffee. Craig was currently sitting around a bonfire with a bunch of guys she didn't know. Was he choosing another victim from his group? Or would he venture away and find someone random? She still couldn't believe she was stalking her ex-lover in the hopes that she could stop him from chopping up another person. She stared at him as he laughed and drank beer, not even having the slightest inkling that they were watching him. She still couldn't look at him and see a killer. All those lazy nights together in bed, listening to the sounds of the waves crashing outside—never mind the time he taught her how to surf. Looking at him now, she just grew angry inside—angry that he had fooled her and even angrier at all the destruction he had caused on the island, the lives he had ruined, and the families who would never be the same again. Tears pooled in her eyes as she thought of Keri leaving the island tomorrow to attend the funeral of her sister and brother-in-law.

"Harley, are you okay?"

She jumped slightly, startled out of her thoughts. "God, yeah. Sorry. I got lost in my own world there for a moment."

"Totally understandable. This is nuts, sitting here waiting for someone to do something heinous. It's a rush."

"Yeah." She turned and looked at Rayland. "Thanks for coming with me. It's nice to have someone with me through all this madness." She couldn't help but think about her dream, though, and she hoped that it wasn't an omen.

"I wouldn't want to be anywhere else." He handed her a cup of coffee. "You should probably drink this; we might be looking at a long night. He looks pretty comfortable."

She glanced over at Craig as he cracked open another beer. She accepted the coffee gratefully and took a sip of the bitter concoction.

"So, what do you have in that bag?"

He smiled as he pulled out muffins from the bag.

"Just about the best muffins that you will find on this island."

"There are no mushrooms in it, right?"

He laughed. "Not that I'm aware of, why?"

"Never mind it's a long story." She grabbed one of the muffins and took a bite out of it. They were pretty good actually. "You may be right."

"Uh, Harley?"

"Yes?"

"He's on the move."

"What?" She spun around to see Craig saying goodnight to his friends. He poured the rest of his beer into the sand and started walking down the beach. He walked like someone with a purpose, not the casual gait of someone on vacation. Had he always walked like that? She couldn't quite remember. Being with him seemed like a lifetime ago.

Harley tossed the muffin into the bag and stood up. She watched Craig from a distance before she started moving. They made their way down the beach, being careful to stay near the treeline to avoid being spotted. He made his way toward the hotel, and she was sure that he was going to grab another victim. It was getting late and she suspected that was when the killer went for his victims, snapping up one of the leftovers that didn't know enough to go home early. That way, no one would notice they were gone because the night was so quiet. If he grabbed someone that night, she would be able to see how he did it, how he chose them. She wouldn't let him get away with it, though. It was over for him; it was just a matter of time.

She put her hand out to stop Rayland, and they stood at a distance and watched Craig as he made his way to the front of the hotel.

"Maybe he's heading in for the night."

"Maybe he's meeting someone," Rayland whispered.

"Possibly." But she wasn't too sure about it. They watched him enter the lobby.

"Let's go and see who he's meeting."

Rayland grinned at her and she couldn't help but laugh. He seemed to be enjoying the game of cat and mouse. Being a businessman back home, he probably wasn't used to this kind of action. They hurried to the front of the hotel and quickly went through the lobby. Craig had gone into the dining room and she felt her heart beat fast. This was it. It was really going to happen. Her ex-lover was about to do the unthinkable, she was sure of it. She moved to the side of the door that led to the dining room and motioned for Rayland to stand back. She peered into the dining room and saw Craig go up to a girl at the bar. She looked at him in surprise as he asked if he could buy her a drink. Harley watched in amazement as the girl giggled and threw her hair back, clearly into Craig. He was making his move. He hadn't come there to meet her—she was just some random girl that he was buying a drink for.

Harley watched them chat and considered her next move. Technically he was doing nothing wrong; she would have to wait and see if they were going to leave together. He wouldn't wait long; he would want to get on with things. He wasn't in for a night of drinking. Harley looked behind her at Rayland who was peering into the dining room with interest. When she turned back to Craig and his lady friend, she gasped.

"Oh shit," Harley said as her stomach plummeted.

She watched as Keri ran up to Craig and started speaking to him animatedly. It was clear that she was filling Craig in on the fact that he was a suspect. She watched as shock registered on his face and then anger—the kind of anger she saw the night that she dumped him at the hotel. He grabbed her by the shoulders and started to shake her. Then he caught himself and stopped. He apologized and ran his hands through his hair. Keri was trying to get him to calm down.

"That does not look good. Isn't that your friend?"

"Yes, and she's totally fucking this up. Dammit!"

Craig was in the process of freaking out and Harley knew the stakeout for the evening was over. If he was going to kill someone tonight, his plans had definitely changed. She had never seen him so angry and she wondered if he would be looking for her that evening. Maybe he would have a victim after all. Not that she ever intended for that to happen.

"We better go before he comes out here," she whispered to Rayland. The two made their way out the lobby and into the warm night air. She was frustrated beyond belief and felt a sense of betrayal from Keri.

"How could she do something like that to me?" she said as they made their way back to the beach. They parked themselves underneath a tree in the dark to see if Craig was going to leave the hotel or go up to his room. The last thing she needed at that point was for him to see her. He was angry enough as it was, and she would want him cooled down if they were to ever have a confrontation.

"She obviously thinks you made a mistake; I'm sure she didn't do it to hurt you."

"What if I'm not wrong and she lets a killer get away? My God, he could be responsible for her own sister's death."

"So, what now, Harley?"

"I don't know. I'm worried that he's going to flee the island now and then we're really screwed. I'm going to have to figure something else out soon and hopefully get the slip on him. He's been tipped off now, though, so the element of surprise is gone."

She was pissed; she couldn't believe that Keri would go behind her back and do something like that to her. She felt betrayed. Keri had no idea what she was playing with and she could very well have helped a killer get loose. She looked up at Rayland who was looking down at her with interest. He really was something else, willing to be there with her as she tried to spy on a killer. He must think she was insane. Maybe that was a good thing, having someone around that didn't care if you fucked up or had a meltdown. Someone that wanted to be there no matter what madness you got yourself into. She had never had anything like that. There he was, standing and waiting for her to tell him their next move, and she didn't have a damn clue.

"I don't know what to do," she whispered, admitting defeat.

He grasped her hand in his and squeezed. "It's not over. You can still get him. You are one of the smartest women I know. Take him down. What do you want to do next?"

"I have to get into his room. The sooner, the better."

His gaze clouded over and then he smiled. "Good girl."

She pulled out her phone, making a call to Ned. She spent fifteen minutes talking to him about what their next move was and how they were going to get that search warrant. She clicked off the call and looked over at Rayland.

"There isn't anything more that I can do tonight so we might as well call it a night. The search warrant should be here tomorrow."

He smiled. "You have quite the career. I couldn't imagine having so much excitement."

She smirked. "Well, it's not always this exciting. But I should probably call it a night."

He nodded before he bent down and kissed her softly on the lips. She opened her eyes and looked up into his. It was a nice end to the evening.

"Can I walk you to your room?"

"No. I'll be fine besides, I want to be alone."

"Good luck tomorrow."

It was her turn to nod as he turned away and she watched him walk towards the beach. She made her way back to the hotel. She wanted to take another look at the case files before she retired for the night.

She was crossing her fingers that they would get into Craig's hotel the next day.

TWENTY SEVEN

A LOUD BANGING ON THE door tore Harley from her sleep. She looked around the room, frantically trying to understand where the hell she was. What was that noise? She couldn't determine if it was pounding in her head or somewhere else in the room? She had opened a bottle of wine when she returned to the hotel room and had sat out on the balcony thinking about the case and how it could have all gone up in smoke at that point. She rubbed her bleary eyes and they finally focused on the room around her. She was lying in her hotel bed wearing a rumpled t-shirt. She groaned at a headache that was slowly revealing itself to her. She looked up as the banging continued. It was coming from her hotel door—someone was clearly anxious to talk to her. She looked around for her phone and realized she had a lot of missed calls. What the hell was wrong with her? What time was it? She had been up most of the night going through her files, trying to find the connection she was missing about what turned Craig into a killer. She had thought about how often he had talked about his family with jest and good humor, but maybe none of what he had told her was real. His family could have been the breeding ground for his hate—though it was well-known that serial killers were usually born that way, not made through their environment. It was just as likely to have a serial killer come from a good home as a bad one. That was the scary part.

Rayland had wanted to come back to her hotel with her and help her out, though she imagined he had a little more than that in mind. She had sent Rayland back to his own room after their failed stakeout attempt. She had wanted to work the rest of the night and she knew she would get nothing done if he were in the room with her. She wiped the sleep out of her eye as she smiled. Yes, she would have got nothing done.

She quickly crawled out of bed, tripping over a glass she had left on the floor. She slid on the files she had left out the night before and wiped out on the floor. Embarrassed she slowly got back up, feeling like she had been drugged the night before. A lack of sleep did nothing to help her get to the door faster. She unlocked it and swung it open to find an exasperated Chief Aat on the other side of the door.

"Have you been sleeping this whole time?" he asked as his hands flung in the air. He stopped then and took one look at her, his gaze causing her to look down at herself. She was in panties and a t-shirt that looked like it belonged to a homeless person. His eyes trailed back up to her face and she instinctively started touching the top of her head to see if she had sprouted horns overnight.

"What the hell are you looking at?"

"Jesus Christ, Harley. You look like you've been dragged behind a pickup truck half the night. Did you go on a bender?"

Her mouth fell open and she wished she would have gone to the bathroom before answering the door. "I was up all night working the case. What time is it?"

"It's 10 am. I would have been here sooner, but you know how these bureaucrats like to dick us around. You'd think they don't want us to catch the killer or something."

"Holy shit. I didn't realize how exhausted I was; I could have slept all day."

Chief Aat looked down the hallway at someone. "We are going to need a minute." She wondered who he was talking to—was it Ned? He stepped into the hotel room and slammed the door behind him.

"Get dressed, we have to go."

She spun around and headed for her dresser, pulling out a clean pair of panties, tank top and shorts. She hurried into the bathroom as she called behind her, "Where are we going?"

"I got the search warrant, Harley. We are going to Craig's room and see what our man is hiding." She quickly dressed, feeling a frenzy kick up inside her. She was excited to see what was in the room. The clue-finding was her favorite part; she liked digging in and figuring out how someone's mind worked.

She glanced at herself in the mirror and did a double take. Her hair looked like she had been electrocuted and her mascara was smudged underneath her eyes. She did look like she had been dragged by a truck—or at least had really good sex. She splashed water on her face and quickly scrubbed. She grabbed the brush and pulled it through her head, stunned that she had slept for as long as she had. She wondered if Rayland would be on the beach, taking a break from his morning surf. The day was about to prove very interesting indeed, and she couldn't get out of the bathroom fast enough. When the chief saw her, he smiled.

"Now that's an improvement."

She stuck her tongue out at him and grabbed her phone, keys, and purse before following him out the door.

"Wait." He turned and she almost ran into him.

"What is it?"

He pulled a gun out from the back of his jeans and held it out to her. "This is off the record, and I will deny giving it to you, but I'm not about to see you killed on a technicality. I want you to be protected; things could get ugly. I will deal with the paperwork later."

She nodded. My, how things had changed between them. "Thank you." It had been a while since she had held a gun. It felt good, familiar, something she hadn't thought she would feel again. It helped to steel her resolve about bringing Craig down for good. She slipped it in the back of her shorts and pulled her tank top over it.

"What if we don't find anything?" muttered the chief. She stared at him and realized this was just as much his fight as hers. It was a huge case for him and it could certainly break his career if they failed. Never mind the economy the tourists brought in, the Mayor must be having a meltdown. No one liked a tourist attraction that had a serial killer running loose in it.

"Then we bring him in for questioning. That is, if he's still around. We bring him in and we rattle his cage. I know him, I was intimate with him, I can push his buttons if I have to."

He nodded. "I'm glad you're here, Harley. I know I was a real dick when you arrived, but we would never have come this far without you. I may have had my head in the sand, since I never believed anything like that could happen here."

She smiled. "Let's go see what Craig has hidden for us."

They went down the hall and she saw that there were a few officers waiting for them at the elevator. Ned was one of them. She was suddenly thankful they didn't all come to the door to get her. She nodded at Ned as they all piled into the elevator. She wondered if Craig would be there when they arrived or if he had already fled the island. She wasn't sure what to expect there, but she hoped they would be able to close the case. There had already been so many senseless deaths—people she had known and cared about taken away long before they had to be. She wanted it to end. She wanted to be able to sleep again without seeing torsos and limbs in her sleep. The killer had to be brought down. Craig had to be brought down.

When the elevator stopped and the doors opened, there stood Keri on the other side of the elevator door, on Craig's floor.

"Harley—!"

Harley took one step toward her and slapped her across the face. Keri gasped as the men stood around her, stunned.

"You bitch! How could you? Do you have any idea what you may have done?" Harley hissed at Keri. She felt the old betrayal creep up again inside her and she wondered why her friend had gone behind her back when she had trusted her with the information.

Keri held her face. "I'm sorry, Harley. I was coming to your room to explain, to apologize."

"Well, it's a little late for that. I trusted you with that information and I told you it to keep you safe. Now Craig may be gone, possibly forever."

"I know. I realized that after. I just couldn't believe it was him and I wasn't thinking. I'm sorry."

Harley stared at her and suddenly felt bad for slapping her. She had reacted irrationally. She was scared that Craig was going to get away and had allowed her anger to get the best of her. "It's fine. Don't worry about it."

"I'm leaving today, Harley. There's going to be a funeral; my family wants me home. I just wanted to say goodbye."

Harley nodded. "I'm glad to hear that. At least I will know you will be safe. I will let you know what we find out. I promise I will find who killed your sister. I promise."

Keri nodded with tears in her eyes. They quickly hugged and Keri walked away from them, heading toward a world that would be missing her sister. She would probably never get over what happened on the island. Harley turned to the chief and his men, feeling mixed up and flustered.

"Let's go," she said as the chief once again took the lead. She followed behind him while the officers were a few steps behind them. They walked down the hallway until they got to his door. The was a chance since he had been drinking last night that he had blown the whole thing off and decided to talk to her first before leaving. Especially if he believed he could convince her that he was not the killer. Serial killers loved that sort of shit. Sitting across from a detective in an interrogation room, seeing which one was the cat and which one was the mouse. They were smart and it wouldn't be the first time a killer walked out of the room free because they didn't have enough evidence.

Her heart started to beat hard as she wondered if he would be inside. She remembered how angry he had been the night before. She had never seen him that mad and she found it unsettling. She and the chief moved silently up to the door and went on either side of the door, guns drawn. The other four men stayed a few steps back and watched the place. There were a few people in the hallway staring at them. One of the officers barked at them to get into their rooms.

The chief knocked loudly on the door. "We have a warrant to search this room. Open the door."

Harley stared at the chief, her heart racing; she listened for any sign of movement in the room. This was it. The chief nodded at her and she stepped back and kicked in the door. The two moved in quickly, their guns drawn. There was no one there.

"The bathroom," she whispered. She looked around the room as he made his way into the bathroom. She didn't see anything that was necessarily odd or out of place, except for the smell. It smelled like death. She choked on the air she was breathing. How could he live in there with that smell?

She started to go through his dresser and the papers that were on top of it. In one of the drawers, there were newspaper clippings from old murders dating back a few years. She shuddered as she realized that they were probably victims. How long had he been doing this? Tears threatened to come, but she fought them back. He had been a monster all along, and she had let him get close. The last clipping was one of her and she stared down at it in shock. It was a scene from the police funeral they gave for Chris. She was standing alone at the gravesite. Where the hell had he got it from? The article discussed her shooting and everything that had transpired after. The blood in her veins felt cold as she realized he had known her before they met. Had he planned their initial meeting? Had she been a mark? Their first meeting couldn't have been accidental. The whole time he had known she was a detective and he had been playing her ever since. Her stomach roiled and she fought the urge to vomit. He was calculated alright, so why hadn't he killed her? He had more than enough chance to. All these thoughts ran through Harley's mind in a matter of seconds.

"Holy shit."

She didn't process the words coming from the bathroom as she stared down at the article. He had known her the whole time. Had he kept her close because he was killing people and wanted to keep an eye on her to get information?

"Harley, get in here!"

She turned toward the bathroom with the clippings still in her hand and hurried over. She pushed the bathroom door open and the smell hit her first. "What the fuck is—" Her words were cut short when she turned slowly around the room. The chief had his face in his sleeve as he pulled the shower curtain open with his other hand. The rest of the room had looked just as she remembered it, but not the bathroom. The bathroom was like a scene out of a horror movie. There was no blood, no, it was too late for that. But it was like a macabre museum exhibit. There were heads, decaying heads piled in the bathtub, all staring up at her. All the heads from the missing torsos. There were flies all over the bathroom, landing periodically on the corpse heads. She stared in disbelief when she looked at what had to be Katie's rotting head. These were her friends, just tossed aside in a bathtub as if their lives didn't matter at all. She would never be able to tell Keri any of this; it wouldn't be fair. Keri had trusted the same monster that Harley did, and finding out about him would crush her. The heads were all in various forms of decomposing. She shook her head, not wanting to believe that the same man that held her at night had done these horrible things. The scene was hideous. The chief pointed silently to the sink and she turned to find numerous fingers laying in the sink. She had seen enough; she turned from the room with Chief Aat following behind her.

Don't puke, don't puke, don't puke, she chanted in her head. The search was over; they didn't need any more than that. She walked right out into the hallway, taking in a deep breath. Tears streamed down her face as the chief yelled for one of the officers to retrieve the manager. She opened her eyes and looked around. There were people in the hallways, staring. They had no idea what was lying just a few feet from them.

Everyone would remember this vacation, seared into their memory forever. She heard the chief tell Ned to start questioning people in the hotel about whether they had seen anything suspicious, or if they had seen Craig leaving the room.

She sat down on the hallway floor and Chief Aat sat beside her. She handed him the clippings. She wished that Rayland was there, as just seeing his face would have made her feel immensely better.

"What is this?"

"I found them in his dresser. I think he kept them from previous victims. If that's the case, there are a lot more victims out there, hundreds maybe."

He shook his head. "You're in here."

"Yeah, I know. I guess he was playing me from the beginning."

"He's good. He's been doing it so long that he probably doesn't know himself any longer. It might not be safe for you to return to New York until he is caught. He could be obsessed with you."

"Wonderful." She remembered how he had camped outside of her hotel room, desperate to get back together. She sighed deeply. "Why would he bring those heads here? They haven't always been here. I would have known."

"They may have been stored or even sealed before now. The fact that they were there and out in the open was obviously to send us a message. He certainly wasn't trying to hide them anymore."

"He's gone, isn't he?"

"Probably, but maybe we can get him before he goes too far."

The manager was a small thin man who approached the room tentatively. He had been informed that the room would be searched. "What's in the room?" Chief Aat pulled him aside and explained the situation to him. He would probably never get that room rented out again unless he set it up as a freak show. Harley continued to stare at the wall, wondering where Craig had gone. If he left last night, he could be on a completely different island, but she would have to bet that he would go to Bangkok so that he could get right out of Thailand. Once his picture was sent to the news stations, he wouldn't be able to hide in Thailand. He would have to change his identity and possibly his appearance. They had a small window of opportunity to catch him.

She glanced over at the chief and the manager, who was now white as a sheet. The chief patted him on the shoulder and he walked away. The chief sat back down beside her.

"The medical examiner is on his way with his team. The manager said that the room was paid for this morning. He assumed it had been cleaned out of personal items."

"He left this morning. So maybe he didn't get as far away as we think."

She picked her phone up and looked for a signal. When she found it, she made a call to her captain in the U.S. He answered almost immediately.

"Harley, good to hear from you. I wasn't sure if I would get to talk to you again. How's the vacation? Some weird stuff has been coming over the news in that area. Are you okay?"

"That's what I'm calling about. I need you to put out an APB in the United States for Craig Torrens. We found the killer, but he got away. Anything you can do on your end would be great. He has been watching me and may end up in New York."

"No problem, Harley, we'll do what we can."

She clicked off the phone and turned back to the chief. "We need to stop him at all travel depots, especially the airport. He obviously has means to travel, and who knows how many passports he has. We need to send his picture out immediately."

Chief Aat got on the phone and Harley turned back to the room, unable to get the gruesome scene out of her head. Who the hell were they dealing with?

TWENTY EIGHT

HARLEY SAT IN THE DINING room with the chief as the crime scene investigators were taking care of the room upstairs. They were now trying to preserve as much evidence as possible. You never knew, maybe they would get lucky. People were being escorted out of the lobby so the bodies could be taken out. She was happy that she wasn't there to relive that scene. She wasn't sure she would get the image of that bathtub out of her head. She would constantly be checking behind the bathroom curtain in hotels for a while, that much was for sure. The murders were shocking the whole island—it was not a secret any longer. Even the officers and medical team had never seen anything like it before. Not too many people did. If you ever got that up close to a killer before, you rarely made it out alive. She had limited experience with dead bodies, and she had never seen anything more vicious and brutal than those Thailand killings.

The search for Craig had come up with nothing so far, and she was terrified that he had slipped through her fingers. Her blood pressure went up every time she thought about it. How could she have been so stupid as to tell Keri what they were doing before they got their hands on him? She would have never forgiven herself if something had happened to Keri because she didn't warn her. In the end, it had bitten her in the ass and made her look unprofessional. But she needed to stop living in the past. Beating up on herself had never helped her in the past before—if anything, it had strangled her.

The killer was an intelligent man and had been clearly doing it for a while, long enough that she had to wonder if he was gone for good. It couldn't possibly be the first time that authorities had come close enough to catch him. Could he really have remained under the radar that long? She shuddered at the thought that he would turn up in a different city and start over again. Maybe he would turn up in New York looking for her and she could bring him down then. There were no guarantees of that, of course. The idea that he would just keep killing was a little more than she could bear. So many dead people—how many were there, she wondered?

"Are you okay?"

She looked up from her coffee. Chief Aat was looking at her with concern. She took a sip of her coffee, feeling like an ass. "I'm sorry that I told Keri."

He shrugged. "Probably not the best idea you've

had, but I can't say that I wouldn't have done it myself had it been a friend of mine. He killed her sister. He's literally been picking them off one by one. She could have been killed next, for all we know. You may have saved her life. We'll get him either way; it's just a matter of time."

"I hope you're right, but he could be anywhere right now."

"He may never have left the island, Harley. You know how these sickos are. He could have been watching the hotel get searched the entire time. They get off on this stuff."

"You're right. That level of ego can cause a killer to fail. He's been doing this for so long that he probably doesn't think he can ever be caught. He's invincible, untouchable."

"And he likes you." He smiled sadly.

"Don't remind me. What I saw was just a façade, a character that he wanted me to see."

"He could be somebody else now."

She nodded staying silent.

"That was quite the slap this morning."

She blushed. "Yeah, maybe I overreacted."

"I don't think so. I was pissed when you told me what she did. I can't imagine how you felt. I just didn't expect that from you," he said with a chuckle.

She laughed, shaking her head. "Aat, you really have no idea."

"I'm sure I don't, but one thing for sure is, you are

one hell of an officer. They are lucky to have you in New York. Will you return to work now?"

"I don't know. I wanted to see this through, but if Craig is gone, then I don't know. Maybe I can still check on things from New York."

He nodded. "Finish up your coffee; we are going to check out the other lodgings for the rest of the victims. Maybe we can get a clue on where he's going or how he chooses his victims. I'm starting to think he just chooses his victims randomly."

"I don't know. There are a lot more female victims, if we go by the missing person's reports from the area. There are 70% more women missing. Craig hated Devon, but what if he just got rid of men when they were in the way?"

Aat nodded. "That's possible."

She wondered where Craig was right then. It creeped her out to think that he would still be on the island watching their progress, watching her every move with a smile on his face. He was enjoying this just like he would have enjoyed laying in bed next to her know he was about to kill their friends one by one. Would she have been one of them? If he was still on the island, then they still had a chance of catching him, but if he had already fled, then the best she could do is watch for similar crimes to pop up in the future. It could take years for him to pop back up in the system again. This was her one chance to make sure he couldn't hurt anyone else.

She drained her coffee and they both got up from the table and headed out.

They started out in Katie and Brian's hut even though she had already searched it once. They were hoping to find something that would tie them all together or see if there was something that pointed to Craig's whereabouts. The chief had a checklist that had the items on it that Keri had told Harley was missing from the first search.

While the officers started their search around the room, opening drawers and going through the clothing, Aat pulled out the checklist to go over with her.

"Okay, we know that he takes identification and credit cards, probably any cash they have as well. Those items have been taken from every single victim. Her purse was missing from the hut, but we did not find that or Brian's wallet with the bodies."

"Right, I think that's how he moves around. He definitely has a lot of money, whether that's from his profession or what he takes from his victims. You said he has a record of theft."

"We are watching the credit cards right now; they haven't been used. He probably doesn't need them to get out, though, so we may never see action on those cards. Especially now that he knows we are on to him."

Harley was hoping that something would come back from the airlines—some video footage or someone that saw him trying to leave. But there had been no reports yet. Maybe he was still on the island.

"Now what is this about a dress? Are you sure it wasn't here or misplaced?"

"I can't be sure, but Keri was sure she was wearing it that night. She said that it was her favorite dress and that she always hung it back up on the hanger behind the door when she took it off. The hanger was empty and we looked all over for the dress."

He looked at one of his officers. "Let me know if you find a red dress." The officer nodded.

Harley pulled out her phone and scrolled through her pictures. "This is a picture of the dress; this is on a different night, since she wore it a few times. Like I said, it was her favorite. The dress hasn't been seen since."

He nodded. "You think this was a souvenir?"

"Yes. I think he fixated on it for some reason, maybe something to do with his past or an old girlfriend, maybe even his first love. He was probably compelled to take it."

She looked down at the picture and how pretty Katie looked in her dress, standing beside the love of her life. They looked so happy. She wondered if they would have stayed together had they not been killed. Would they have stood the test of time and gone on to grow old together or would they have been like many other couples who got bogged down by work and children, eventually getting divorced? The question would remain unanswered but looking down at the picture she thought maybe they would have survived where others didn't.

"They must have been so scared together."

"At least they were together."

She looked up at Aat. "I guess that's something."

The huts were small; it didn't take long for the officers to toss the entire hut and come up with nothing more. Harley stepped out of the hut and sat on the porch while they finished up. The killer liked souvenirs, so there was an emotional attachment to what he did. Though his souvenirs, it seemed, came in the form of heads. That could be the only explanation for the macabre collection they saw at the hotel. The way he killed was personal. It took a lot to get close to someone and cut their head off. These killings were personal to him—the question was why?

Where was Craig? She looked out at the beach, and then the tree line that separated the beach from the hotel. Was he out there watching her right then? Knowing that she wanted to bring him down? Was he worried or was he laughing at them?

Harley sat out on her balcony drinking a beer as she felt the cool evening breeze come off the water. She loved the view; she couldn't imagine being in a room without a view—it was such a waste. She had tried to read to get her mind off the day's events because she had no idea how she was going to get to sleep that evening, but nothing was working. Her book lay there unopened and she just stared down at the beach. There were a few people still out on the beach that evening, but she couldn't make any of them out. She didn't know how anyone would want to be out at night after what had transpired on the island so far. People believed bad things just never happened to them. It was kind of sad, but they had all been warned at this point. What happened at the hotel was on the evening news and they were saying it was the grisliest thing they had ever seen happen in the area. Craig's picture was everywhere at that point, but no one had seen him. It made her wonder if he really did stick around. The police department was planning on scouring the mines again in the morning to see if he was hiding out there.

They had found nothing substantial at any of the victim's lodgings. The tourist from Texas had just been missing her identification, while the young girl had some items of clothing missing, though her friends couldn't be sure if they had been taken or misplaced, so that was up in the air. All identification, money, and credit cards were gone. Not one of the credit cards had been used, however, so there was a good chance that Craig had ditched them somewhere. He wouldn't be that stupid at this point. He obviously had a nest egg to use, probably under a different name. Who else could afford to go on vacation for a month at a time? At first, she had found it romantic, the notion of being able to travel the world and go wherever you wanted on a whim. Now everything that he did seemed suspicious to her, red flags that she should have paid attention to. They were looking deeper into his background now and his mother and family were being questioned. They were horrified, of course, and surprised beyond belief. *He could never have done that. He is such a sweet boy. Blah blah blah.* Parents were enablers for the most part. It was rare that a mother would sit down with the authorities and say they always knew their son was a serial killer and they just didn't want to tell anyone. Craig was a master of disguise; he clearly fooled his own mother as well.

One thing that she found unusual was that the heads were clean. She had been thinking about it all night. Clean in the sense that there was no dirt, debris, or anything that would suggest that they were ever buried or hidden somewhere. It was as if he had severed the heads and then just took them back to his hotel and set them on display. Those were the real souvenirs, not the dress, not the passports; he was severing the heads so that he could look at them after. He kept them until they had to be disposed of for fear of rotting or smell. Why did he keep some and not others? She thought back to the heads that were in the room. Devon's head had been with his torso. Then something clicked with her, and she grabbed the file she had of Brian's autopsy. She should have picked up on it earlier. When they found the bodies of Katie and Brian, his head was also with the body, but

Katie's had been missing. When she thought about all the heads in the room, they were all female. That was the link. It wasn't random. He was killing females and keeping their heads as souvenirs. He had no emotional attachment to the men he killed, so they had likely just got in the way. So, their killer hated women—killing them was personal to him. She wondered what Craig's relationship with his mother was like.

He kept the women's heads with him; he had to, which explained why were they so clean. He must have kept them at a different location that he could stop at now and then. Somewhere private. She had been in Craig's room enough times to know that they weren't being kept there at any point. Another thought kept creeping in her mind and it ate away at her. Maybe this was all her fault. What if the killings started after she broke things off with him? Was that what set him off? She imagined heads sitting in the hotel room on ice the whole time while he seethed over their breakup.

Her stomach rolled as she stared down at her beer. She had ordered room service, but she was starting to regret it. She had been starving when she had returned to the hotel, not having eaten for most of the day.

She was looking forward to hearing from Ned or even Aat tomorrow to see if their search came up with anything. It was possible they would find a hideout, somewhere that Craig had laid out for his sick little fantasies. They had found no evidence that the victims had been killed and dismembered in Craig's room, so he must have taken them somewhere else. There's no way he would have been able to pull something like that off with so many people out on the beach. He had another location on the island and she hoped they would find it in the morning. A lair would have a lot to say about a killer; it would be the place that he could be himself, letting it all hang out, so to speak. If they found the place, it was likely there would be something that would lead them to Craig.

She was taking the next day off, as there was nothing more she could do at that point. Chief Aat was more than capable of performing the search. Besides they wanted to see what would happen if she was left alone. She wasn't sure what she would do with the day, but she was curious to see if Rayland would be available to hang out. Aat had the idea that if she was out alone that Craig might try to reach out to her or even approach her. It would be even better if she were with Rayland, as it was possible that they could pull him out of hiding through jealousy.

She wasn't sure if the plan would work, but it was worth a try. She wasn't worried about Craig approaching her; she could handle herself just fine. She relished the idea; she just wasn't sure it would be that easy. She was realizing very quickly that Craig was fearless, and he didn't seem to care that his misdeeds had been uncovered. She was hoping that she would hear from the captain in New York that they had pulled him off the streets, but again that would probably be too easy.

Tomorrow she would go off on her own and see if the killer came to her. Between her and Aat, she prayed they would turn something up so that she could get her hands on Craig.

There was a knock on the door announcing her room service had arrived. She picked up her beer and turned away from the ocean. She closed the patio door behind her, saying goodnight to the view until tomorrow.

TWENTY NINE

BUTCHER WALKED THE BEACH MORE on edge than he normally was because he no longer had the secrecy he was used to. He had to be careful now and he didn't like that—he liked moving freely wherever he wanted. Hiding was for cowards and he was no coward. They thought they could stop him, but no one could—they were all below him. They had no idea who they were really dealing with. He knew they were hunting him, but he needed the blood or he would not be able to sleep. They would not stop him from getting what he wanted. He hadn't slept in a while and he would need his rest for tomorrow. He had big plans, delicious plans that excited him so much that he wished he could fast forward to the next day. It was going to be one of the best days of his life. It made him smile just thinking about it.

He had to focus, however, as he had a task at hand and he needed to get to it while he had some measure of privacy. He usually liked to hunt on the beach by the hotel, but that was a hot spot right now, so he had to hunt on a less populated part of the beach. Not that it mattered. No one looked at him; they wouldn't expect a killer on the run walking the beach as if he wasn't afraid. It wouldn't matter if they did know—he would still snatch them in the night.

He loved watching Harley throughout the day, imagining her walking into the bathroom and seeing his prizes. He would have loved to have been in the room with her enjoying the view. When she came out of the hotel, she was white as a sheet. She knew what he was and she was in awe of it. She knew just how powerful he was—that he wouldn't be taken down by a bunch of small-time cops. No, he had been doing it far too long for that.

He saw a shadow in the distance and knew that there was someone up ahead walking along the beach. He took a quick look around to make sure that there was no one nearby. The last person he had seen was still quite a distance away. They would not be able to see him clearly. He smiled when he saw a woman stumbling along the beach singing some pop song under her breath. He moved quickly and when he was close to the woman, he moved to the side and smashed the side of her head with his elbow. The woman dropped like a stone. Butcher heaved her over his shoulder and continued to walk the beach. He didn't have far to go this time. Carrying a woman was far easier than carrying a man.

Butcher paced in the abandoned hotel, trying to relax with his glass of whiskey. He had *Chopin* playing from his iPhone in the background. The atmosphere irritated him, but he couldn't exactly drag an unconscious woman back to where he was staying after the debacle on the beach that day. He wouldn't be on the island for much longer, as it was coming to the time that he needed to move on to a new place. But he wanted to see Harley before he left, to get close to her again. It was all he could think about. He would not be able to leave without seeing her again.

He finished off his whiskey and set the glass on the ground. He stared at the woman before him in the chair. Butcher had made all the arrangements ahead of time. The plastic, the chair, his tools—they were all laid out in just the way he liked it. He normally preferred to pick out his women, someone who fit the profile of his own mother, but he no longer had the freedom he once had. His mood, however, was stormy; he would have preferred to be in the hotel room, relaxing. That was the way it was supposed to be. The police and their meddling had ruined that for him, and if he could make them pay in some way before he left, he would do it. The one benefit to it was that the woman's wallet had a lot of money in it. He would use them to leave the island eventually. They would never find this body and he would be gone before they even knew the woman was missing. They would never think to come out all this way to find the abandoned hotel.

"I'm sorry about our surroundings. It wouldn't have been my first choice, I assure you. I don't typically take my guests to such filthy places. Not at first, anyway. But at least we have the music."

The woman across from him looked at him in disbelief. One side of her face was bruised from where Butcher had struck her. She was so scared that she was sweating, with drops of sweat dripping down the side of her face. Unfortunately for her, Butcher would be taking a lot of frustration out on her. He would leave that abandoned hotel relaxed and in peace. The woman started screaming and Butcher smiled sadly. The poor girl. Even without the music, she didn't have a prayer of being heard by anyone where they were. No one had been out there since Butcher was on the island, he had made sure of that.

He looked down at his tools and picked up a drill. He was feeling anxious and knew he had to get started before it got any worse for him. He started walking toward the woman and turned on the drill just before he got to her. The screams became desperate and shrill and Butcher closed his eyes briefly to take it all in. He loved hearing the screams; they made him feel whole again. He pushed the drill into the woman's leg and watched as it disappeared into the skin. The woman suddenly stopped screaming and looked down at her leg in shock. The color drained from her face and Butcher wasn't sure if she was going to pass out or not.

"It's always excruciating until my frustration goes away and then I will make it quick, I promise."

The woman slowly looked up at him, sweat pouring down her face. There was a brokenness about her eyes, a helplessness; she had already given up. Butcher was disappointed in her—she was so unlike his mother. She had no fight in her; she was a weak woman who angered Butcher even further. He bent down and came eye to eye with the woman and let out a yell in the woman's face in the hopes of instilling terror into her life. The woman started to shake so badly in front of him that the chair beneath her clicked against the cement flooring in a rather pleasing way.

He stood back up and returned the drill to his toolkit. He smiled down at all the tools, knowing just what he was going to do to the woman before ending it for her. He grabbed the ice pick and turned back to her. The screams started once again and they were better than the classical music. Butcher started toward her, feeling better than he had all day.

Cleanup was a lot easier that time around as Kingpin just buried the dismembered body on site. He didn't make it too easy, however, separating the body parts and making various burials throughout the hotel. By the time he was finished, however, he was exhausted and longed to be back at the hotel. He packed up his tools and headed out.

He was sleeping somewhere else that night just to be safe; he wasn't taking any chances this time. He didn't want to run into Harley before he was ready for her.

He thought about where he should go next in his travels. He could visit his mother who must miss him so much. He hadn't seen her in years. The last time he saw her, they got into a terrible fight. She had said some unforgivable things, and he had left instead of doing to her what he really wanted to. He wondered if his mother would be proud of him if she knew what he really was and if she saw what he was capable of. She had never been proud of him before; she feared him.

These days she would have no choice to admit what a powerful man he had become. He was not the man she thought he was. Maybe it was time to return to the States, possibly stop into New York as well. He finally arrived at his lodgings and went inside. He showered quickly while thinking about his insatiable thirst, which had finally quieted down for the night. He couldn't stop if he wanted to, and he didn't want to. When he was finished showering, he crawled into his bed and fell asleep with a smile on his face. He was very much looking forward to tomorrow.

THIRTY

HARLEY HAD A HARD TIME focusing on the beautiful walk on the beach when all she could think about was what Aat might be discovering out on the island. She probably should have just gone with him instead of driving herself nuts wondering all day, but she knew that he would call her as soon as he had anything important. She wanted to believe that they still had a chance to catch Craig before he left the island. It was her job to lure him out if he was, in fact, watching her and the rest of the team. She often felt like she was being watched and she wondered what kind of sicko the guy had to be in order just to sit back and watch as they scrambled around finding one body after the other. He must feel pretty confident about himself.

She was happier still that she didn't have to spend the day alone. She was walking the beach, hand in hand with Rayland, looking more handsome than he had the last time she saw him—or maybe she was just really glad to lay her eyes on him. She had called over to his hotel room that morning unsure of whether or not he would be out surfing. The beach had opened up early again that morning—God forbid the police department do anything to ruin the tourist's vacation.

"I can't believe there are still people out on the beach drinking and having a gay old time."

Rayland laughed. "Well, most of the people here spend their whole year backpacking around. They budget what they can to last throughout the year. They aren't going to pack up and go until it's time to go to the next place. Others are too high to care while others still believe that nothing bad will come their way. I'm sure you've seen the same thing on the force. If someone isn't directly affected by an event, then it doesn't shape their lives or their decisions."

"Yes, I know. I just wish I could go down there and shake each and every one of them."

"I'm glad you called me this morning. I was worried about you yesterday, and then word traveled fast about what they found in your boy's hotel. I was happy I had finished surfing by the time the crew came in—people were saying it was a pretty gruesome scene."

"You have no idea; I shudder every time I think about it."

"I'm just happy you're okay and I get a chance to spend some time with you. I imagine you will be heading home soon now that this is wrapping up?"

"Yes, I only planned on staying a couple of days.

There's not much I can do now if Craig has flown the coop. I'm not really in the mood to try a vacation again, not here, anyway. I can just try to watch the case from New York and hope that we get some new leads. What about you?"

"Oh, I'll be heading out soon myself. I've surfed my brains out and now it's time to get back to reality. Besides, it's not going to be the same here without you."

She blushed, feeling the same way about him. She couldn't imagine lying on the beach or going into the surf without him there. All her friends were gone, so it would be wrong to be there. She wasn't sure she would ever be able to return to the islands again. Keri probably felt exactly the same way that she did.

"Why don't you come back home with me for a while. I would love for this to continue to a more serious level. I've grown to care quite deeply for you and I have one hell of a penthouse suite."

She laughed, as she definitely felt the same way about Rayland. She was crazy about him in ways that she had never felt with another person before. The idea that they were falling in love made her warm all over. "I'll think about it, but it does sound pretty amazing."

Her stomach growled and she thought about going back to the hotel for an omelette, remembering the time they went to the restaurant looking for mushrooms. She smiled sadly when she thought of the look on Devon's face when he took that first bite. Craig had been there the whole time that they ate, and he had laughed, drank beer, and surfed with them all the while knowing he was going to kill some of them.

"Are you okay, sweetie?"

"Yes, I'm sorry. I was just remembering my friends and the fun times we had together." She took a bit of her omelet as she fought back the tears.

"It's a tragedy, I know. I'm very sorry."

She shrugged. "It's okay. It's all just hard to believe sometimes."

"Of course, but time heals all, as they say."

She needed to get a plan in motion for the day, but she didn't want to let Rayland in on it. She didn't want him to know that they might be expecting Craig to show up that day, as she didn't think he'd be able to act the part of not knowing something was going on. Besides, he was so excited to see her that she didn't want him to think that it was the only reason they were hanging out.

They could probably spend the day on the beach or have a picnic; she certainly wouldn't be against going back to her hotel room for a while.

He smiled at her and she asked, "So what do you want to do today?" *Please say hotel room, please say hotel room*, she thought to herself.

His smile widened into a grin and her heart started beating fast. "I thought that we could take a boat to one of the other islands. There's one that isn't far and it's cooler than this one. Plus, I think it would help take your mind off things if you aren't surrounded by all the things that remind you of death. It'll be a little getaway for the day. We'll have a blast I promise."

"Wow, really? That sounds fantastic, but I don't know if it's the best idea. What if the chief needs me or tries to get a hold of me?"

"C'mon, Harley, I think the chief can handle things on his own for a day—you said so yourself. Let go for a day. We aren't going far, and you have your phone if the chief needs to get a hold of you. I will bring you right back if something important is going on."

"You're right, I'm sorry. Of course, I would love to go."

It looked like Craig would have to be a little more creative when it came to finding her after all. She had faith in him, though, as he wasn't the type to just let things go. The idea of jumping to another island was certainly appealing. Every time she looked at the beach by her hotel, she was flooded with memories of her friends as well as what happened in Craig's room—the very room that she used to spend the night with Craig in. Yes, she would definitely grab the opportunity to see a different view.

"Great. Let's split up and I'll let you grab a bag for the day, and we will meet down at the beach. I rented a boat. Don't forget your bathing suit."

They stopped walking and she turned to him. She kissed him full on the mouth. "See you soon."

Harley had her bag packed when she headed out of the hotel lobby to meet Rayland on the beach. Her phone buzzed and she looked down at it, surprised to see a message from Keri.

> Keri: I think my face still hurts from that slap. :P Funeral is today and I haven't stopped crying.
>
> Harley: God, I'm sorry about that. I usually don't go around slapping people. I wish I was there for you today. Hugs.
>
> Keri: No worries, I'm pretty sure I deserved it. It's all so surreal you know?
>
> Harley: I know. Trust me, I've been there. It won't always feel this bad.
>
> Keri: Any news???
>
> Harley: Craig seems to be gone. No news yet. I will let you know as soon as I do. Give my love to your family.
>
> Keri: ☹ Will do.

Harley put her phone in her pocket and checked her bag once again to make sure she had everything she needed. Her gun was placed in between the towel.

Craig could be anywhere, and she wasn't taking any chances on her life or Rayland's. She hurried to the beach where she found Rayland standing on a dock beside a fisherman's boat. It wasn't very big but more than big enough for what they needed it for. It still had a small cabin below that had small living quarters and a bathroom. They were only using it for travel, so they didn't need anything extravagant.

Rayland looked tanned and relax in board shorts and a t-shirt. His biceps stretched the sleeves of the shirt, causing a stir inside of her. She ran down the dock with a huge smile on her face.

"Hey, beautiful," he said. "Ready to go?"

She nodded and kissed him, excited for their day of adventure. She always had a great time with Rayland, mainly because their chemistry was so good. He helped her into the boat and she sat down on a side bench while he talked to the owner of the boat. She watched as the two men untied the ropes that secured the boat to the dock. Rayland jumped on board and the other man helped to push the boat away from the dock. Rayland got behind the wheel and they started off toward another island.

"Just let me get this sucker on course, and then I'll set the autopilot and we can talk a little. You can grab a drink from the cooler if you want to."

She reached over and opened the cooler, grabbing a bottle of water out of it. She noticed that there was a chilled bottle of wine inside the cooler as well. He must have quite a day planned for them and she realized that it had been a long time since she had thought about someone in the long-term sense. She had been single for a long time because she had wanted to be with Chris. She had always hoped that he would take the blinders off and see her as more than just his partner. It had never happened, and then with the shooting, dating seemed to be the last thing on her mind. Now that she met Rayland, she wondered if things could be different for her this time around.

She settled back in her seat and gazed out into the ocean. The sun was hot that day and the breeze from the water felt delicious against her skin. What a perfect day for a boat ride. The water looked so perfect, so fresh and clean. She leaned over to see if she could see any fish. Suddenly Rayland was beside her, which startled her, and she gripped the railing so she didn't fall over.

"Whoa! Easy there. You don't want to fall over."

She laughed, a little shaken. "Wouldn't that be a real date killer. I was just trying to see some fish. You scared me."

"Sorry, I have the boat on autopilot now." He leaned in for a kiss and she wondered how reckless it would be if she took him downstairs while the boat drove itself.

"I think we should have lingered in the bed for the morning."

He chuckled. "Maybe you're right. I was so excited to get you out here. But that doesn't mean we won't get there later."

She giggled. "I just want to get as much of you as I can."

"You don't think this is the end of it do, you?"

"Really?"

"Harley, I would love to continue spending time with you to see where it goes. If that means coming to visit you in New York, then I would gladly do that."

She grinned. "I love the sound of that."

He kissed her again and their lips lingered together.

"There's a lovely restaurant on the island I thought we could check out."

She smiled. "That sounds great. Where is the washroom by the way?"

"It's downstairs. Don't be too long; we will be arriving shortly. I'm just going to check on the coordinates."

She got up from her seat. She steadied herself on the boat with a laugh and then made her way down the ladder to go to the lower quarters. She held onto the railing to steady herself while she got down. She looked around at the tight quarters and saw what could be a bedroom. Rayland had his suitcase on the bed. She found the rumble of the boat soothing as she sat down on the bed. She was nervous about being there with Rayland, but she was excited about their little adventure together. She heard a phone ringing and she quickly dug into the pocket of her shorts and grabbed her phone. It was Ned. Excited, she answered the phone to see if he had found Craig.

"Ned, what's up?" She hoped he had some good news for her.

"Harley, where are you? What is all that noise? I can barely hear you."

She was smiling as she absently opened Rayland's suitcase, lifting the lid. The contents were just like you would expect from a man's suitcase. She pulled out a shirt and smelled it. She loved the way he smelled. It was then that something caught her eye.

"I'm on a boat. What's going on?" she muttered distractedly.

"It's not Craig!"

There was static on the line and she wondered if she heard him correctly. "What did you say?"

"It's not Craig! Jesus Christ, we were wrong, Harley. It's not him."

She suddenly was having difficulty breathing. "What the fuck are you talking about?"

"We found his body, just like all the others. God, it was so much worse than all the others, it was like he hated him. Tell me where you are!"

Harley's heart was beating out of her chest as she attempted to catch her breath. There was a roaring in her ears as she tried to comprehend what Ned was saying to her. He had to be wrong. She slowly looked down at the suitcase and fingered a piece of red material underneath his shorts. She pulled at it feeling the luxurious fabric between her fingers. She pulled it all the way out of the suitcase, staring at the red dress before her.

"Oh shit." She could not take her eyes off the dress. "Fuck, fuck, fuck."

"Harley? Harley? Where are you? I'm coming to get you."

"I'm on a boat. I don't even know where the fuck I am. We're going to another island."

"Who are you with, Harley?" The static was getting worse on the phone. "Harley, dammit, are you in danger?"

Her eyes slowly looked upward as she imagined Rayland up on deck. She kept hearing the words Ned had said: *God, it was so much worse than all the others, it was like he hated him.*

She was in danger. Horrified, she thought of how he would have access to the dress. The things that were done to those bodies, the heads in the bathtub. He must have put those heads in Craig's tub.

She was holding a dead girl's dress. She tossed it on the bed as if it had caught on fire. He couldn't be the killer. *Not him, please not him,* she thought. She could hear Ned yelling at her on the other side of the phone.

"I know who it is."

"Dammit!" Ned yelled into the phone.

"Harley, are you okay?" Rayland called from above.

"I have to go," she whispered into the phone.

"Harley, don't you dare do this—"

She clicked off the call and threw the phone on the bed. Her mind was racing as a hundred different scenarios went through her head, none of which ended with her getting off the boat alive. Her gun was upstairs in her bag, of zero use to her at the moment. She wouldn't be able to stay down there for very long before Rayland would come looking for her. She took a deep breath and centered herself. The man that she was crazy about was a sadistic serial killer. It was impossible. It had to be. The man upstairs was clever, intelligent, and evil, and she would have to use all her wits to figure out a way to get away from him.

THIRTY ONE

THE MORE SHE THOUGHT BACK on conversations and actions of Rayland's, the more pieces started falling together. He had known all about their suspicions of Craig; she had even allowed him to follow Craig around. She had practically given him all the information he needed to know to frame Craig. When their stakeout had failed, he had listened to her on the phone talking to the chief about the search warrant he was getting the next day. He had all night to make a plan to have the force really focus on Craig while he did what he wanted. Rayland must have gone after Craig when she left him behind, killed him, and then planted the evidence in his room. Poor Craig—he died believing that she thought he was a killer. It all made sense. There were too many thoughts going through her head at once, she was trying to put all the pieces together and she just didn't have the time for it.

She moved to his suitcase. She stopped to listen

for Rayland, but she couldn't hear any footsteps. She looked down in the suitcase and started to move things around. She moved his towel and swim trunks and noticed that there was a small zipper pouch at the bottom of the suitcase. It was heavy when she picked it up and opened it. She spread the opening and her hands started to shake.

"Oh shit, I'm dead." The pouch was filled with passports and credit cards. She pulled a few of them out and glanced at them. Some of the pictures she recognized while others she didn't. There were so many of them, not all of them could possibly have been from the island. He probably kept them with him because he didn't want them out of his sight for a minute. How many bodies were out there that were never found? She continued flipping through the passports. She opened the last one and looked down at Craig's picture. She felt a wave of despair at what he had endured for no reason whatsoever.

She felt high on the terror she felt. It fed off her like a living, breathing entity. If she let it have control of her, if she even let it in a little, then she would not be able to get her control back. Every nerve in her body was on edge, alert and aware of the abhorrent evil that she had let into her life. Her body knew well before her brain the kind of danger she was in. Her mind was stuck between shock and disgust, prohibiting her to fully understand what she was up against.

"Well, you certainly got yourself in one fine fucking

mess now, didn't you," she whispered. She placed the pouch back where she found it and closed the suitcase. She ducked into the bathroom and flushed the toilet. That would allow her some excuse for taking so much time. She turned toward the mirror and remembered Katie's red dress. Tears pooled in her eyes as she remembered the mutilated body of her friend. He had some dead girl's dress in his suitcase, and she felt bile rise in her throat. Her whole body shuddered, wishing that she could remove the image from her head. She couldn't help but think whether he took it off the body before or after Katie died. Was that his souvenir?

Both hands gripped the side of the sink. She closed her eyes and took a deep breath. She needed to get her shit together if she was going to get off the boat alive. There were people on the island; if she could just get there without causing suspicion, then she could find someone to help her. She thought about the gun in her bag and wondered how easy it would be to get her hands on it. If she knew Ned, he would be trying to triangulate her cell phone location, but she couldn't depend on that. She was on her own for now.

She jumped at a knock on the bathroom door.

"Harley, are you okay?"

She stared at the door, fear taking over every part of her body. The man on the other side of the door was capable of horrifying things. "Yes, Rayland. Sorry. I think I got a touch of seasickness. I'll be out in a second."

"I'll get you a ginger ale. Maybe that will help settle your stomach."

"Thank you. That's sweet of you."

She needed to ignore the fact that she had slept with a serial killer long enough to get herself out of the mess. If she dwelled on it, she would start to feel useless and he would see that she changed. She needed him to believe that she was the same girl and that she had no idea who he really was. She washed her hands and wiped at her eyes. Everything was going to be okay.

She stepped out of the bathroom and he was gone. She glanced at the suitcase before making her way back up the ladder. She took a deep breath and plastered a smile on her face.

"There you are." He smiled at her when she got back on deck. Everything seemed to be just as she had left it, except that her bag was missing. She didn't see it beside the cooler where she had left it.

"Sorry, I think breakfast just didn't sit right with me. Where is my bag?"

"Oh, I just put it under the bench seat. We can grab it when we get to the island."

She wondered if he happened to find the gun she had inside. He didn't appear to be acting any different—though she hadn't realized he was a cold-blooded killer either, so there was that.

He handed her a glass of ginger ale and she gulped it to wash down the bile that kept threatening to come up. He smiled down at her and leaned in for a kiss. She steeled herself for it and when his lips met hers, it was like something was alive and crawling against her skin. *Keep it together, Harley*, she thought. It was no longer the feeling of butterflies or passion that the kiss arose in her, but instead she had the strong urge to choke the life out of him. When they parted, she took the opportunity to sit down and glance out at the ocean. She could see the island at a distance and felt a rush of relief.

"Is that where we are going?" she said breathlessly.

"Yup, that's it. You look gorgeous, by the way. I should have told you that from the beginning."

She stared at him a moment, as his words felt like a punch in the stomach. She glanced down at the pretty sundress she was wearing and thought of Katie's favorite, and she tried not to snap. She looked back up at him, smiling. "That's sweet, thank you."

She glanced back at the island willing the boat to go faster.

THIRTY TWO

THE BOAT PULLED UP TO the dock slowly, so slowly that Harley began to feel like she was losing her mind. She wanted more than anything to step off the boat. She thought there would be someone there to meet them, but there was no one on the dock. In fact, there was no one anywhere on the beach at all. There were trees lining the whole length of the beach as if it was a private island. Was there a chance that he took her there to kill her? She had expected that there would be people lounging on the beach that she could turn to for help, but there wasn't a soul around.

"Where is everyone?"

He pulled the boat beside the dock and turned off the engine. "Oh, this island is a little more remote than the other one. That's what makes it so great. We have to walk down a trail to get to the action. The restaurant is through those trees, and on the other side of it is a beach more incredible than this one. Trust me, you'll love it."

She didn't trust him one bit, and whether there was a restaurant beyond those trees or not, she wasn't taking any chances. She needed to get away from him before they got into the trees. For all she knew, he was leading her to her death. There were a few other boats lining the beach, so she knew there were other people somewhere on the island.

She watched as he tied the boat to the dock. He stood up, looking proud of himself. She took the opportunity to start searching the bench seats for her bag. She went through one after the other, but there was no bag. Suddenly he was behind her and she gasped.

"Rayland, you scared me."

He chuckled. "Sorry. It looked like you needed some help over here. If you are looking for your bag, it's on the other side of the boat."

She watched him go to the other side and open up one of the bench seats, pulling out her bag. She almost laughed with relief when she saw it.

"Oh, thanks," she said as he handed her the bag. The bag felt heavy, so she was confident the gun was still in there. She smiled sweetly as he turned away from her and grabbed the cooler. He started walking away from her and she followed slowly behind him. He turned, quickly catching her off guard.

"Can you hold this for a moment and pass it up to me?" he asked, holding out the cooler.

She stared at him, unsure of whether he was on to her or not. Finally, she said, "Of course I can."

She grabbed the cooler from his hands and waited as he lifted himself onto the dock. She passed it to him and he quickly set it down on the dock. He held his hand out to her and she let him hoist her out on the dock. She needed a moment to make sure the gun was still in the bag, but he wasn't allowing for it. She didn't want to take the chance of confronting him until she was sure that the gun was still in the bag.

When she saw him bend down and grab the cooler again, she slowly slid her hand into the bag feeling in between the towel. Her hand grazed the cold metal of the gun. She almost cried with relief but kept her breath even while he walked down the dock.

She pulled out the gun and stopped, pointing it at him. "I know who you are."

Rayland stopped suddenly on the dock and stood there for a beat before turning around. He wasn't more than a few feet from her. "Holy shit, Harley, what are you doing?"

"Or should I say, *what* you are?"

"What are you talking about?" he said as he took a step closer to her.

"Stay right there."

"Harley, I think there has been some misunderstanding."

"Don't bother. It's over. I saw the passports. Or do you have some excuse for that?"

In the blink of an eye, his face changed and the real Rayland came out. "Yes, I suppose I shouldn't have brought them with me, but I was planning on leaving right after our little getaway."

"Are you out of your fucking mind? What you did to my friends, to Craig—it's madness."

"Now, that's not very nice. Craig was beneath you. He was weak—you should have seen how he cried like a baby."

Her hands started to shake. She didn't want to think about the agony of what Craig or any of her friends went through at Rayland's hands. She couldn't believe the man she had been falling for was the same twisted man standing in front of her. He took another step toward her and they were practically face to face, the gun pointing right at him.

"You take one more step and I'll blow a hole right through you."

"I'm a little shocked by your reaction. I thought we had a connection—I know you felt it."

"I fell for someone who doesn't exist. I didn't know who you were."

"Yes, you did. The night we made love on your desk, among the crime scenes photographs, we were connected in every way. I knew you were falling in love with me, with the man capable of what's in those files. That's why you read them over and over again. You weren't disgusted. You were in awe of the kind of man that could do anything he wanted to and never get caught. You fell in love with my intelligence and my power."

"No," she choked out. "You're wrong. I had no idea. I was only interested in bringing you down and ending the killing."

He smiled then and he looked every bit of a maniac. "It's never going to end, Harley. If anything, it's just beginning."

"How could you? The things you did…" She let the sentence trail off, not knowing where she was even going with it. She felt betrayed. He was the worst kind of human being and yet she longed for the man she had at breakfast that morning. He was gone now, though—if he was ever really there in the first place. The time they spent together was all a joke now.

His eyes glazed over. "It's like a symphony, Harley. If you just tried it, you would see how good it makes you feel—how relaxed you become after. You're so much like her."

"Like who?"

"My mother. She had your strength, your beauty. I knew it from the first moment I saw you."

She couldn't believe what she was hearing. "Jesus Christ, you have mommy issues? Big surprise. So, you kill women to get even for what your mother did to you? How bad was it? Did she lock you in the closet when you were bad? You're a fucking monster," she spat out at him.

"No, she didn't love me, just like you."

Without notice, the cooler came flying at her, and she fired off a shot. She knew she didn't get her shot as she tumbled back into the boat, the contents of the cooler falling all over the place. She hit hard on the deck, her head hitting the bench seat, and the gun went flying out of her hand, sliding across the boat. Her hand went to her head as a wave of dizziness came over her. She didn't feel any blood. She looked up to see Rayland hop down into the boat and come toward her with a knife. When he got close, she threw her leg up and took out his right leg, toppling him. She rolled over, her vision clearing even though she still felt dizzy. She saw the gun and moved toward it, crawling on her hands and knees. She reached out for the gun, but he grabbed hold of her ankle and yanked it hard. She fell onto her stomach, and he kept pulling. She rolled over to face him as he plunged the knife into her chest.

She gasped immediately as her lung collapsed. She stared up at him in shock, trying not to panic.

"I'm sorry it has to be this way. It will happen quickly for you. You will die, and I will move on to be a God in your world."

She looked at him in horror as her vision blurred. She was not going to pass out, not now. He bent down to kiss her, and she struggled against him. He kissed her mouth.

"Don't waste your energy, Harley, you're going to need it."

She suddenly felt faint and she couldn't believe how much the collapsed lung was sucking all her energy away. She was gasping for air but wasn't getting enough of it.

He stared down at her and suddenly his eyes glazed over. He was staring through her, not at her. She was going to die and the last thing that she would see was his eyes. She would see only evil before she died.

"Mom?" He touched her hair softly.

Surprised, she sputtered, "What?"

His eyes focused and the break in his reality terrified her more than anything. She wasn't sure what other horrors he was capable of.

"Hey! Are you guys okay?"

Rayland looked behind him at someone on the beach. The man must have heard the gunshot and come running. He had no idea what he was getting involved in.

Rayland looked down at her disappointed. "I wish I could stay here and finish you off, but we have company."

She used the last energy that she had in her and choked out. "Run!" She started coughing and blood hit the deck of the boat.

Startled the man's mouth dropped open and he turned and ran, disappearing into the trees. Maybe help would come.

Rayland glared at her. "This isn't over, Harley. No matter where you go, I will find you. I will come for you when you least expect it and we'll have our moment together. You are mine. We'll have the ending that I've always imagined. You can't escape destiny." He left her and ran downstairs, coming up a few minutes later with his suitcase. He hopped out of the boat and ran down the dock. Harley sat up and started coughing. She knew exactly what was happening to her. Air was getting in and causing her other lung to compress. It wouldn't be long until her second lung would collapse under the pressure. If that happened, she was done for. It would happen quickly, and she needed to get some help quickly. Air and blood flowed into the cavity where her lung had resided. She raised herself up to peer over the deck; Rayland had ran into the trees after the man. She hoped the man got away.

Panic rose in her and she tried to remain calm, knowing that freaking out would only make things worse. She had to focus or she would die on that deck.

She saw Rayland come out of the trees. He was coming back to finish the job. She watched as the monster ran down the beach where a speedboat was docked. The boat was a lot faster than the one that they came in. The man must have got away and Rayland was on the run. He was going to get away while she died in some stranger's fishing boat.

She looked down at her chest where the knife was sticking out of. Once she took it out, she wouldn't have a lot of time. She put her hand around the handle and slowly pulled it out. She gritted her teeth as she tossed the knife aside.

She slowly stood up, feeling wobbly on her feet. She coughed, her chest feeling like it was about to explode.

Blood splattered on the bench in front of her. There was a lot of pressure on her other lung as well as her heart. Air was getting in, but nothing was coming out.

"Oh fuck," she rasped, her voice leaving her. Her chest was filling up with blood. She didn't have a lot of time. She knew if she didn't release the pressure that her other lung would collapse. She knew she was in trouble and her eyes welled up. *Don't you be a pussy*, she thought. She leaned against the wheel on the boat trying to think of what the hell she was going to do to get out of the mess she was in. Did she have any hope? She couldn't possibly drive the boat; even if she could, she would be dead before she got to the other island. She felt the pressure on her lung, not to mention she was losing a lot of blood. She needed to take the pressure off her lung long enough for her to get to the hospital. She was gasping, and she could barely catch her breath.

Then suddenly like a light going on in front of her eyes, she saw Chris, in the cruiser with her, laughing. She thought she was hallucinating until she realized she was remembering the time he saw the documentary of the man with the punctured lung. Could she really cut into herself? She was likely to cause more damage than good, but at that point, what other choice did she have? She would have to move quickly because it was not going to be an easy procedure. She opened the bench seats to see what she could use. She scanned the items before her, making a mental checklist. She pulled out tape, a long nail, and straws. She coughed, and more blood splashed against the bench. She was scared, more scared than she had ever been. She thought going up against Rayland had rattled her but knowing that her life was hanging by a thread brought clarity to her mind like she never experienced before.

She took the nail and looked at it closely, thanking God that she'd had a recent tetanus shot. She cut along the seam of her dress, opening the whole side up—that wasn't what she really needed the nail for, things were about to get much worse. She felt along her ribcage, counting her ribs one by one until she got to the fifth and sixth one. She felt underneath the bone between the two. She took a deep breath, trying to give herself the courage to do what she had to do. Tears streamed down her face and she cursed as she pierced her skin with the nail, crying out. "Oh shit. Oh shit." She moved the nail in a circular motion opening the wound. She felt woozy and worried that she might pass out before she got the job done. She tried to remember just the way that Chris had explained things. She hoped the opening was big enough for the straw to do its thing. *Well, this is it,* she thought. Her breathing was becoming labored and she had the taste of copper in her mouth. She screamed, feeling more pain than she had ever experienced and most of it was self-inflicted. She quickly picked up the straws, the kind you use with large milkshakes, and slid one through the hole in her side and push in as far as she could, leaving some of the straw hanging out. She started coughing hard again and then it stopped as she watched fluid drain out the side of her body. Blood and pus pooled on the wooden floor beside her and the sight of it scared the shit out of her. She felt a rush of air come out of her side and she felt the instant relief of pressure in her chest—thankfully, she got to it before her lung burst. The lung was able to expand and contract normally once again. Tears streamed down her cheek in relief, but she knew she wasn't out of the woods yet. She would need to keep the straw inside her for the time being and secure it properly.

She looked over at her bag and gingerly walked toward it. She pulled out a t-shirt and rolled it up. She pulled out a lifejacket from the bench seat and set them beside her. She grabbed the tape, and as she took pieces off, she placed them around her wound and against the straw, closing up the hole around the straw. Her hands started to shake; she was losing a lot of blood. When she was confident that the straw was not going anywhere, she took the rolled-up shirt and pressed it into her chest wound. She applied as much pressure as she could. She would need more to move around properly. She quickly slipped into the lifejacket and fastened the front of it. She made sure the t-shirt was still rolled up and secured over the wound underneath the jacket. She released the valve on the lifejacket and it inflated causing pressure against her chest.

She felt like shit, but it was the best that she could

do at that point before she could get to the hospital. A wave of nausea rolled over her and she felt dizzy. *Don't you dare,* she thought. She would not pass out now, she would not pass out, she would not…

THIRTY THREE

"OH MY GOD, I THOUGHT you were dead."

Her eyes fluttered open as she looked up at a man she didn't know. She felt weak, as all her energy had zapped out of her body. She tried to sit up but her whole body ached—God, she needed to get to a hospital.

"How long have I been out?" She was in a fragile condition, so she couldn't exactly take the time to sleep it off.

"A few minutes, maybe. I heard the gunshot and came right away. I called for a helicopter. There's someone dead on the beach, but he can't be saved. I thought you were dead too."

"I feel dead. I need my phone."

He looked around and found it on the deck near her bag. He brought it back to her.

"Can you dial the number for Ned?" she asked him. "It should be in my contacts. Then can you give it to me?"

He nodded as he went about looking for the number. She pulled herself off the deck, sitting up. She was perspiring heavily, and her energy was going down by the minute. The man handed her the phone.

"What's your name?" she asked.

"William."

"Thank you, William."

He nodded as she turned to her phone, hearing the ringing on the other end. Ned picked up immediately. "Where the hell have you been? We tried to trace your cell, but the signal has been bouncing off all over the place. Where did you go, the Bermuda triangle?"

"Shut up, Ned!"

There was a pause. "What's wrong, Harley?"

"It was Rayland. He just tried to kill me. Hell, I'm in pretty bad shape either way."

"Who is Rayland?"

"Ned, I don't have a lot of time. I found a ton of passports." She listed off all the names she could remember and told him to check the airports.

"We will have to run some names and see what pops up in the database."

"We don't have time for that. Send someone to the airport, just in case."

"Where are you? I will come and get you. What happened?"

"I have a collapsed lung."

"How could you fucking go off without me? You

could have got yourself killed. You need to get to the hospital."

"I'm not going anywhere. I don't think he will go to the airport right away. It's too easy, and he's not a fool."

"Don't be ridiculous, Harley. He can't just hang around here."

"He wouldn't go to the airport." She turned to see William talking to her. She focused on what he was saying. "He would hide out somewhere secluded until he could slip away," William said.

"Hold on, Ned." She nodded at William. "Where would that be? Where could he hide?"

"There's an abandoned hotel not far from the beach on the other side of the island. It never survived the Tsunami."

Harley nodded. "He's there. Take me there."

William hurried to the wheel and got the boat started right away. Her breathing was coming out in shallow bursts and she wasn't sure what kind of energy she would have for a showdown, but she was going anyway.

"Ned, I know where he is. The abandoned hotel on the island."

"Harley, you stay put. I will meet you on the beach by the huts. Do not go there without me."

"I can't wait until you get to the island. He already has a head start."

"If you are going anywhere, it's straight to a hospital. I forbid you to go anywhere near that psychopath without me."

"Sorry. I have to do this. I can't let him get away." She couldn't help but think about Rayland's promise to her.

She clicked off the call before he could argue with her further. She had to bring down Rayland; the idea that he would be loose in the world was more than she could bear. She would never sleep again if he were loose to kill more people or come after her. If he knew she was alive, he would only come for her.

"Are you sure you're up for this?"

She turned to William who had them going at a good clip toward the other island. "I don't know, William, but I'm going to give it my best. The name is Harley, by the way."

"Maybe the cop is right. You need a hospital; you look like shit."

"If I go to the hospital, an evil man will probably get away. I can't let that happen."

"Well, I know a shortcut to the hotel. We'll go around instead of just going to the island first."

She sat down, trying to preserve her strength. She had no idea what she was up against, and the blood loss had weakened her considerably.

They pulled up to the beach and she could see the relic in the distance, standing alone like a symbol of war. She supposed it was—after all, it was still standing after a Tsunami hit it. There was another boat parked on the beach and she knew William had been right about the location. He was there, and he might know she had arrived. She couldn't depend on the element of surprise.

She turned to William. "You stay put. Go back to the main hotel and send some help."

"Harley, I don't think I should be leaving you alone in your condition. You seriously need medical attention. How about I just wait for you here."

She nodded. "Fine. But if anyone other than me comes out of that hotel, I want you to get the hell out of here."

"Okay, good luck." He watched with a mixture of alarm and curiosity as she picked up her gun and made her way toward the hotel. She couldn't remember ever perspiring the way she was now, even after a workout. The dress underneath was soaked through and she wondered if she was dying. It took just about all her energy to trot up to the hotel. She leaned against the entranceway as a wave of dizziness passed over her. She needed to catch her breath with only one working lung. The hotel was going to be her grave today, she could feel it. She would be okay with that if she could take Rayland with her.

She made her way in as silently as possible. She expected him to be right there in the entranceway, but he wasn't. She moved into the hotel and stood in the middle of what used to be the lobby, and she started looking around. The upper level was too deteriorated for him to have gone any higher. The flood had taken a lot out of the hotel; it was a miracle it was still standing, especially so close to the beach. She made her way down a hallway and started checking rooms. It wasn't long before she found him in what appeared to be a banquet hall. He wasn't even trying to hide. He sat on a ledge looking out the window, and to her utter shock and dismay, he was drinking a glass of whiskey.

"So, you survived after all?" he said, not even looking up at her. His eyes remained on something outside—or possibly a memory in his mind.

She walked unsteadily into the room, gun at her side. She didn't feel like she survived. She felt like she was on the edge of death, teetering on the dark side. "Are you disappointed?"

"No, thrilled actually. It just proves how much you belong to me. I knew you were special from the moment I met you. You belong to me, Harley."

She laughed. "You just tried to kill me. Not exactly the story of soulmates, is it?"

He smiled at her, that sweet sickening smile of a man so close to madness that he was barely part of the same reality as she was. Just the look of him sent a chill up her spine that made her want to run screaming away.

"Admit it, Harley, you are drawn to me in a way you can't even explain. We both knew we were entwined ever since that time you ran into me in the hallway."

Her eyes threatened to flutter closed, possibly forever.

She remembered that day. Spilling coffee on him, the rush of embarrassment and attraction between them. She would have taken him to bed that very same day if she had the chance, that's how strong the chemistry had been between them. She had thought they were meant to be together, but she had not fallen for his dark side. She had fallen for the man who brought her pastries for the stakeout, the man who had jumped in the ditch to help her out after she crashed, the kind and nurturing man who had huge Christmases with his family. She was not in love with a monster; she was in love with a man who didn't exist. It was just like her best friend used to tell her: all the good ones were gone. She chuckled at the memory, and the fact that she started laughing shocked her. Maybe she really was dying—she sure felt like it.

"Your destiny is to die by my hand just like my mother will."

She blinked slowly as she looked at him. Is that how he saw her? Would that be her fate? He wanted her to believe that this was all his mother's fault, but the truth was, some people were just born evil. Sociopaths were just born with something missing; they held no compassion or empathy for people. The horrible things he did to people weren't his mother's fault. He was soulless—evil incarnate—and he would kill whether his mother was dead or not. She stumbled woozily, trying to make sense of the thoughts going through her mind. She looked up at him again, but she was unable to find the man she had been falling in love with. The one with the kind eyes and the attentive gaze that made her feel like she had finally found a home. It was all gone, just an act to get close to her. He wasn't even capable of love. When she looked at him, she could see a cold emptiness in his eyes; his dark was showing, and she didn't like it one bit.

"How could you sleep with me when you were out killing my friends?"

"Don't take it personal, Harley. I didn't kill them because of you—well, not all of them. Those two boys were not good for you, and they needed to go.

"Things were over between Craig and me. You could have left him alone, and there was never anything between Devon and me."

He waved away her comments. "Craig was a useful tool. It kept you distracted so that you would have a chance to fall in love with me."

If he kept talking, then she was going to be sick. It was just the ravings of a madman. The ego that he had was beyond her. She would never convince him that he did anything wrong. In his mind, it was his destiny. He would just continue to take as many lives as his thirst needed, and there would be endless bodies. He couldn't get away with it.

"We weren't in love. Everything we experienced was a lie."

"It didn't feel like a lie, especially those nights we spent warming up your bed."

"You monster." There were tears streaming down her cheeks. She was exhausted and talking to him was taking more of a toll on her than the stabbing had. She would never get the answers she wanted. He was enjoying the fact that she was upset by their circumstance, that he had fooled everyone. He was incapable of feeling anything, much less remorse for breaking her heart and playing her for a fool.

"How many are there?"

He looked surprised by her question. He took a sip of his whiskey and thought about it. She raised her gun slowly and shot the glass right out of his hand. "How many are there!" she screamed. She wobbled from the exertion the scream took from her damaged lung. Her chest was on fire, her throat raw.

Standing up, he shook the glass shards from his hand. She could tell she wounded him and it made her feel good. He seemed enthralled with the sight of his own blood. He rubbed the blood between his fingers. He looked up at her with an impressed expression on his face. "Very nice, Harley."

She waited while he stared at her. "I don't know an exact number. After a while, they all blur together. The people are meaningless; all that matters is the blood. You forget things that don't really matter after a while. If I had to guess, I would say a few hundred at least."

She stared at him in disbelief; it was worse than she thought. Maybe he had been doing it since he was a kid—a teenager for sure.

"You sick sonofabitch. You've always been a monster. Your mother should have drowned you at birth."

Something snapped in him—she had hit a nerve. He glared at her in a way that showed the evil inside of him. It was probably the same look his victims saw before they died. "It's time for me to go, Harley. By the look of you, I won't be able to take you with me. You're no doubt on death's door, and I must be leaving now." He started toward her, moving fast. She went to lift the gun to shoot him and it was like she lost all use of her arm. The gun was so heavy and her energy was gone. He was upon her in seconds and struck her hard across the face. She fell to the ground and he was on top of her. He wrapped his hands around her neck and stared down at her. She saw that glazed look come across his face again and it scared the shit out of her.

"Goodbye, mother."

He squeezed her throat hard just as she lifted the gun and fired it into his thigh. He screamed and released her. He rolled off her and held his leg where she had shot him. She tried to get up, but she was too weak to move.

"Freeze right there, Rayland," a voice commanded. "It's over."

The last thing she saw before she blacked out was Chief Aat and his men pouring into the room. They had him—she could go now.

She woke up in a room she didn't recognize. She would have assumed she was dead if her entire body wasn't wracked with excruciating pain. She turned to the side to see Ned sitting in a chair beside her bed.

"Harley? Are you awake?" He got up quickly to retrieve a nurse. It wasn't long before he returned with one in tow.

"It hurts," she whispered.

"I don't doubt that," the nurse replied. "We are going to give you something for that." She administered a needle and within minutes a certain numbness came over her. There was nothing like being high to numb the pain—they must have given her morphine.

"How long have you been here? Tell me everything before I pass out again."

"You've been out for three days. They weren't sure you were going to make it. You put your body through hell, Harley. They said that the makeshift tubing you put in your ribcage saved your life. You'll have to show me how you did that."

She laughed at that. It hurt to laugh but she was glad she was able to. "I have my old partner to thank for that one."

"It was impressive, to say the least."

She grew serious. "Where is he, Ned?"

"We have him, Harley. You shot him, but he

survived. He's being detained in Singapore until he's sentenced. He won't ever be getting out. It's over."

"He told me there are hundreds of bodies. We may never know all his victims."

"We might be able to get a list from him before they sentence him. He would hope for some leniency. We can try at least."

"I can't believe it's over."

"You are lucky to be alive. You had no business going after him alone, especially in your condition."

"I know, but I couldn't let him get away."

He nodded sadly, knowing exactly what she was talking about. She had fallen for Rayland and he had turned into everything she hated.

"Did you find William?"

He smiled. "Yes, he was waiting at the boat when we arrived. He sent you roses."

She looked over at a vase of red roses that sat among a few other bouquets on the table at the end of her bed. She smiled. "Well, how about that."

"We searched Rayland's hotel room, and he was truly under our nose the whole time. We found rolls of plastic wrap, an ax, and a stun gun. He must have used it on his victims to keep quiet. We found the passports and credit cards you were talking about, as well as his tools."

"Tools?"

"Well, I would call them torture devices. He had them all wrapped in a leather case—everything from an icepick to a butcher's knife to a drill. There is blood residue on all of it even though he cleaned them quite well. The tools tell their own story—a horrifying one."

Harley felt the blackness coming back and she knew she was going to pass out again. He smiled down at her before she went. The last thing she thought of before she went to sleep was not Rayland but Chris.

THIRTY FOUR

HARLEY SAT IN THE COURTROOM awaiting Rayland's sentencing. She wouldn't have missed it for the world, and she had refused to fly back home until she was able to look at Rayland again and see what was handed to him. He sat at the table with his lawyer, looking just as handsome as he did the last time she saw him on the beach. Even an orange jumper couldn't dissipate his looks. She thought she would feel destroyed when she saw him again, but she felt nothing at all. A numbness had settled in her heart every time she thought of Rayland. He had refused to give them any information on his past killings; his ego would not allow him to plead for his life. He glanced back at her a few times and smiled, not the smile of a serial killer but the one of the lover she once knew. She stared back at him stone-faced, refusing to give him any satisfaction.

She had healed up nicely since she left the hospital, with no permanent damage. She had a lot of scars, but she was okay with that—she was a survivor, after all. She had quickly messaged Keri to let her know that Craig wasn't the killer and to explain everything that happened. Keri was broken-hearted to hear that Craig was dead. Harley apologized for not believing her.

Chief Aat had offered her a job, which she declined respectfully, as she was looking forward to returning to New York. As a thank you for all the work she did on the island in bringing Rayland down, Thailand offered her an all-inclusive package to come back and visit them again when she was ready. She wasn't sure when that would be, but she wanted to see Ned again.

Her captain back home had heard about her work in Thailand and offered her a promotion to detective, effective immediately. She turned it down, however. While working the case, she realized that she no longer wanted to work for the department. She had been through hell and back, but she felt like she could take on anything after dealing with Rayland. She was on her own journey of forgiveness for the mistakes she had made, but she knew that the healing would only come with time and she was wiser for the mistakes. She had let go of what happened with Chris and she would eventually let go of Rayland too. She was able to give Keri closure for her family and take a madman off the street for good. She had decided to open her own private investigation company so that she could work on cases of her own choosing. She no longer wanted to deal with drugs; she thought hunting down killers might be better suited for her.

She recognized Rayland's mother in the courtroom as well—the shock of red hair was a total giveaway. It all made sense to her now why Rayland had fixated on her. Aat had filled her in on the questioning involved with his mother. It turned out that he didn't have a big family after all. His father had left him and his mother despised him. She admitted she had always known there was something wrong with "her boy" but had never known he had hurt anyone. She explained his childhood and all the butchered animals in the neighborhood. She had known it was him, that he had done it, but she was afraid of him. She knew he was a dangerous man but his unspeakable crimes were beyond what she ever imagined. She whispered to Harley that she always thought he would come back and finish her off, and she had lived in fear of him for years, hoping that he was dead. She had ordered him out of the house, but she knew he would come back. He had the classic history of a serial killer: born, not made.

THIRTY FIVE

HARLEY SAT BEHIND HER DESK as she watched movers bringing in boxes and office equipment. She was back in New York, setting up her new office. She was thrilled to be back home and working toward a future in a career that she would have a little more control over. She had been the talk of the news for weeks and had been on a talk show or two, and that had already boosted business for her. People were anxious to talk with the woman who had brought a notorious serial killer down.

She had healed up nicely, although she was still pretty sore when she moved around. She had a few clients on a waiting list, waiting for the doors of Wolfhart Investigations to open its doors officially. She had considered taking some time off since the trauma of the island, but in the end, she knew that working was the most healing thing that she could do.

The phone rang, and she smiled. It was the first official call since the phone company had set everything up for her.

"Hello, Wolfhart's Investigations."

"Oh my God, you sound so badass."

Harley burst out laughing at the sound of Keri's voice. "Hi girl, how are you?"

"I'm okay. You know, one day at a time and all that. I wanted to say hi and see how the new office was coming along."

"It's great. The movers are here as we speak."

"You sure you don't want to take a couple of weeks off and come visit before things get crazy for you again? You haven't been out of the hospital for very long. You should take some time off and come and see me."

"I promise you I will. I just needed to get this whole thing started before I talked myself out of it."

"You've been through so much—we both have."

"Yes, we are true soul sisters now." Harley smiled into the phone. She cared a great deal for Keri and knew that she would visit her shortly. They still had so much to talk about.

A man walked into her office with a clipboard. "I need you to sign this." He held it out to Harley.

"Look, Keri, I have to run. I have papers to sign. Let me give you a ring back tonight."

"Sure, no problem. Good luck with the move."

"Thanks."

She hung up the phone and took the clipboard from the man. She read the invoice and signed it. "Thank you."

"We'll just finish up out there and be out of your hair shortly."

"Perfect, thanks."

She started organizing her desk when the phone rang again. She picked it up and said, "Hello, Wolfhart's Investigations."

"Hello, Harley."

"Who is this?"

"I know you could never actually forget me. How crazy was it that both you and my mother were in the same room together? It was like seeing twins. It was like my true destiny revealed. I knew right then what I was supposed to do. If only I hadn't been handcuffed at the time."

A chill ran up the length of her body. It couldn't be.

"How did you get out?"

"Oh, Harley, they could never keep me there. I'm too good for that. Plus, I have so much more work to do. I'm going to paint that new office of yours with your blood."

Oh shit.

A NOTE FROM KIMBERLY

Dear Reader,

I hope that you enjoyed this book and the characters as much as I did introducing them to you. I've been writing my whole life and finally decided to share some of the musings that go on in my head.

If you have enjoyed this book as much as I hope you have, the second and third book will be released shortly after this one. Follow Harley on her journey as a Private Investigator and see the new monsters she meets and whether she catches The Butcher once and for all.

Sign up to my mailing list at **WWW.KIMMILOVE.COM** where you will also connect with my radio show, Hot Girl Shit. My website is where you will find news about events and new books coming out.

If you would like to leave a review for the book and share your thoughts it would be greatly appreciated.

Stay inspired!

Love,
Kimberly

ABOUT THE AUTHOR

KIMBERLY LOVE is a radio host on Hot Girl Shit on and author of *You Taste Like Whiskey and Sunshine, Bare: Love, Sex and Finding Your Soul Mate* and *Divine Vengeance* as well as the CEO of Viking Queens, a membership site that empowers women to find love and live out their dreams.

Her radio show with 30,000 plus daily listeners showcases celebrities, coaches, and entrepreneurs who are an inspiration to women. Hot Girl Shit is about empowerment and helps women to learn to have fun and to go past fear to discover the life that they have always dreamed of.

Kimberly travels the world writing and currently lives in Florida with her daughter.

Find her online:

WWW.KIMMILOVE.COM
WWW.VIKINGQUEENS.COM

Printed in Great Britain
by Amazon